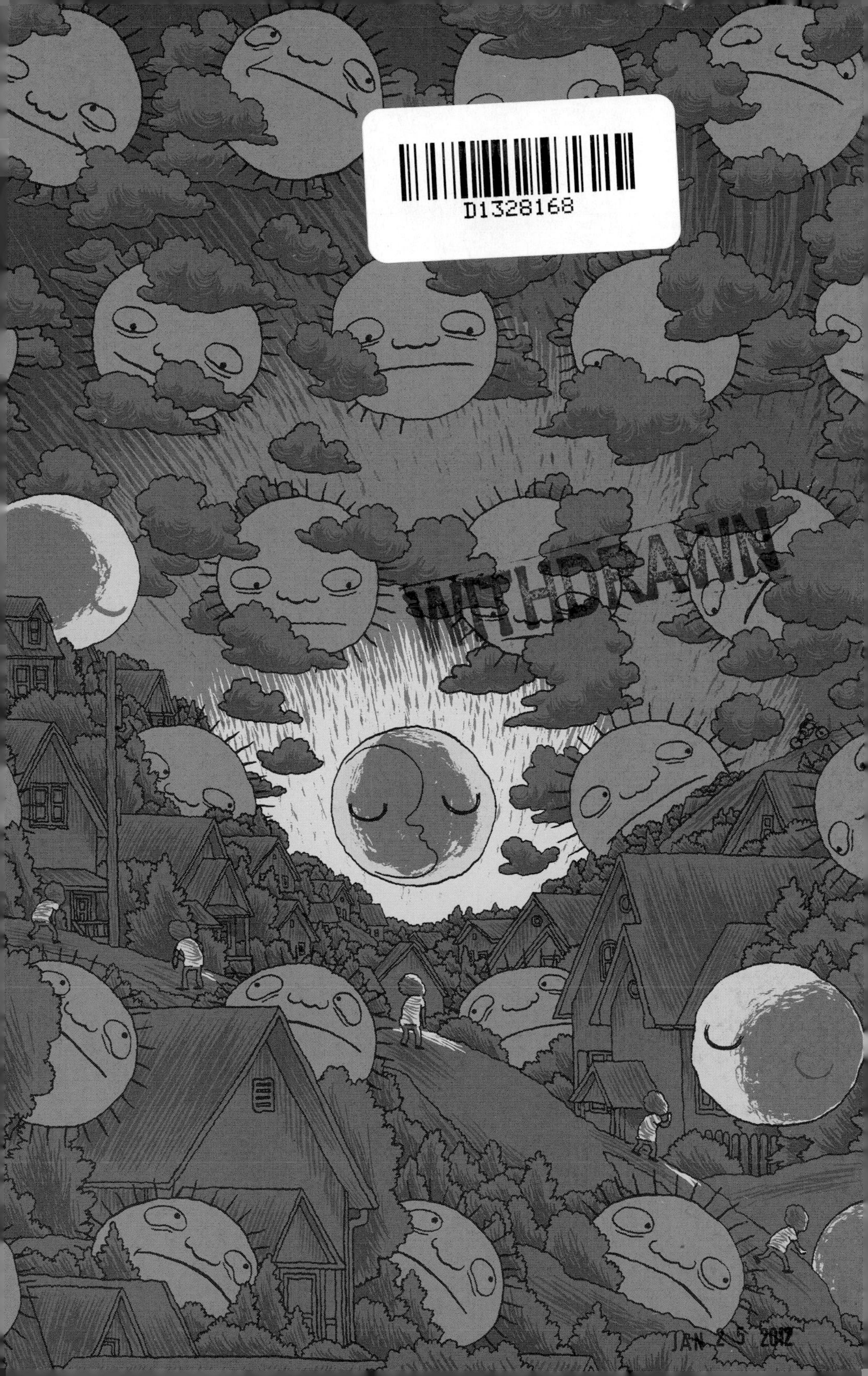

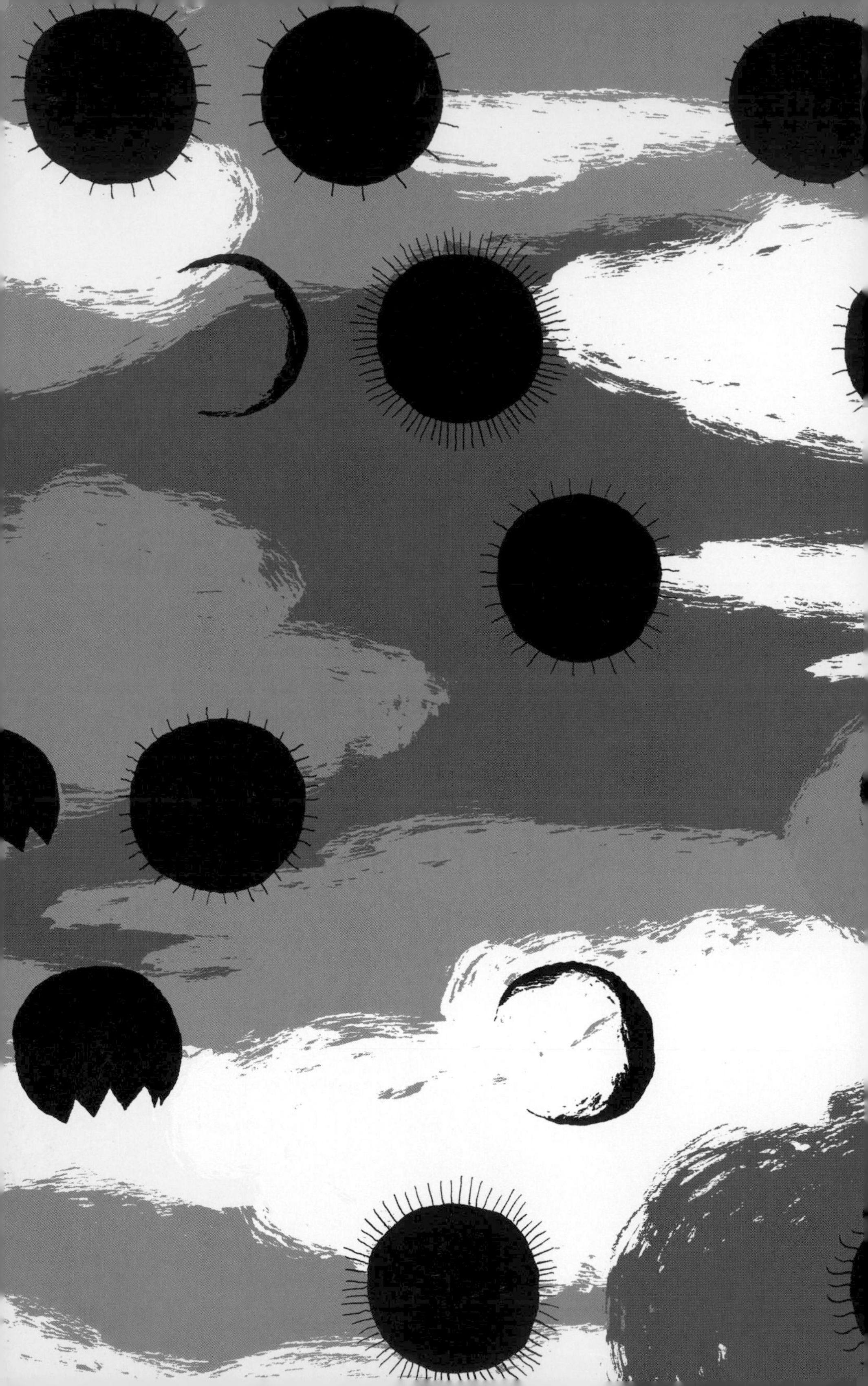

I·WILL
·BITE·
·YOU!

I WILL BITE YOU!

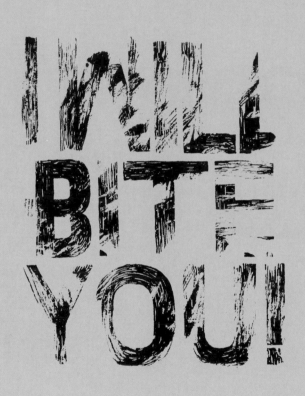

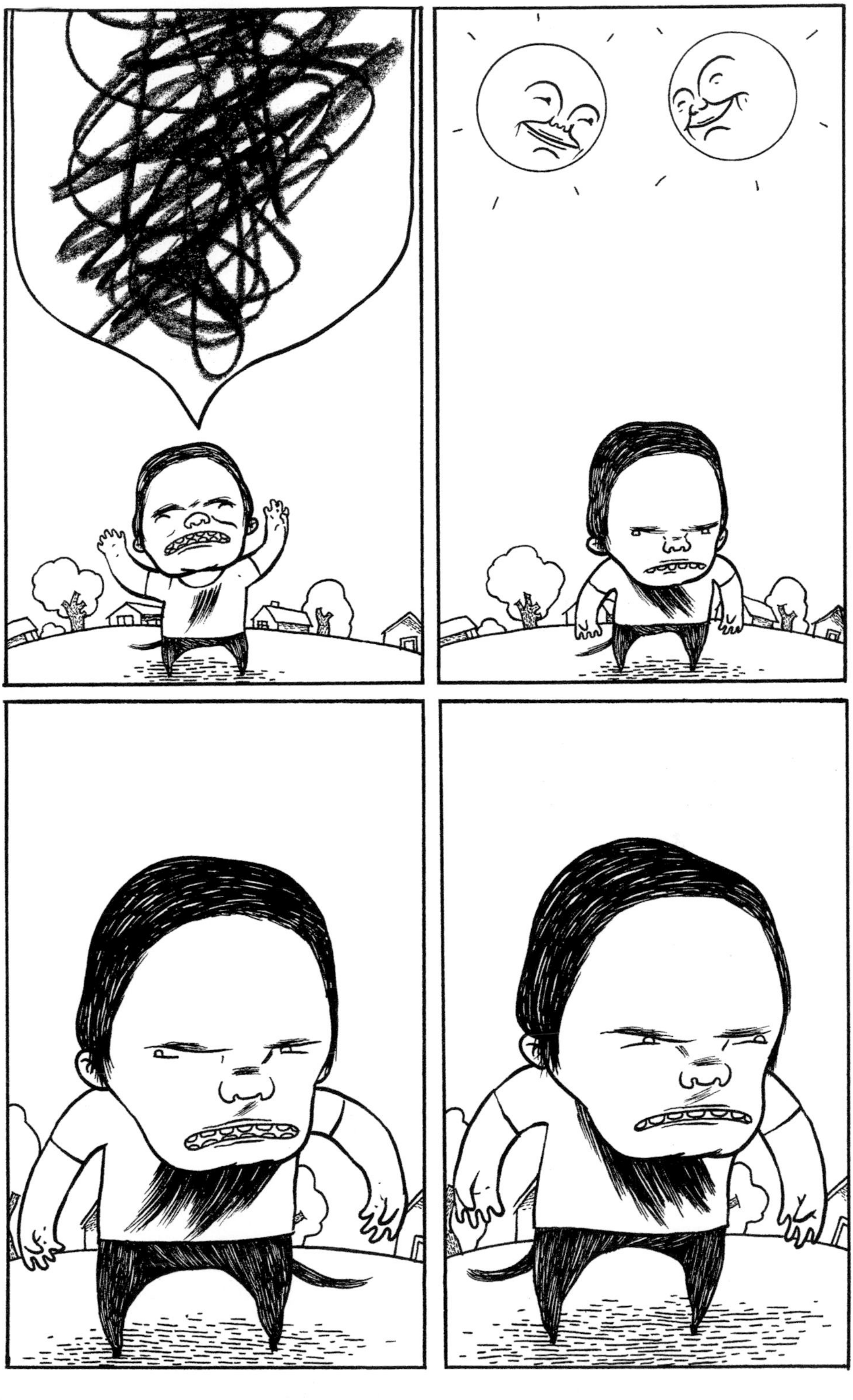

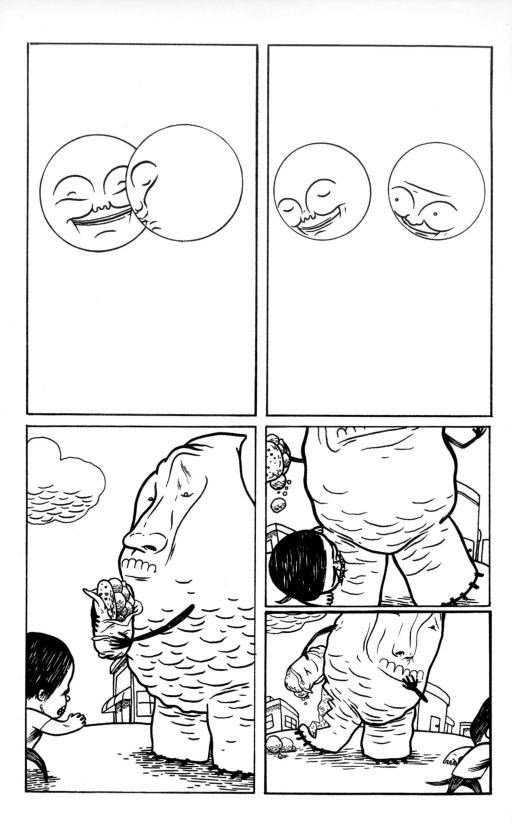

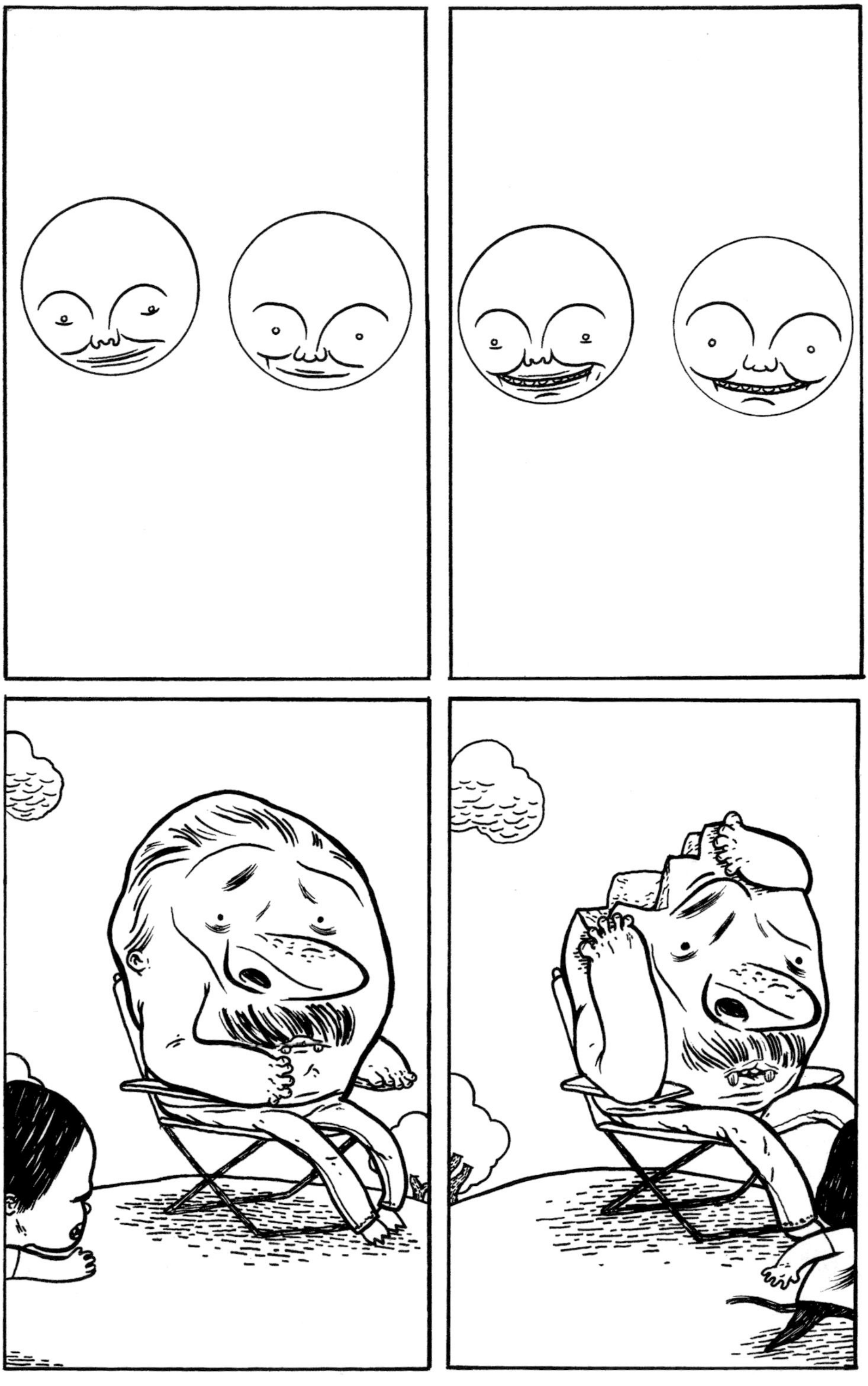

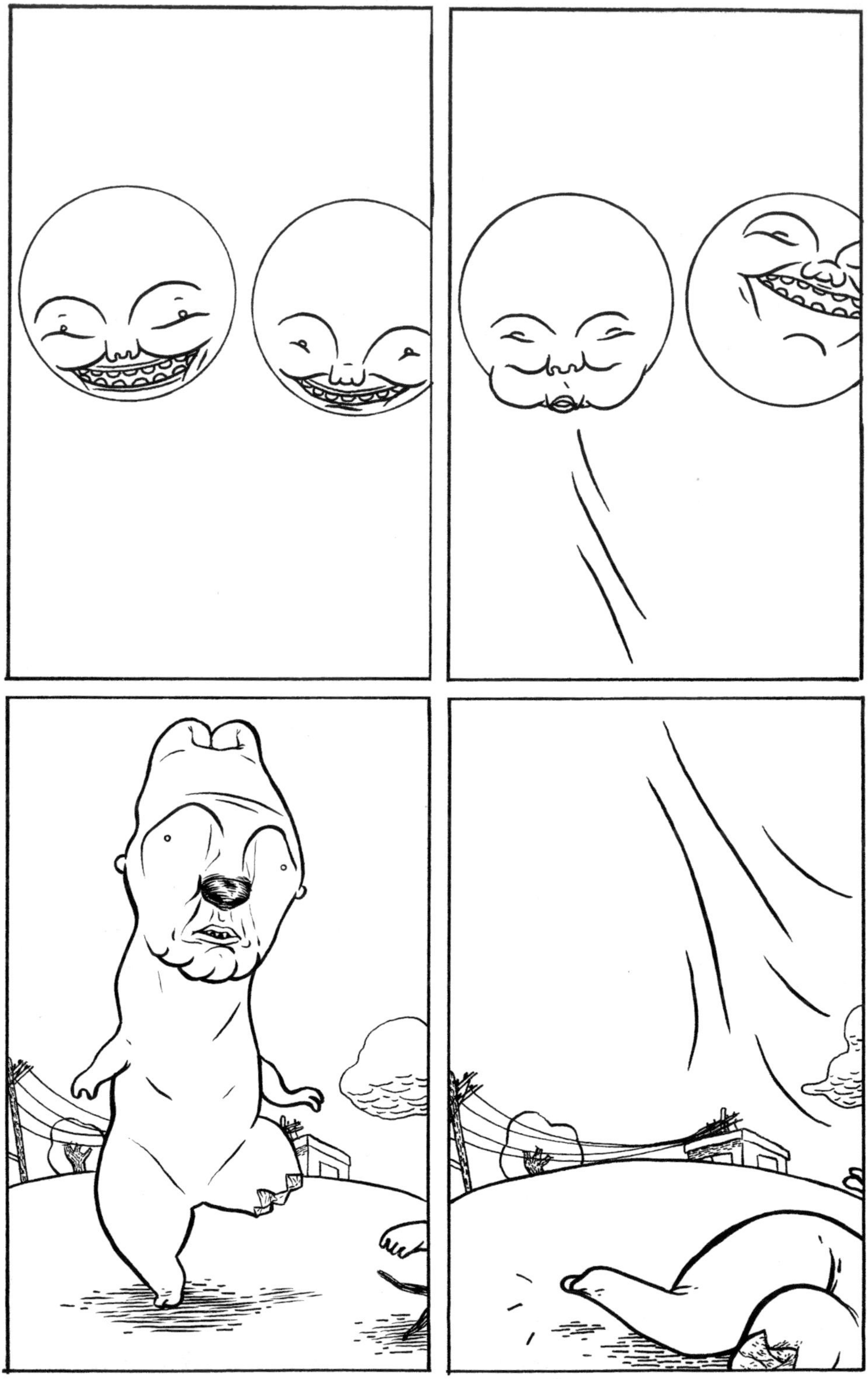

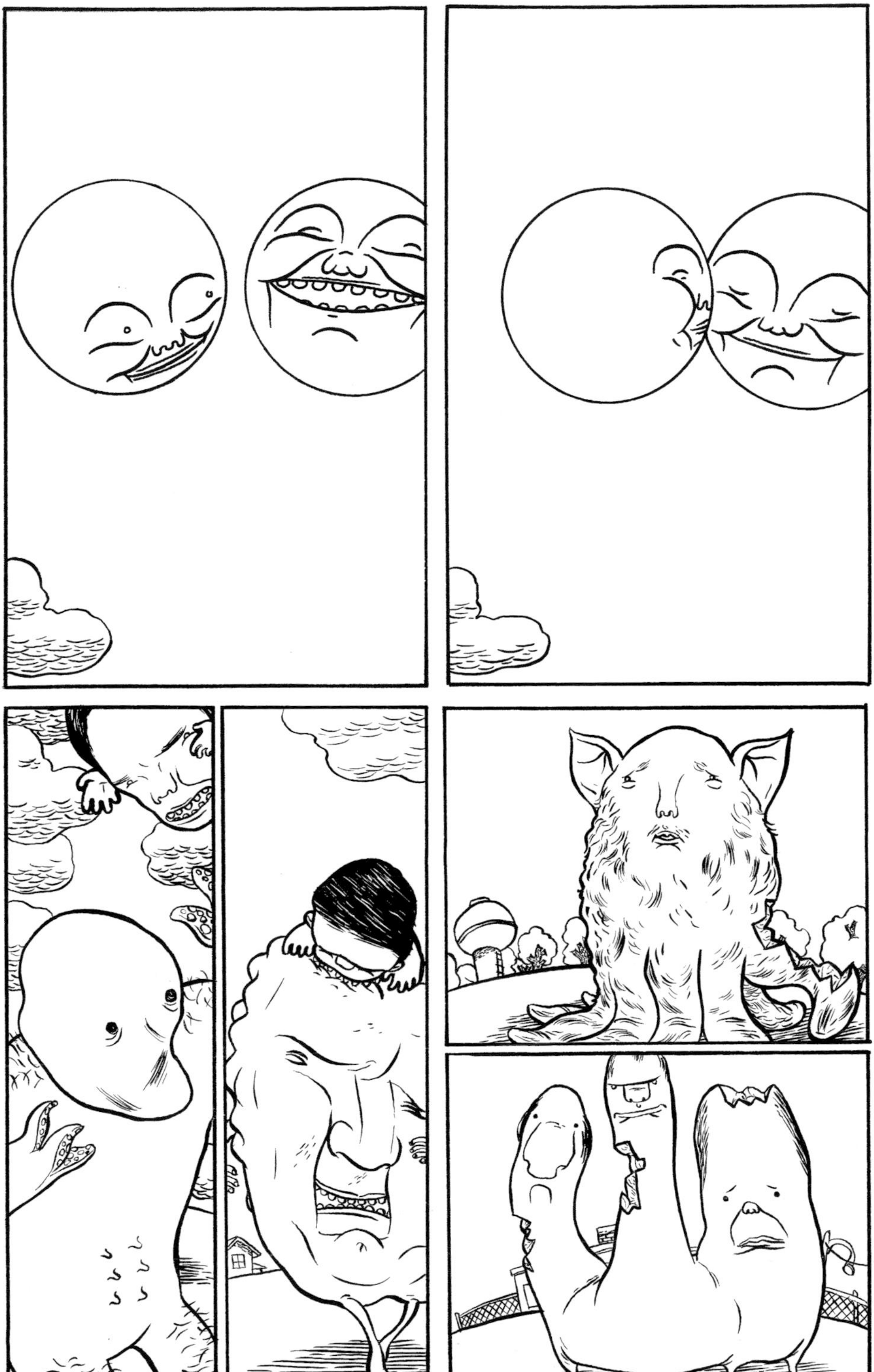

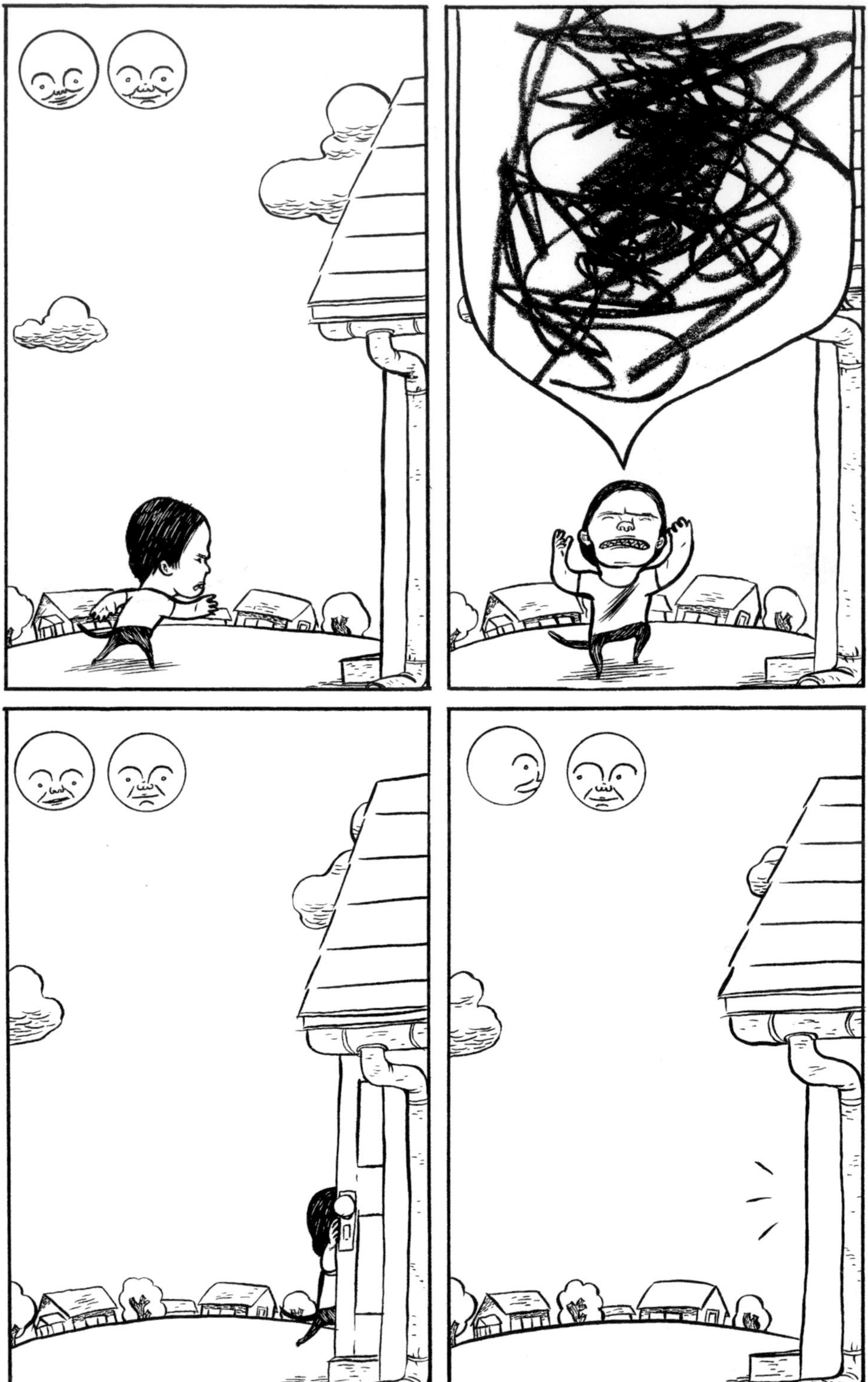

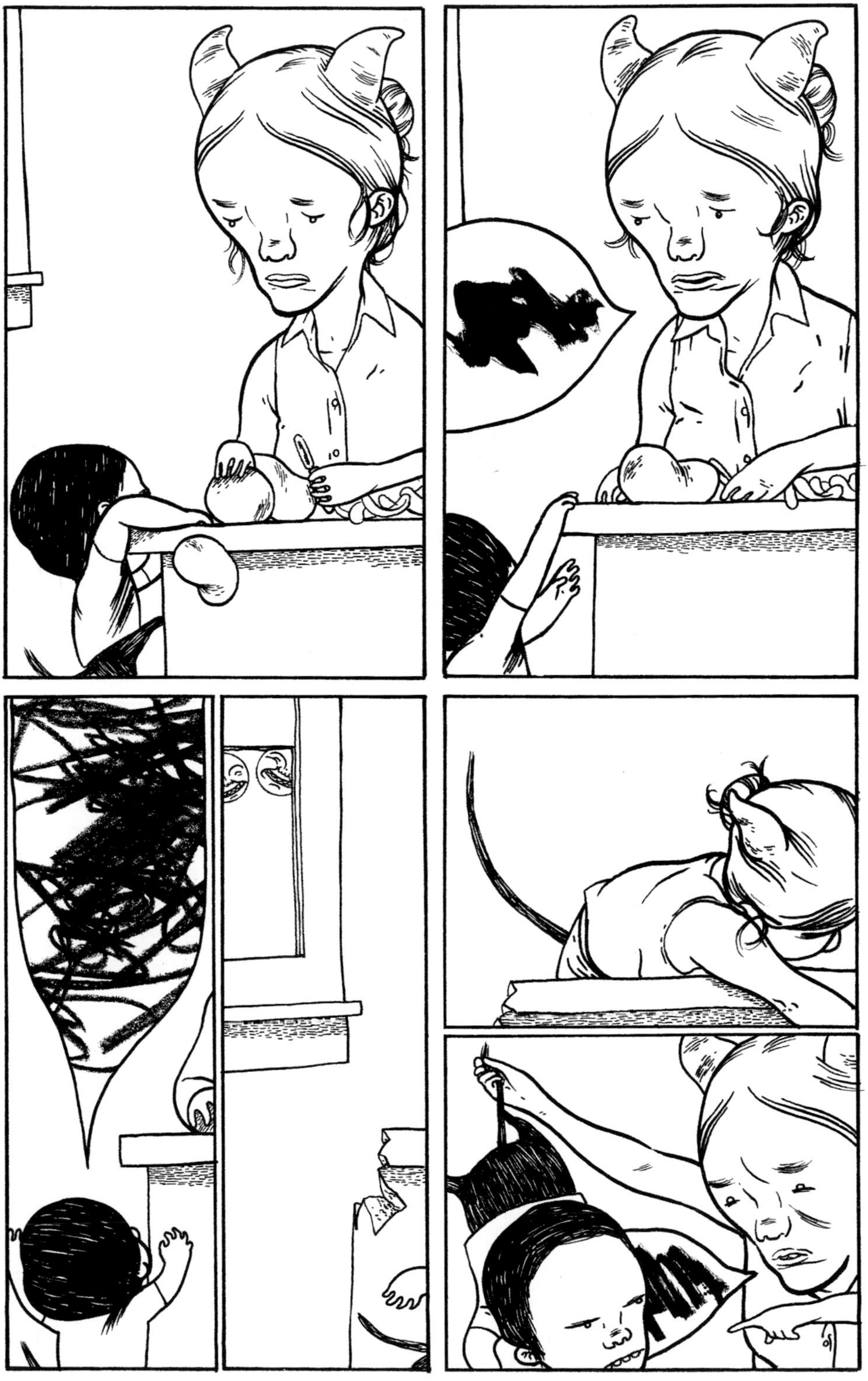

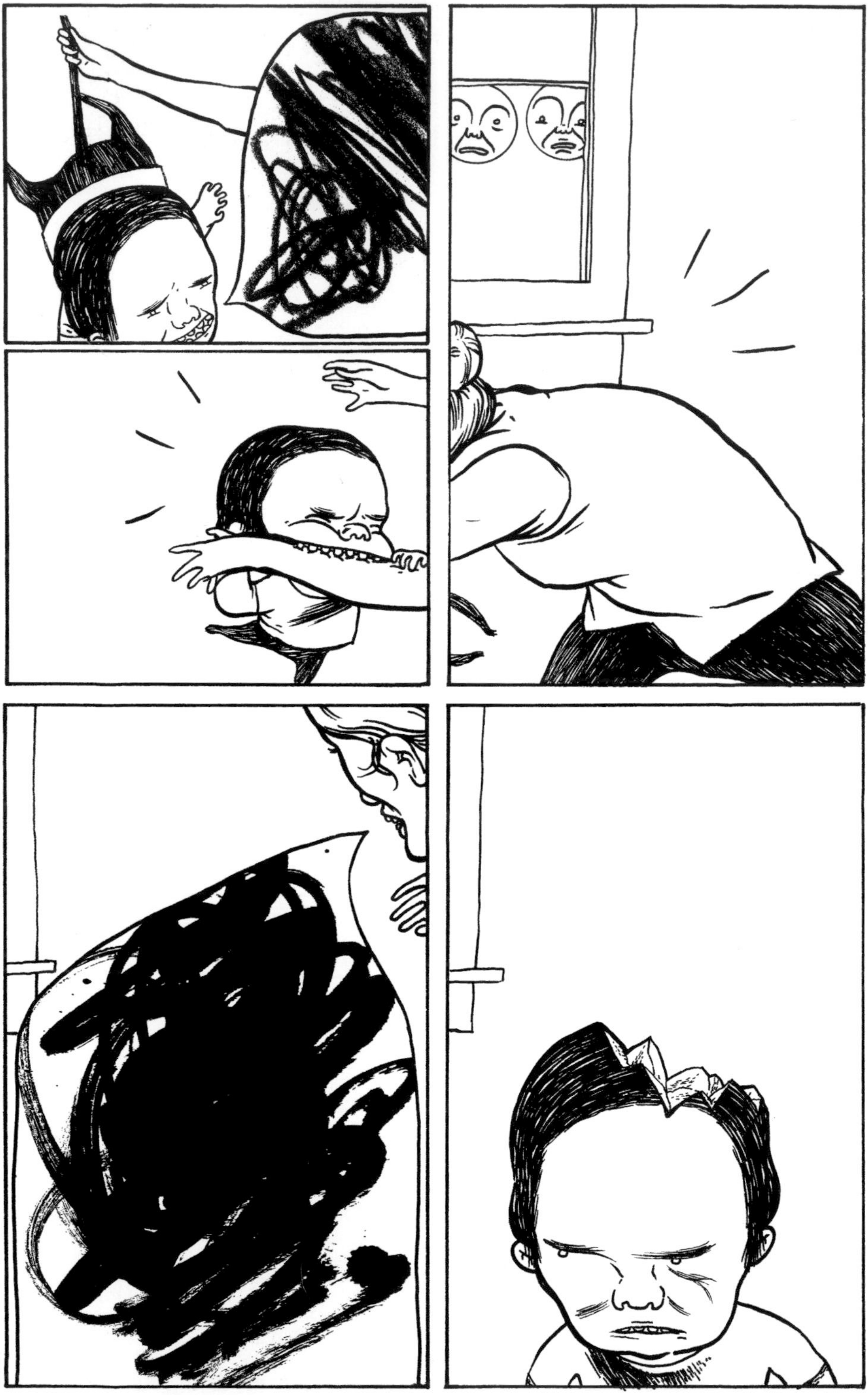

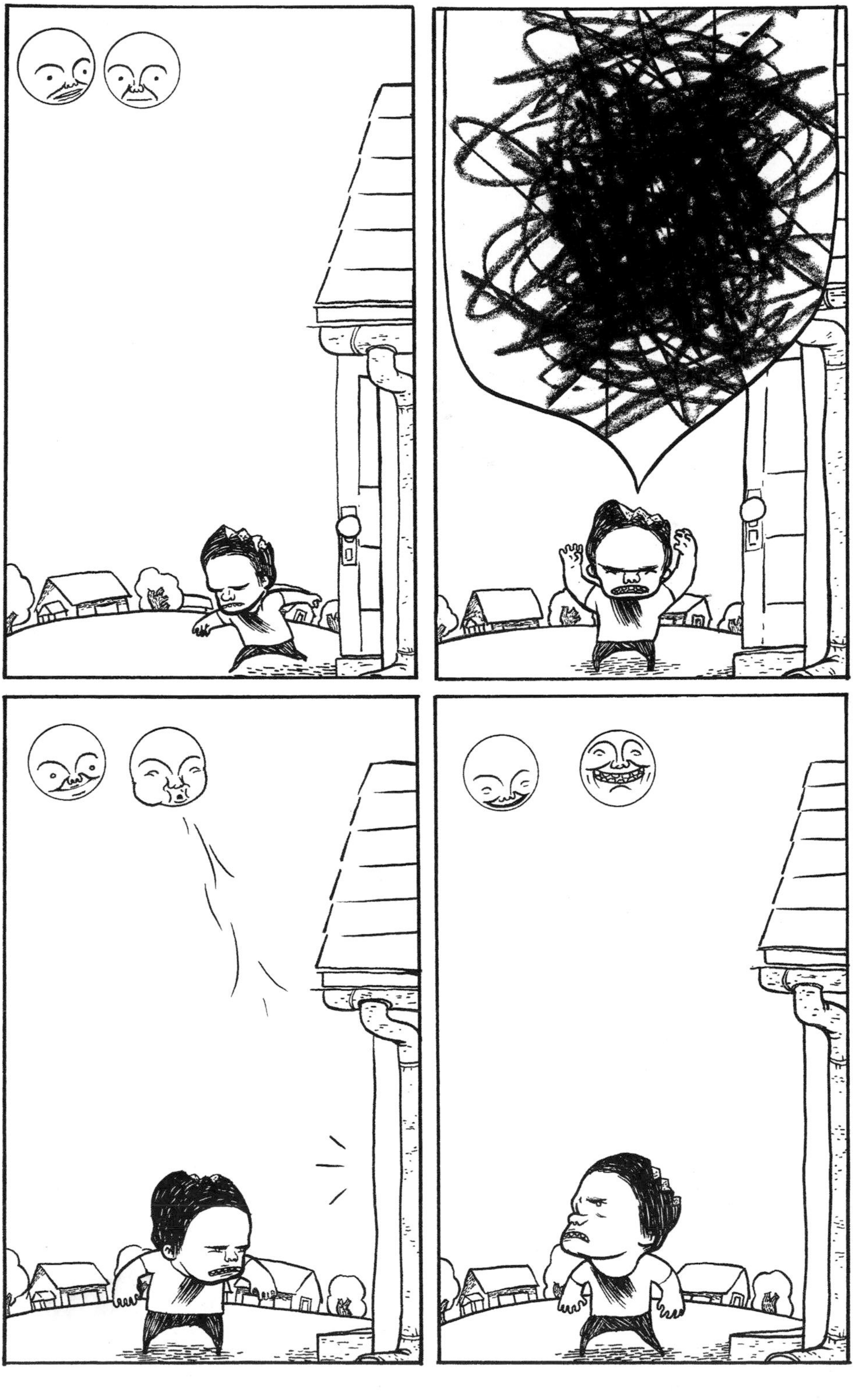

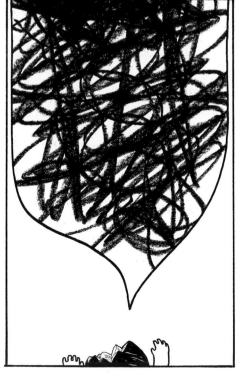

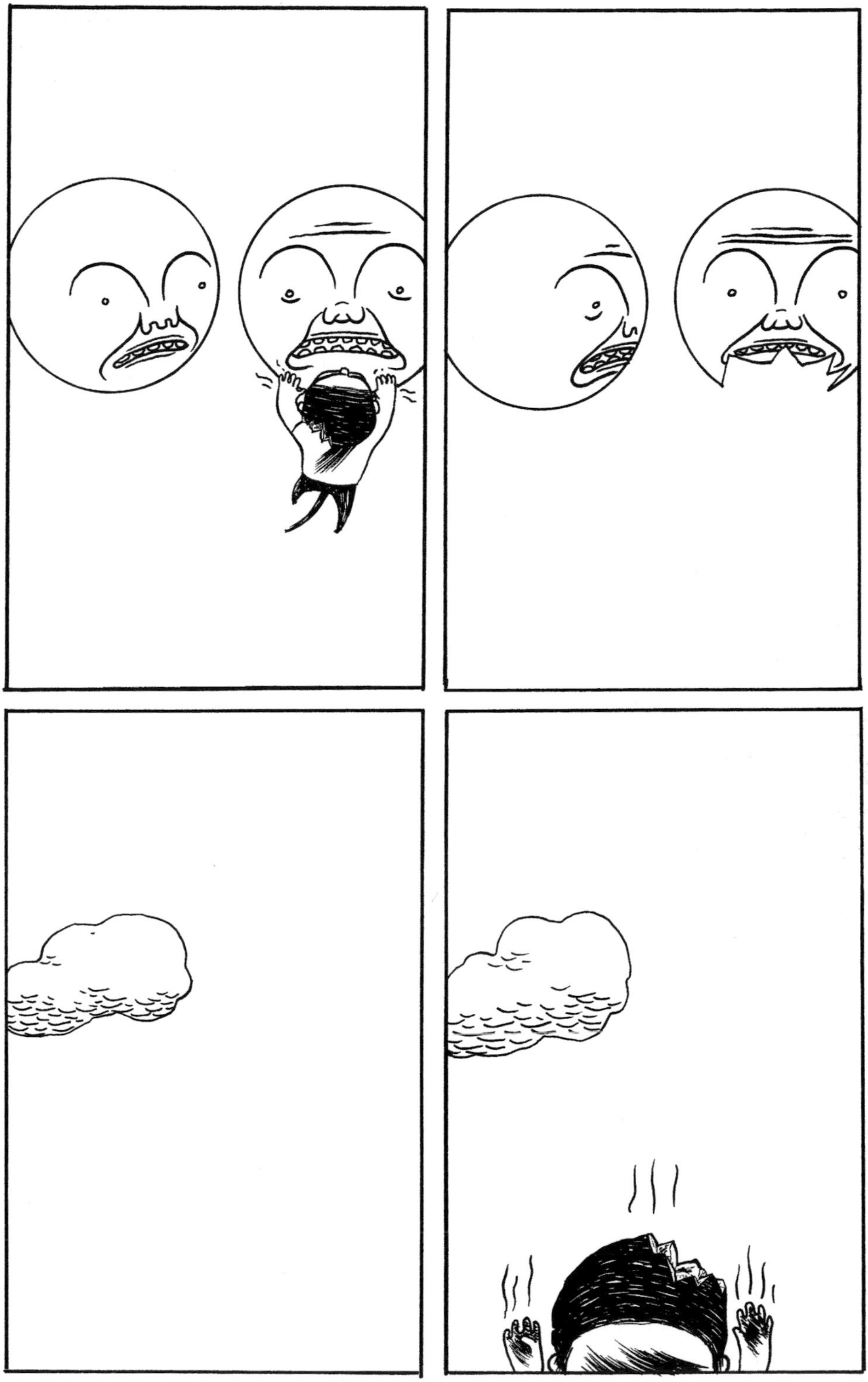

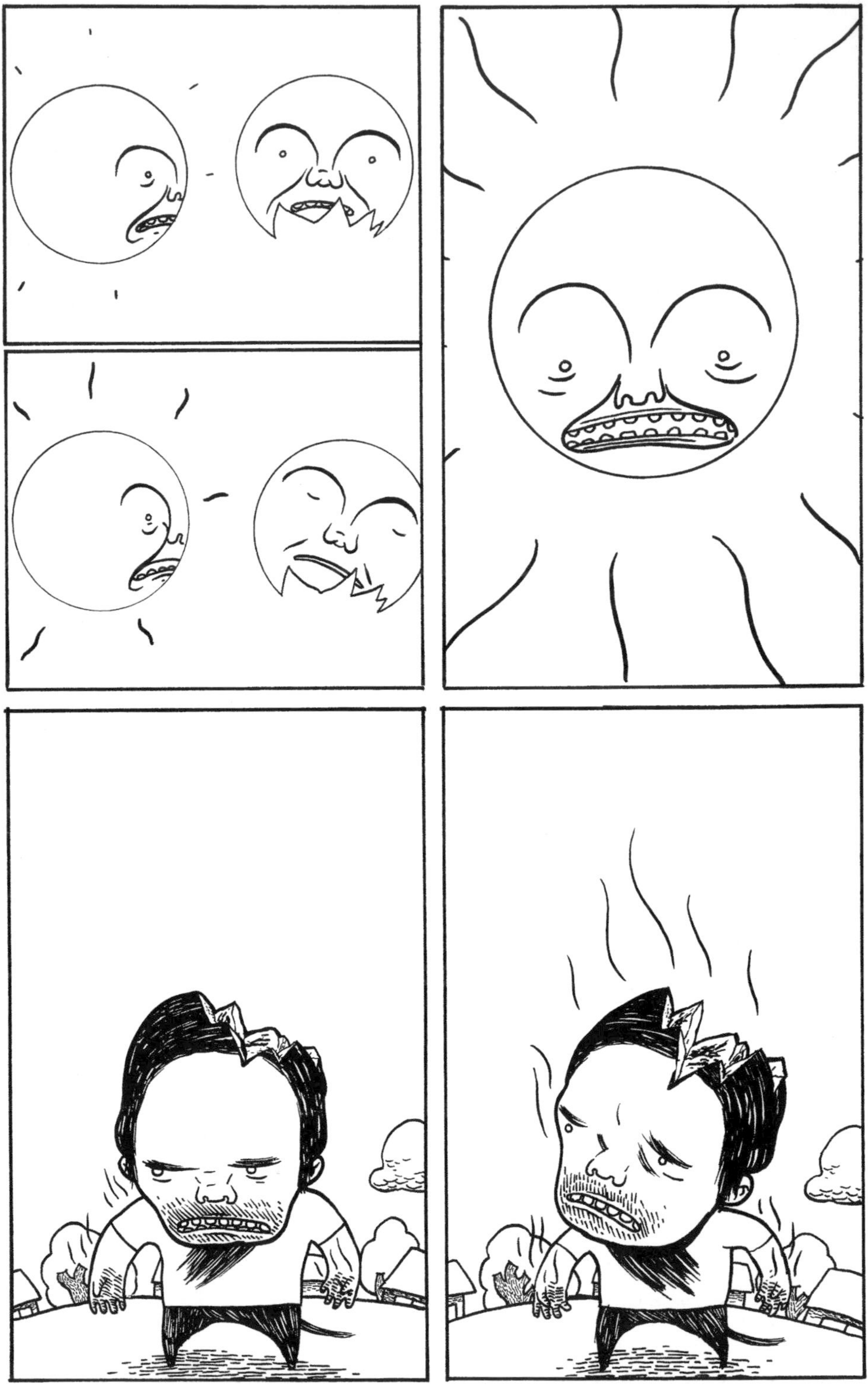

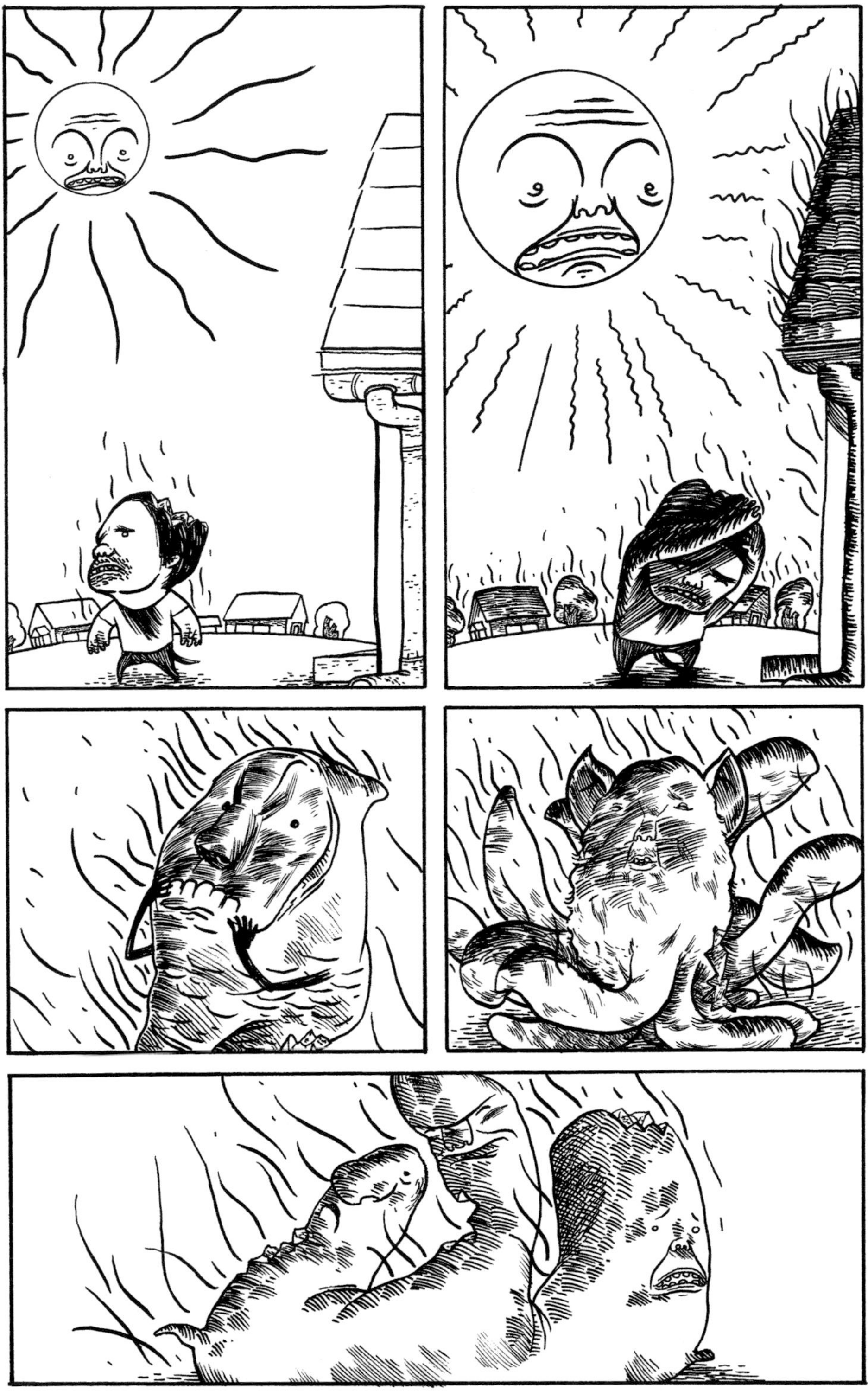

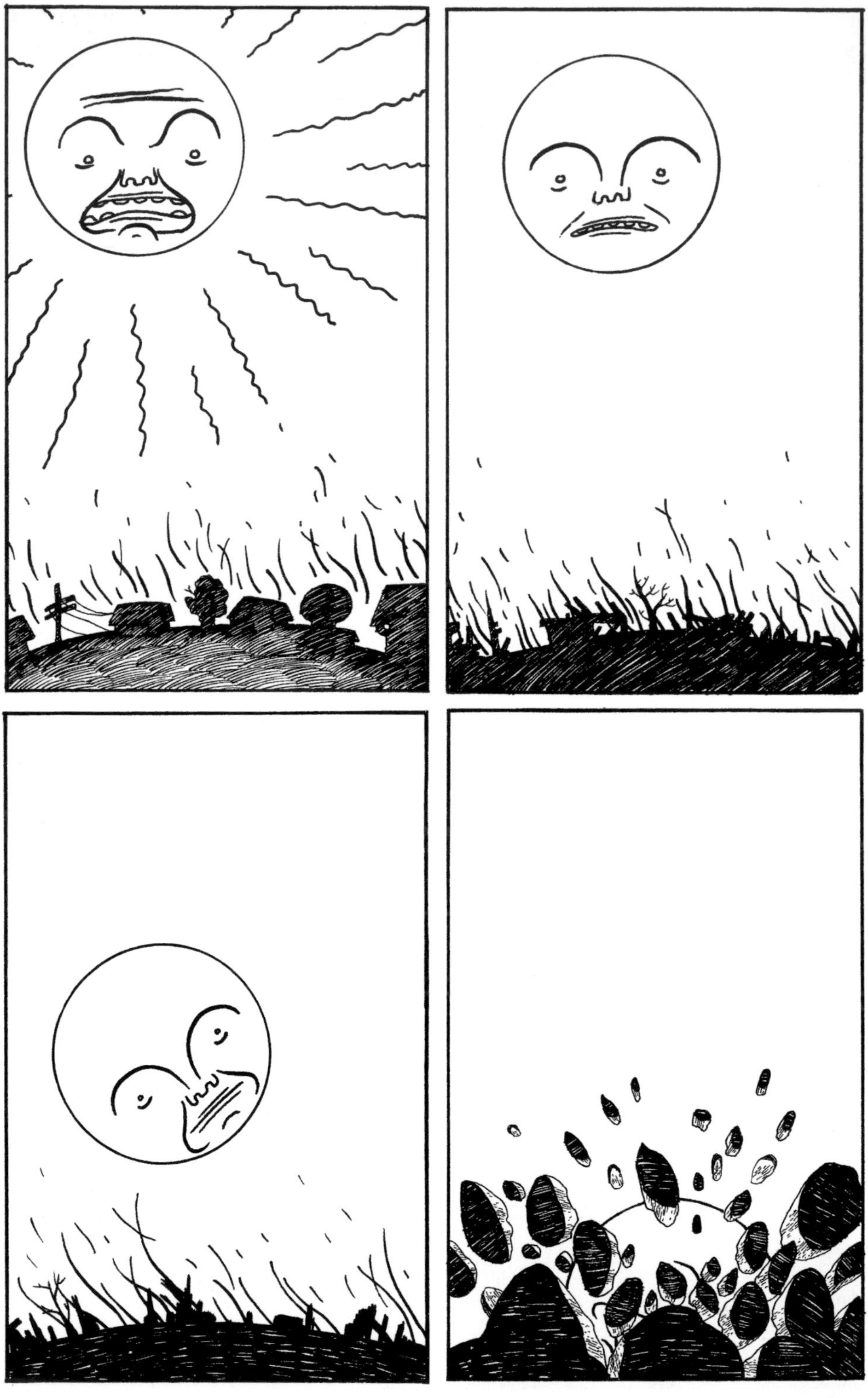

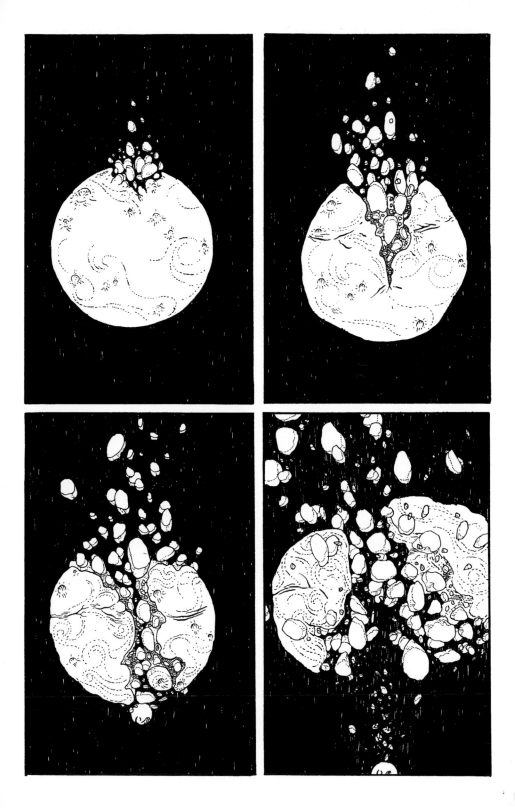

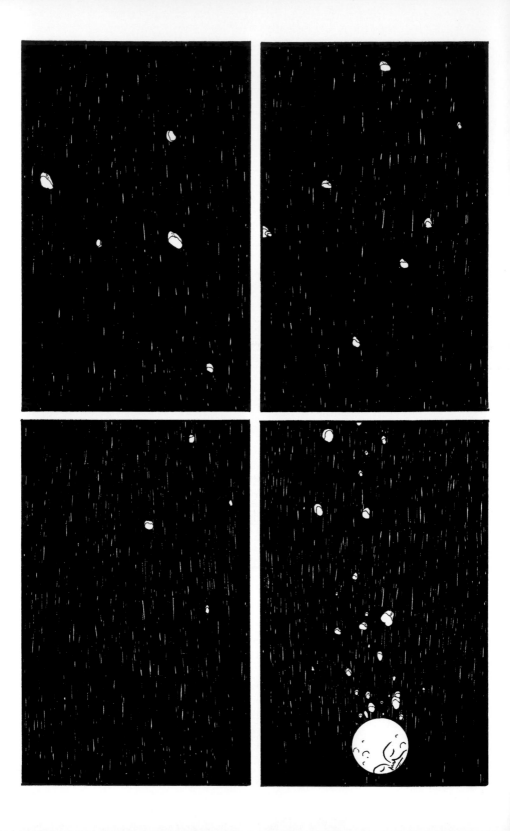

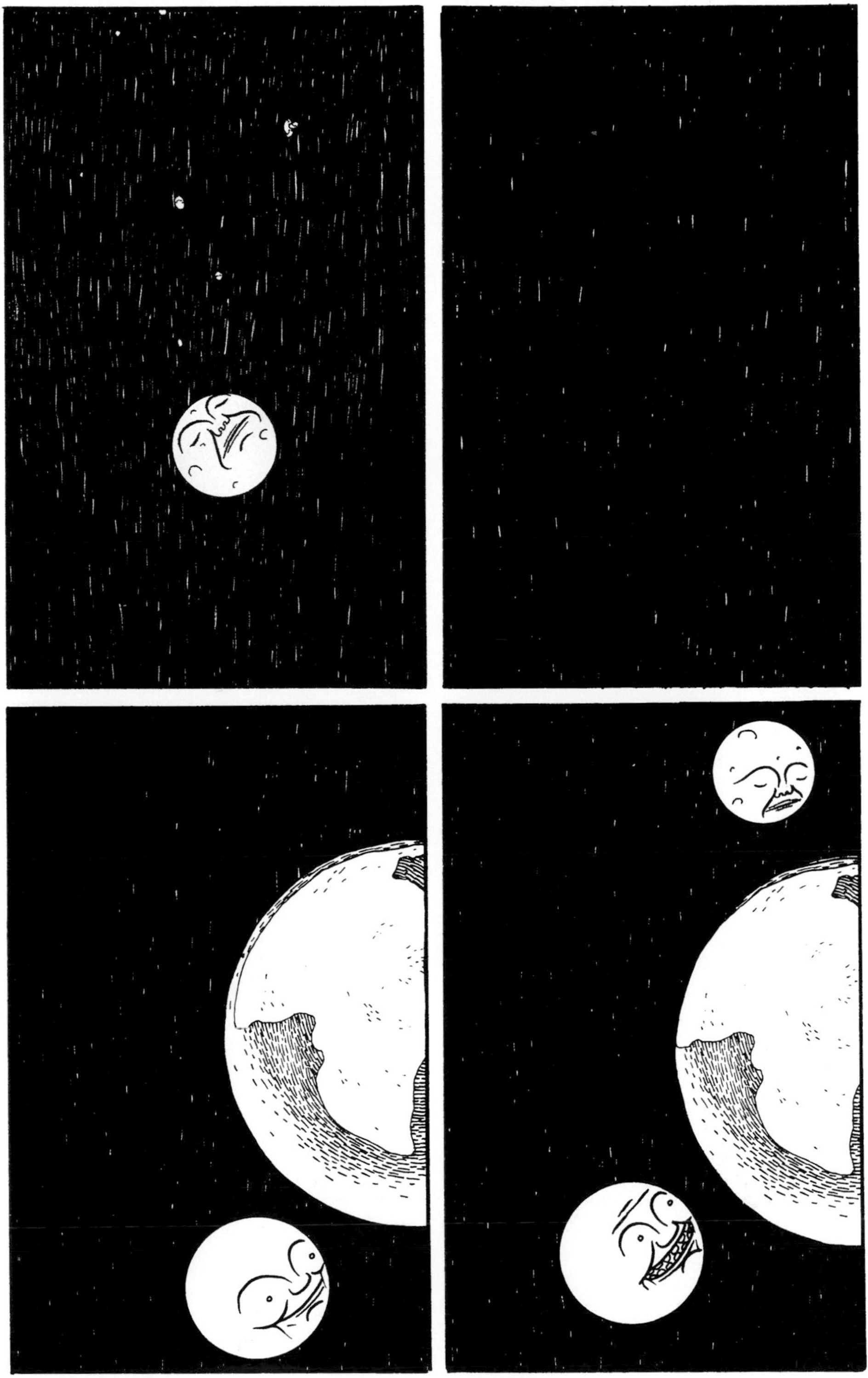

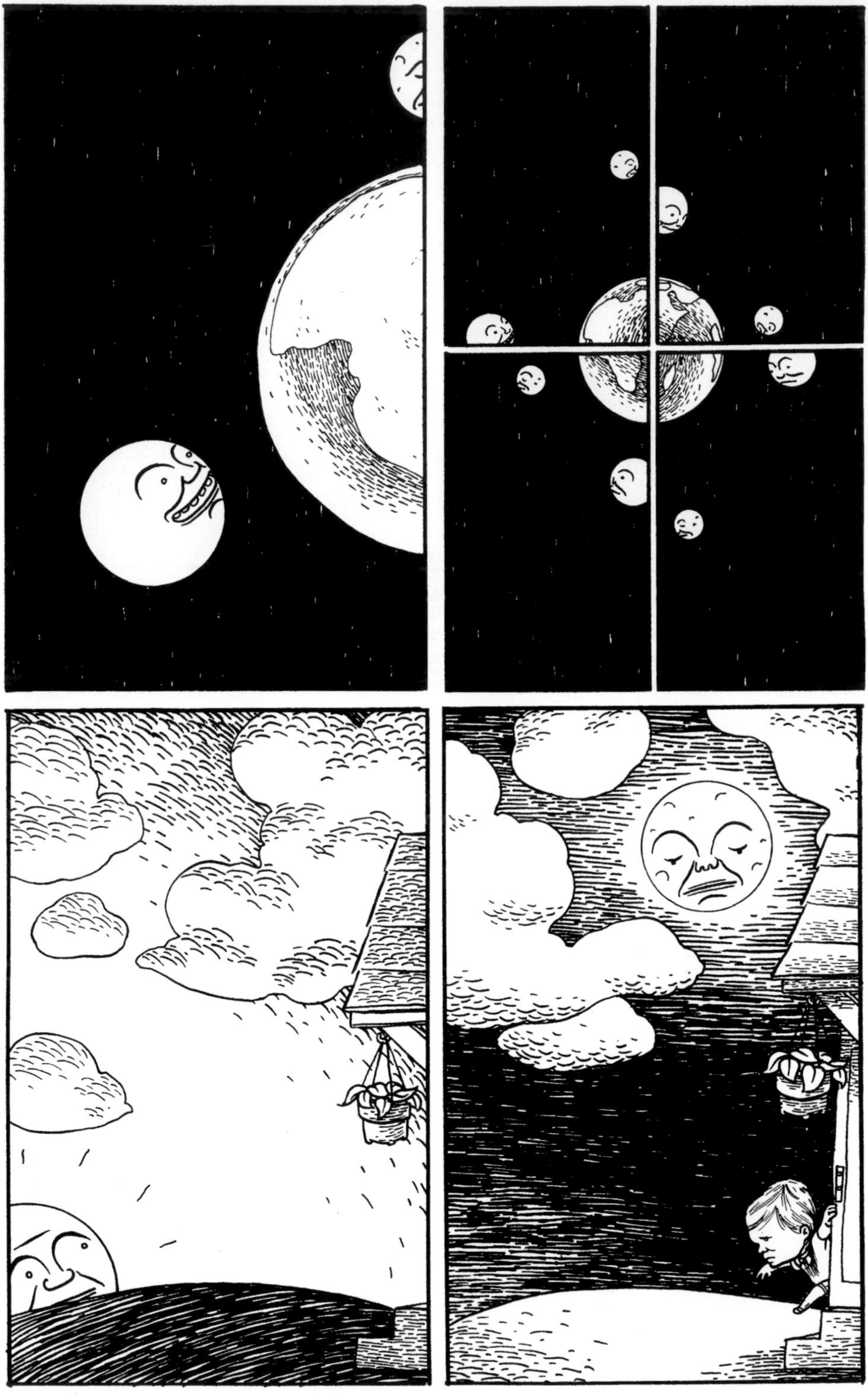

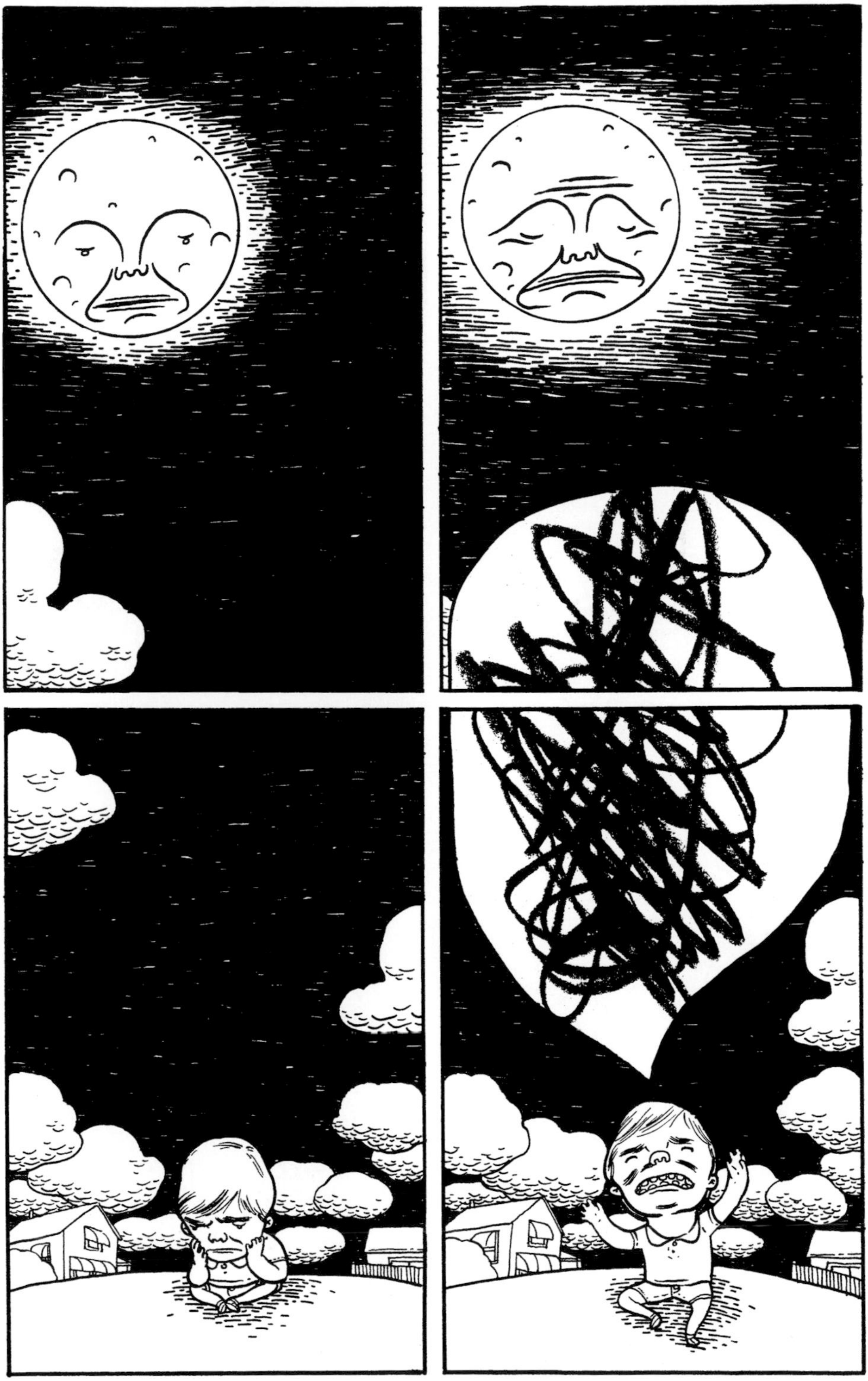

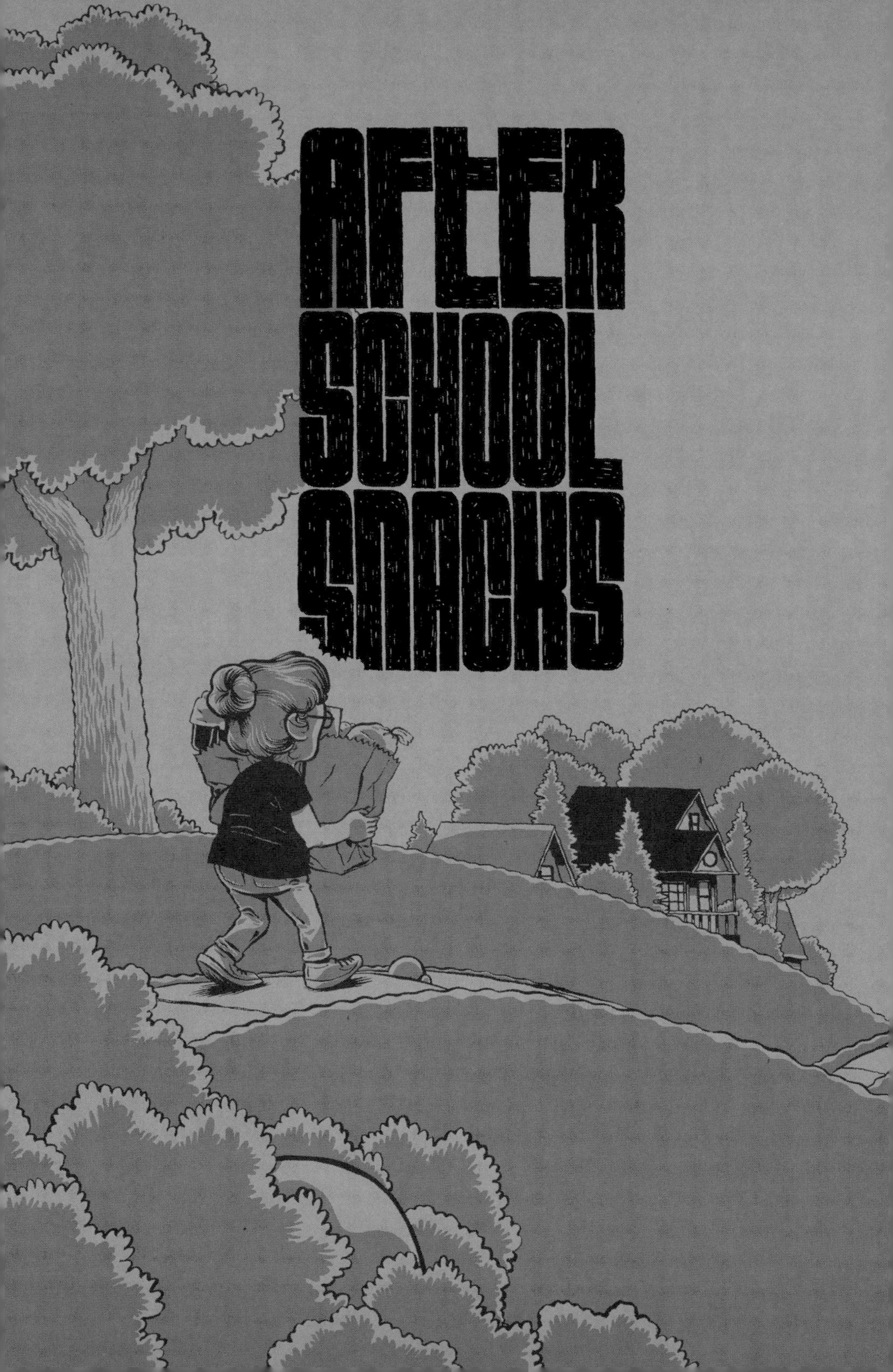
AFTER SCHOOL SNACKS

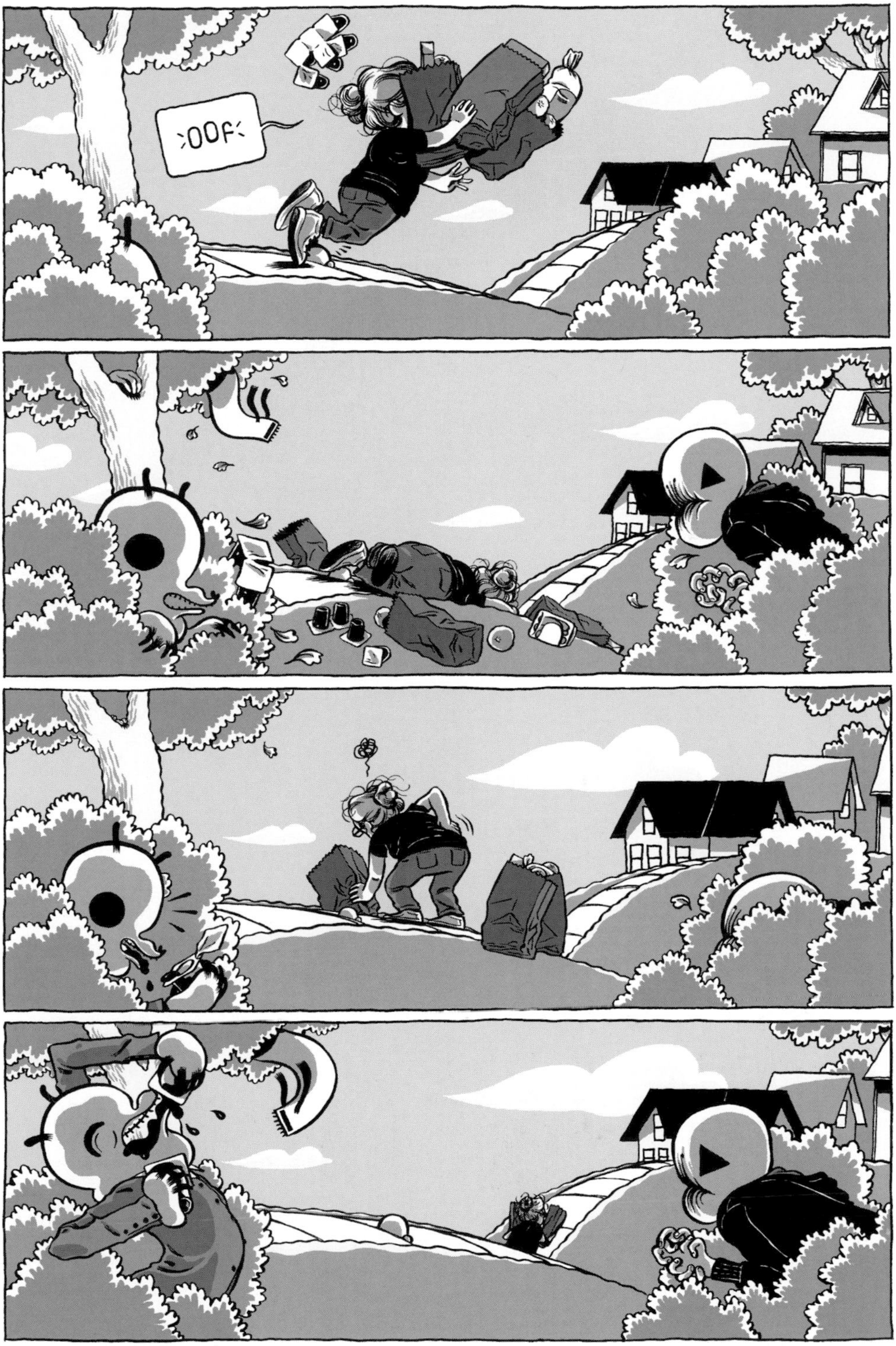
OOF

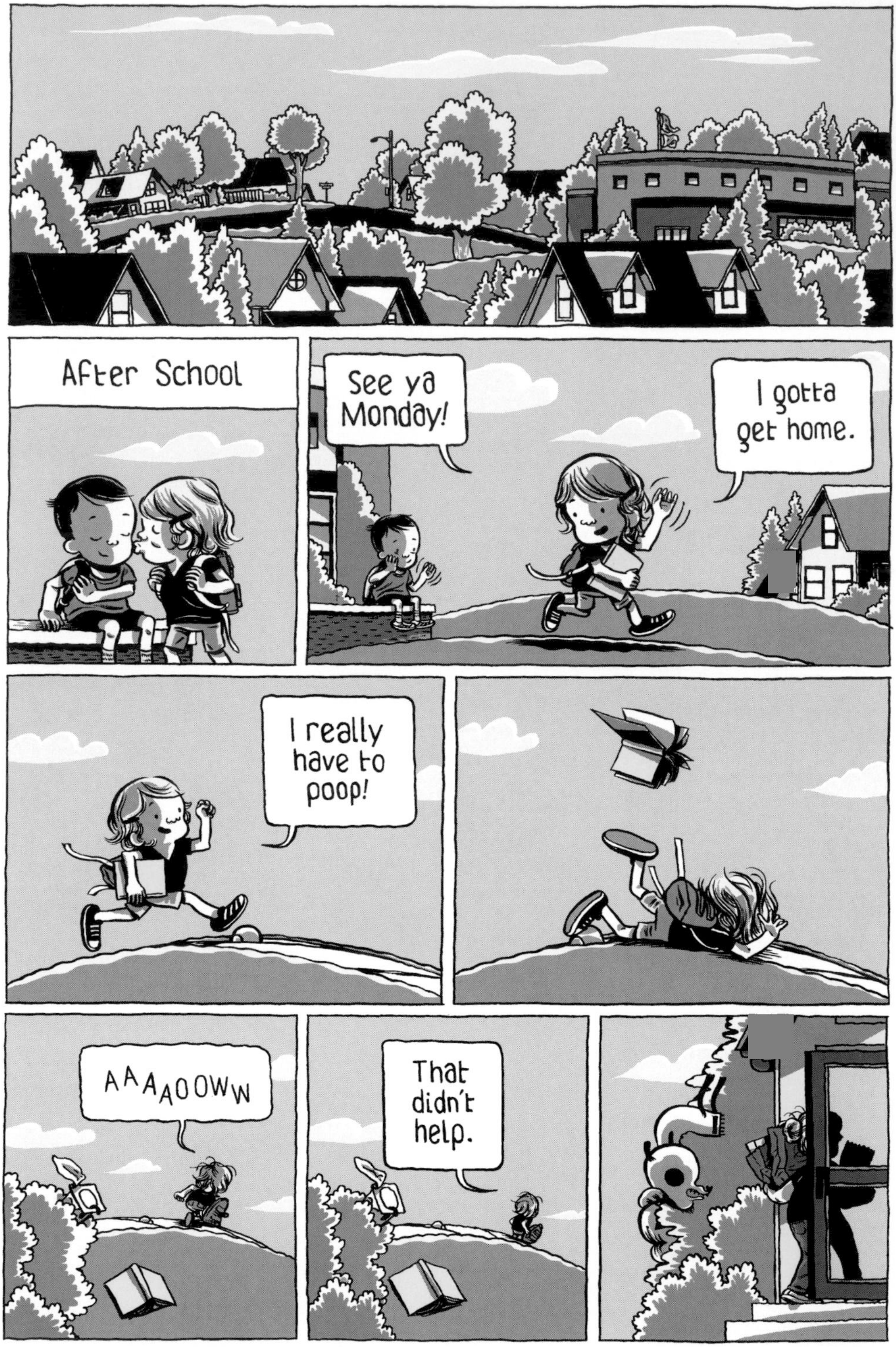
After School
See ya Monday!
I gotta get home.
I really have to poop!
AAAAOOWW
That didn't help.

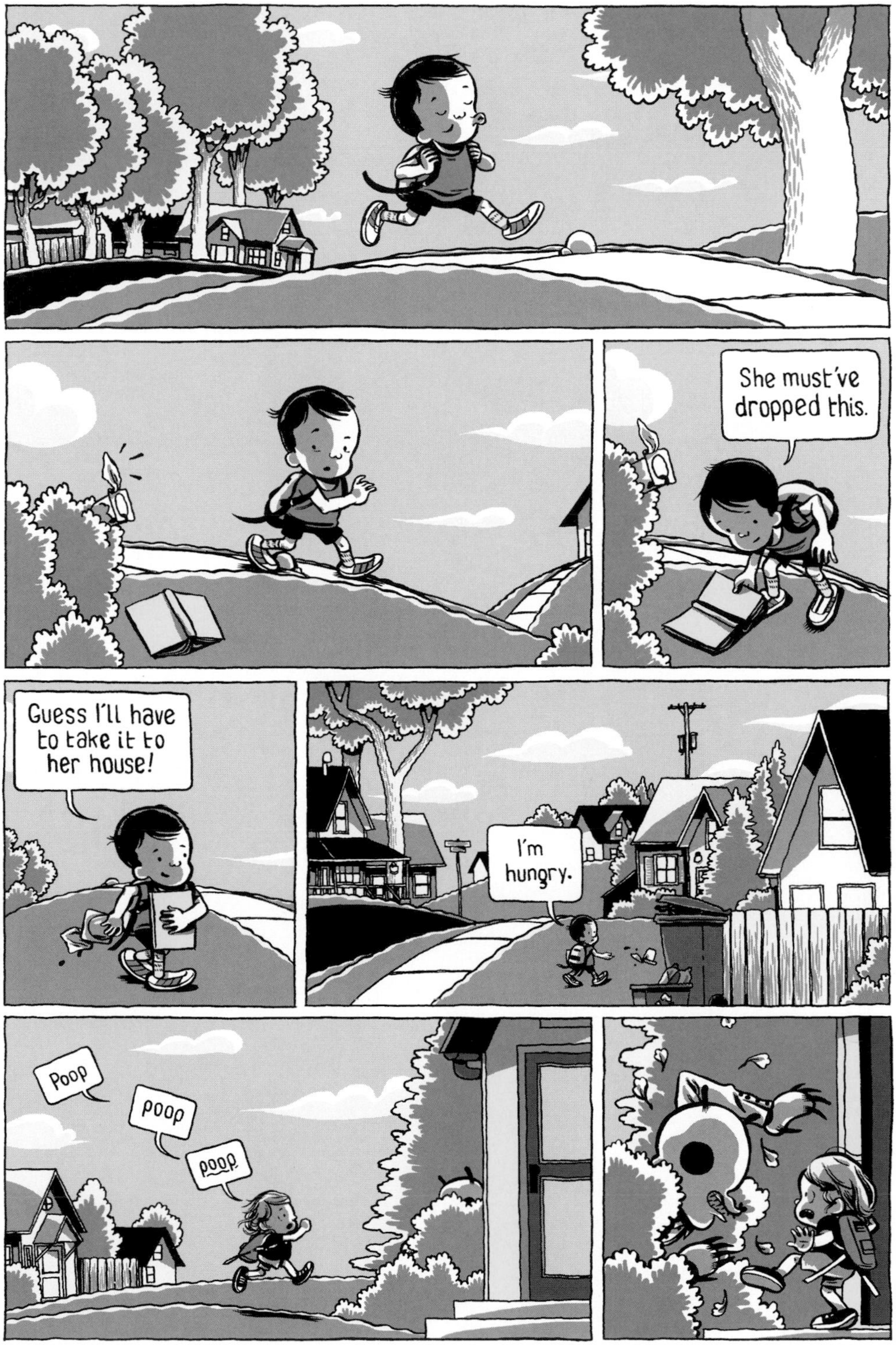
She must've dropped this.
Guess I'll have to take it to her house!
I'm hungry.
Poop
poop
poop

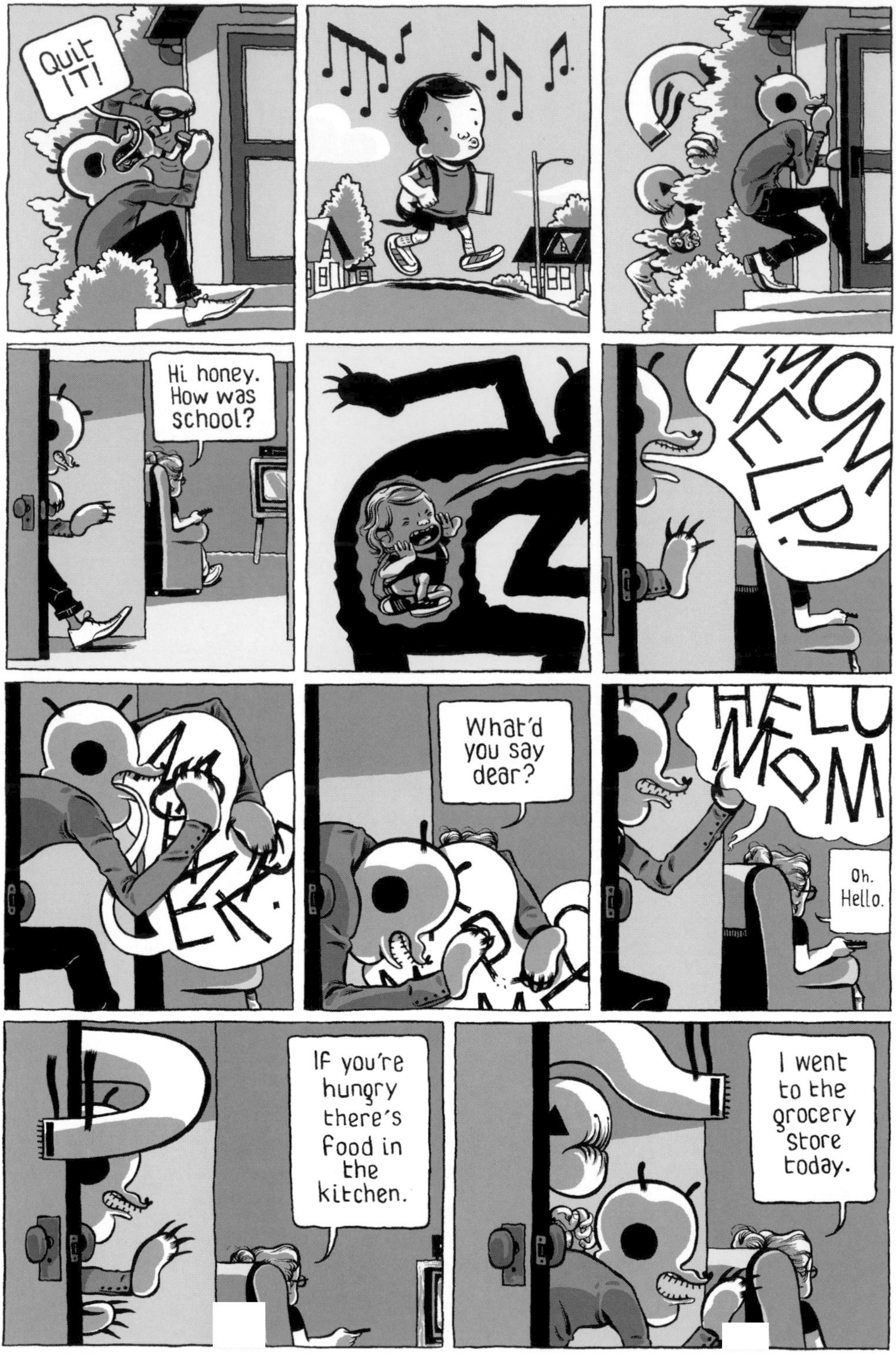
Quit IT!
Hi honey. How was school?
MOM HELP!
What'd you say dear?
HELLO MOM
Oh. Hello.
If you're hungry there's food in the kitchen.
I went to the grocery store today.

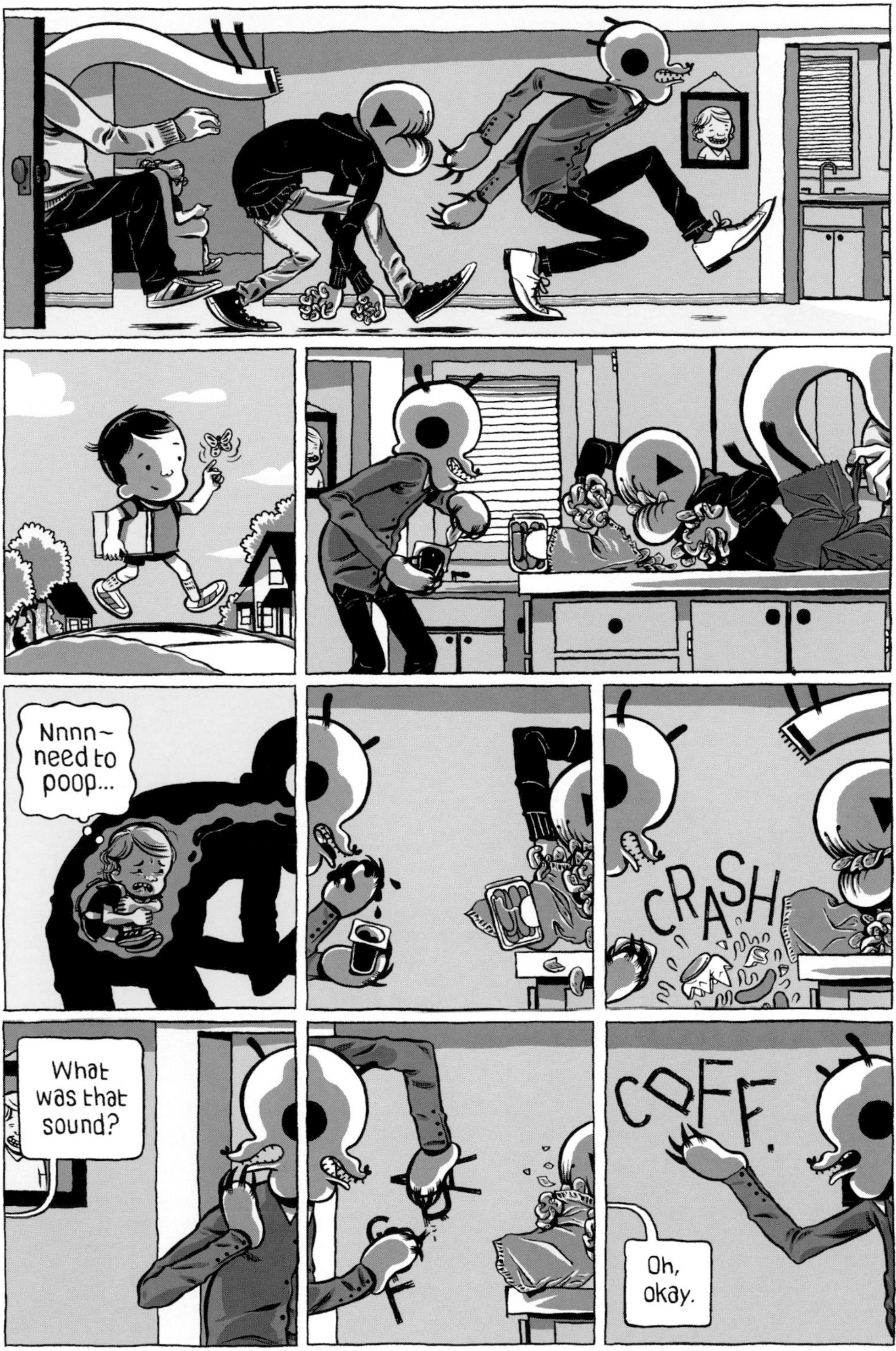
Nnnn~ need to poop...
CRASH
What was that sound?
COFF.
Oh, okay.

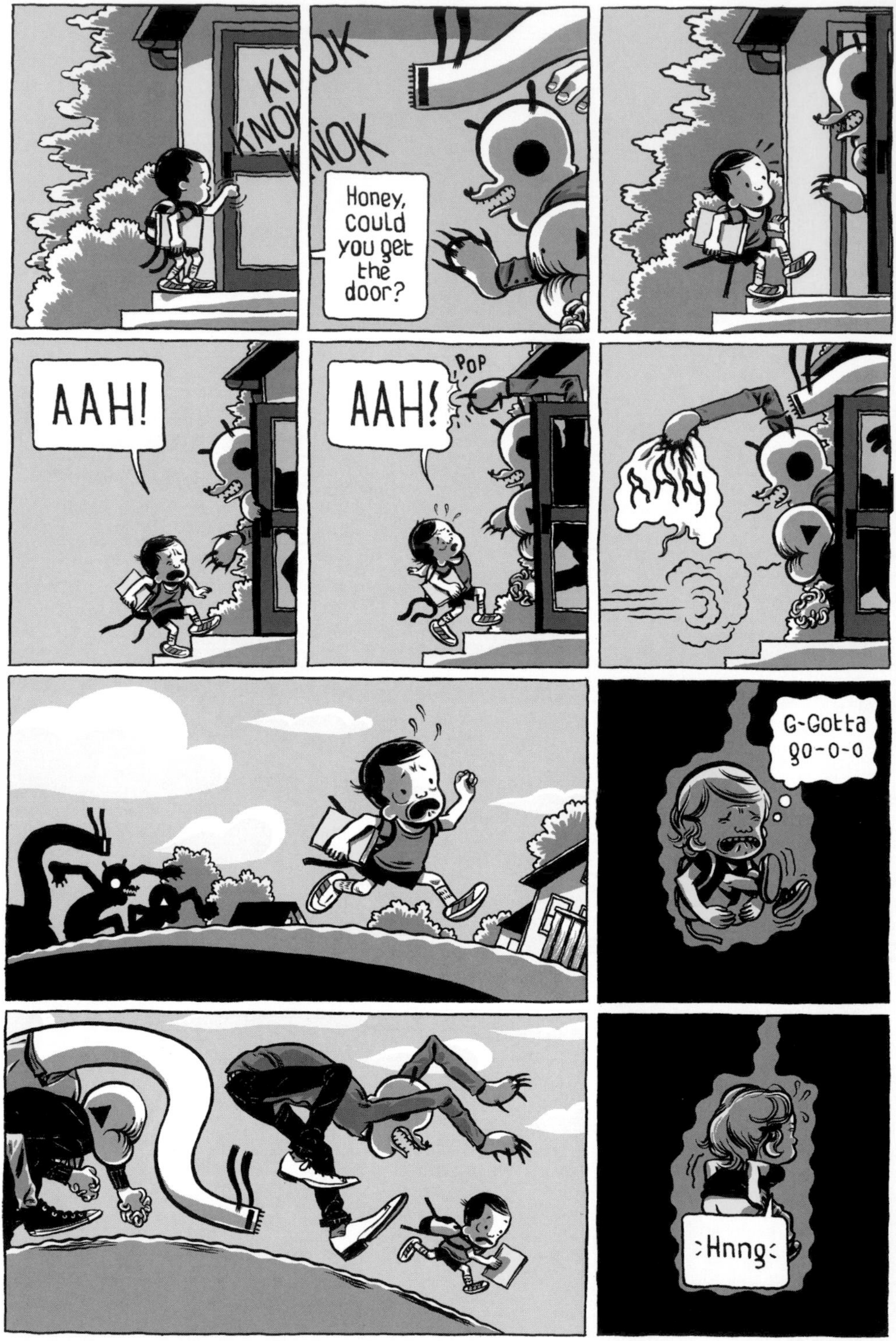
KNOK
KNOK
KNOK
Honey, could you get the door?
AAH!
POP
AAH!
AAH
G-Gotta go-o-o
Hnng

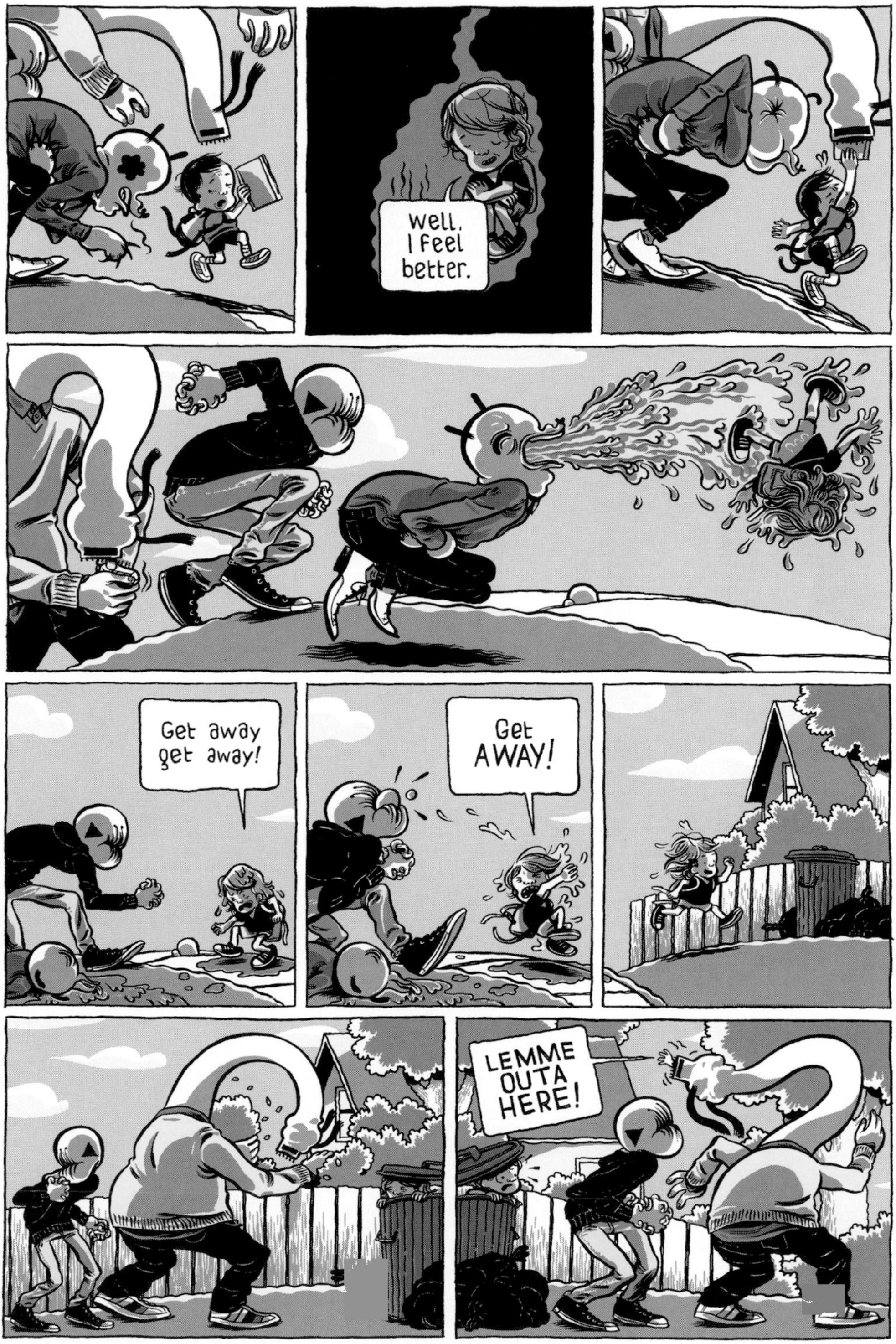
Well,
I feel
better.
Get away
get away!
Get
AWAY!
LEMME
OUTA
HERE!

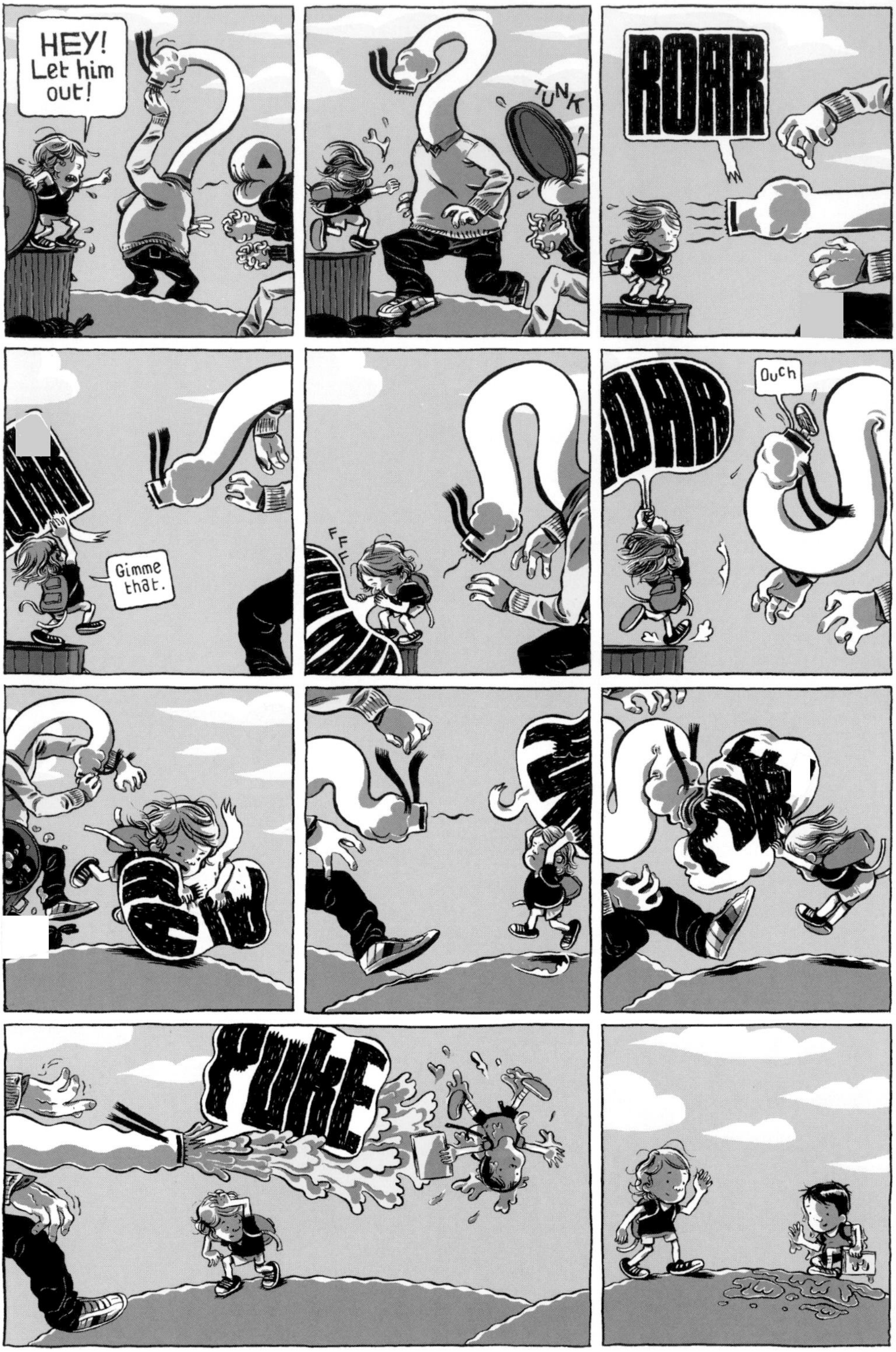
HEY! Let him out!
TUNK
ROAR
Gimme that.
FFF
Ouch
PUKE

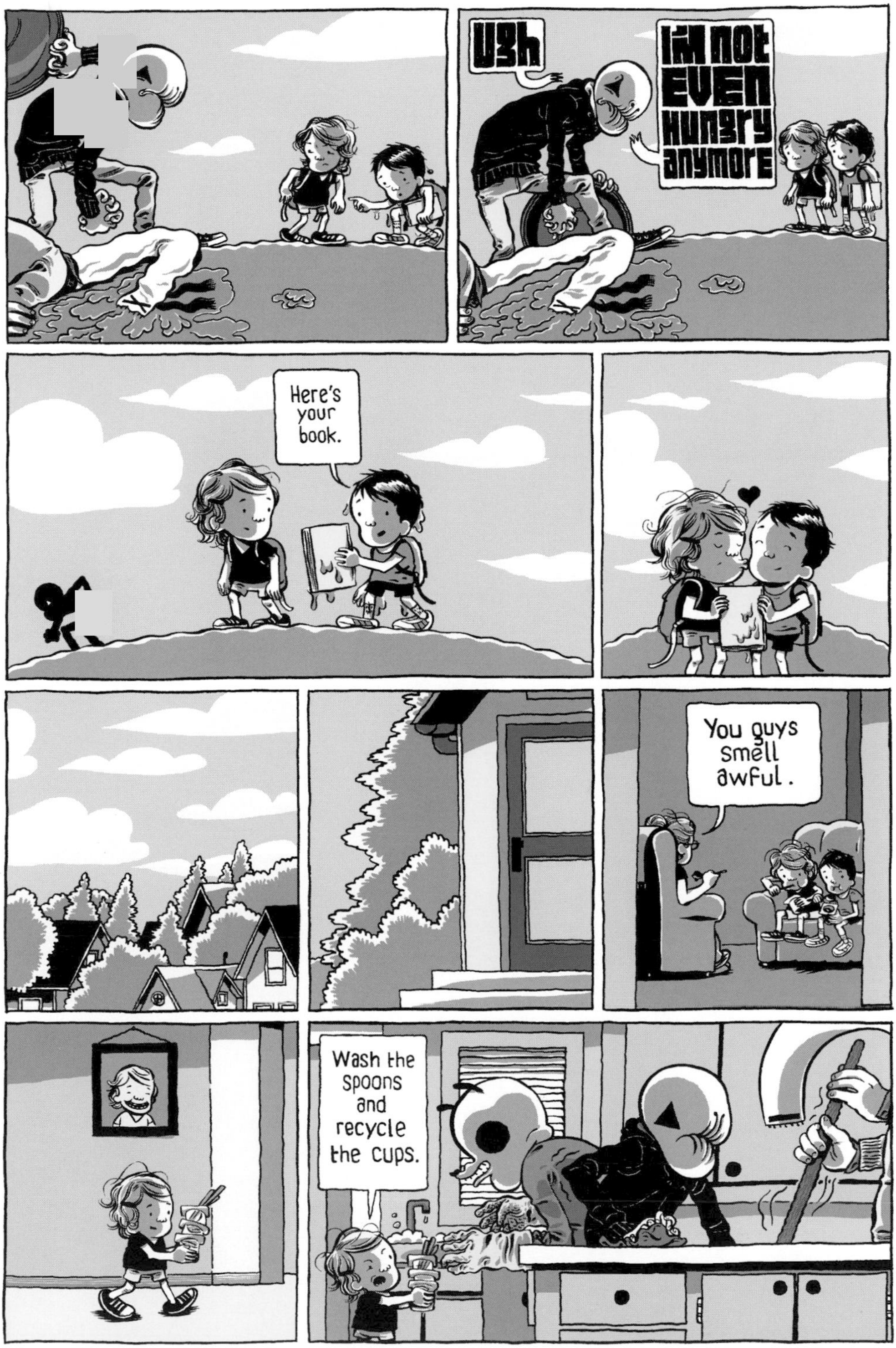
Ugh
I'M NOT EVEN HUNGRY ANYMORE
Here's your book.
You guys smell awful.
Wash the spoons and recycle the cups.

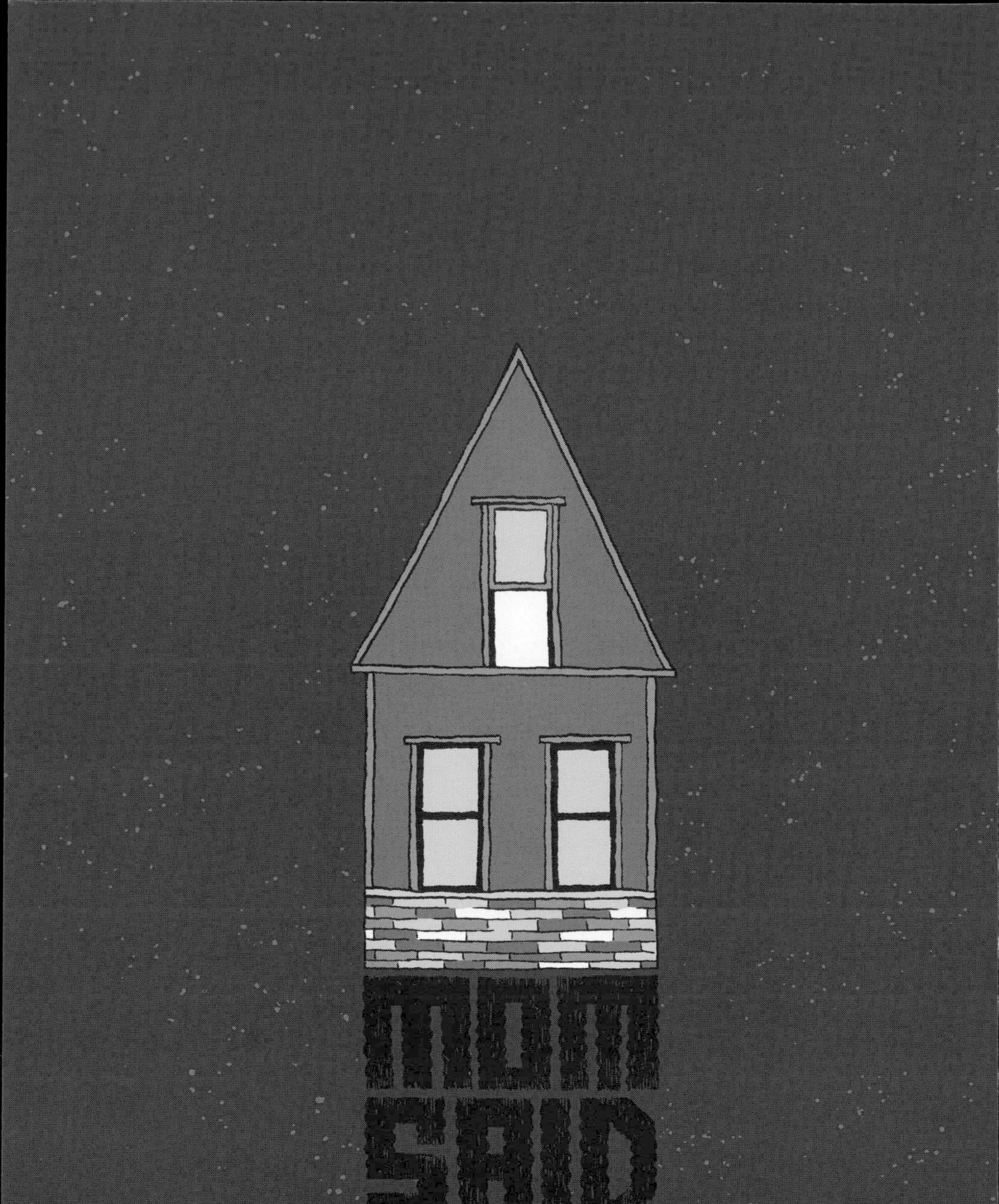
MOM
SAID

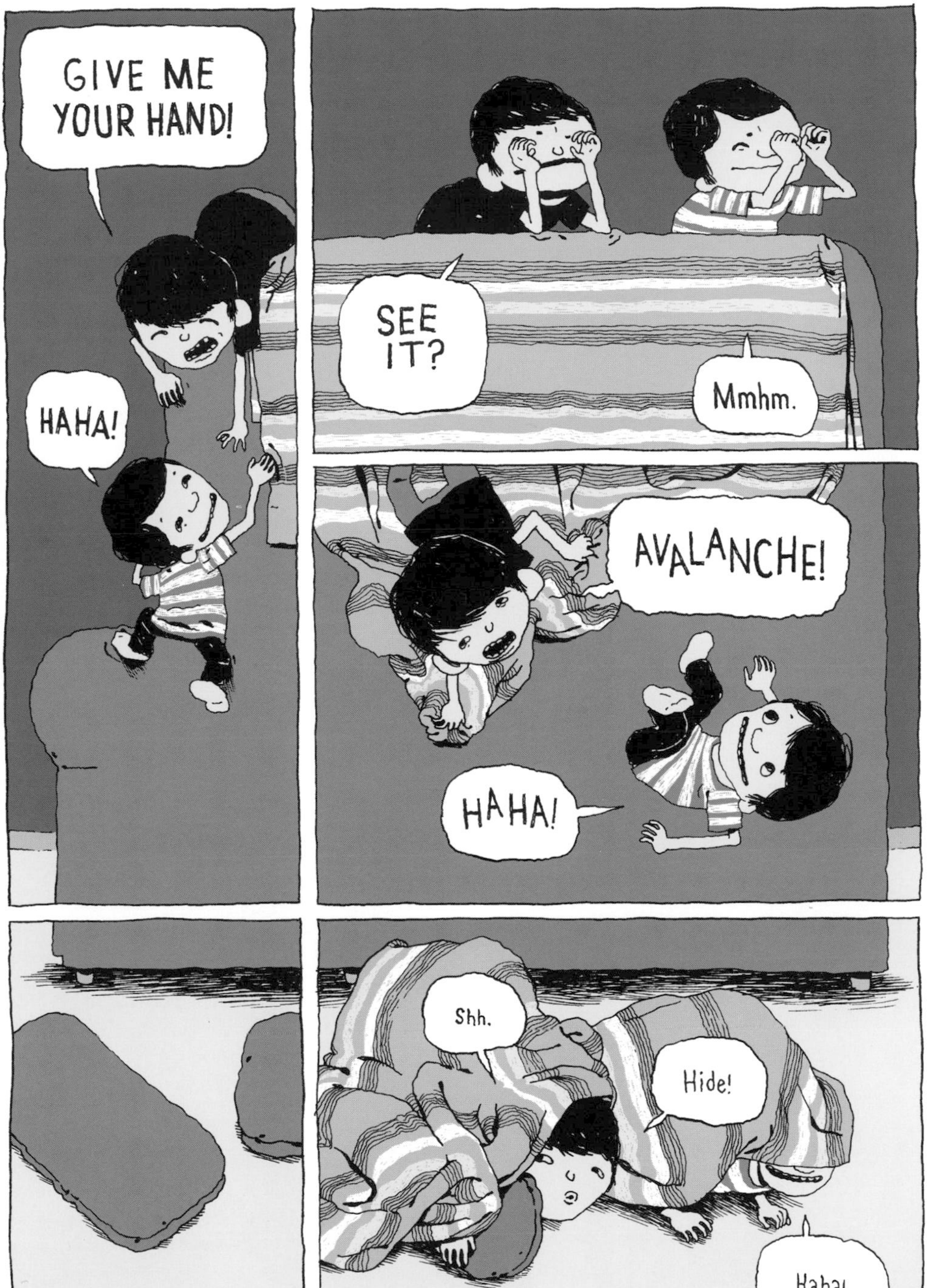
GIVE ME YOUR HAND!
HAHA!
SEE IT?
Mmhm.
AVALANCHE!
HAHA!
Shh.
Hide!
Haha!

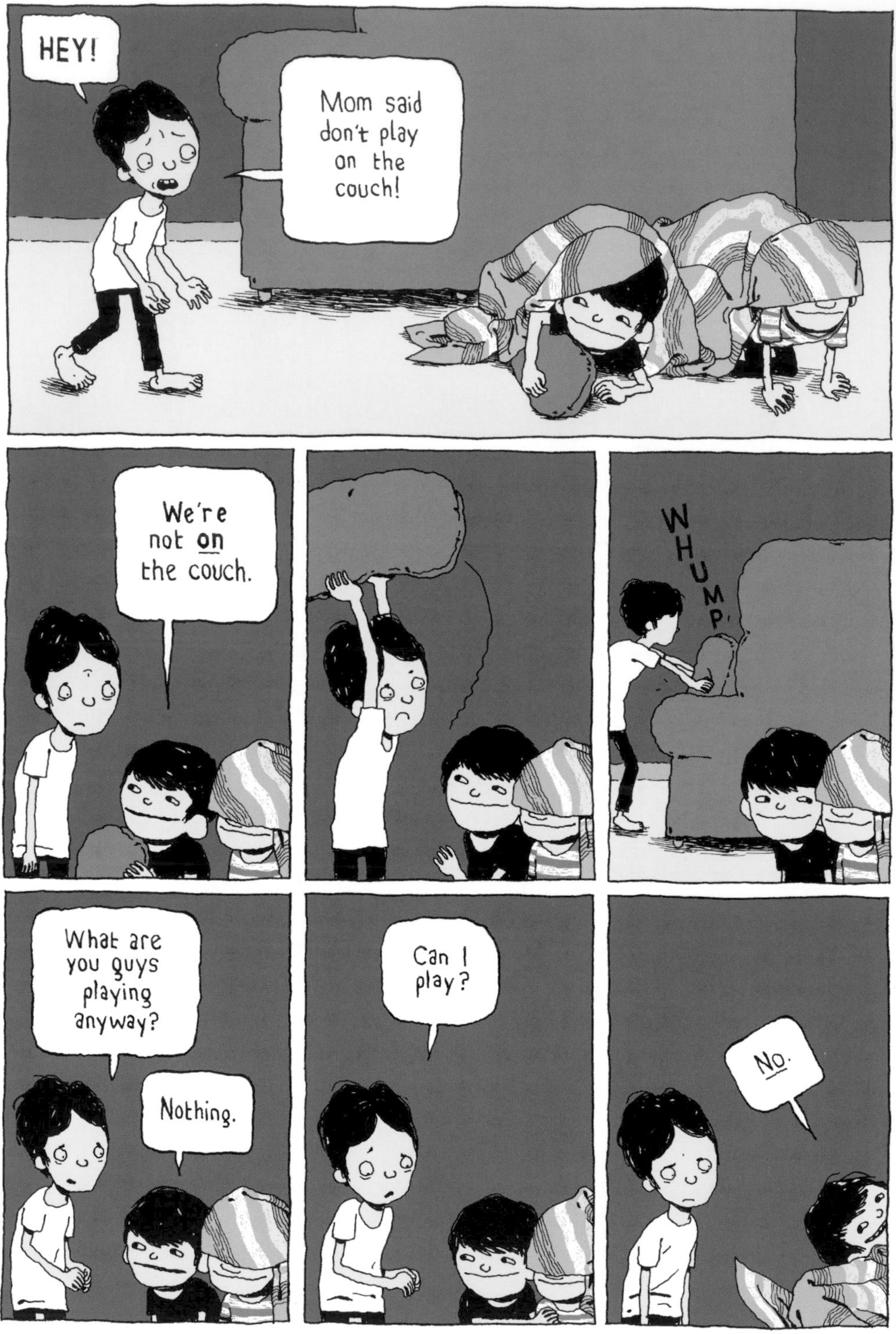
HEY!
Mom said don't play on the couch!
We're not on the couch.
WHUMP
What are you guys playing anyway?
Nothing.
Can I play?
No.

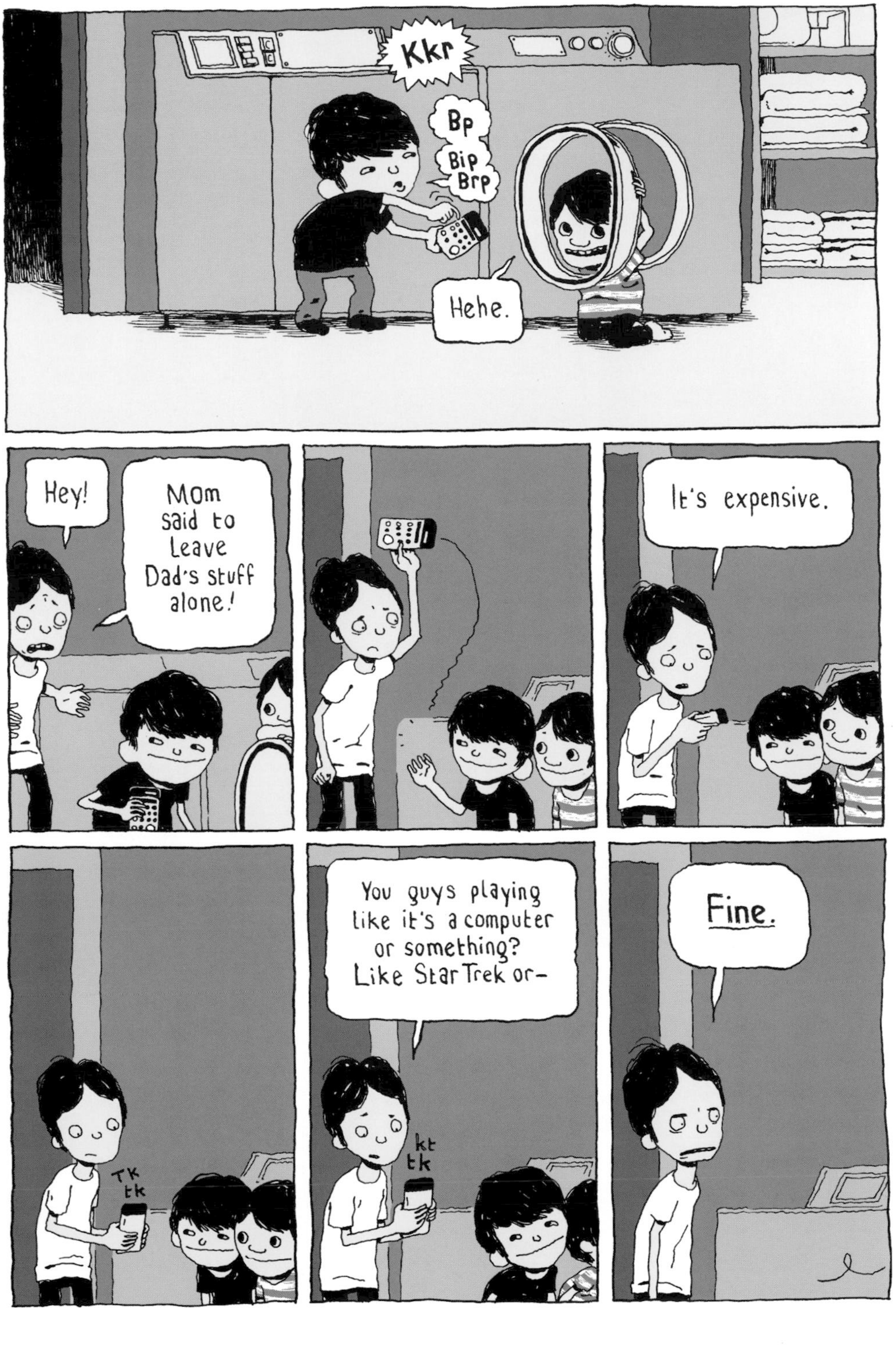
Kkr
Bp
Bip Brp
Hehe.
Hey!
Mom said to leave Dad's stuff alone!
It's expensive.
TK tk
You guys playing like it's a computer or something? Like Star Trek or–
kt tk
Fine.

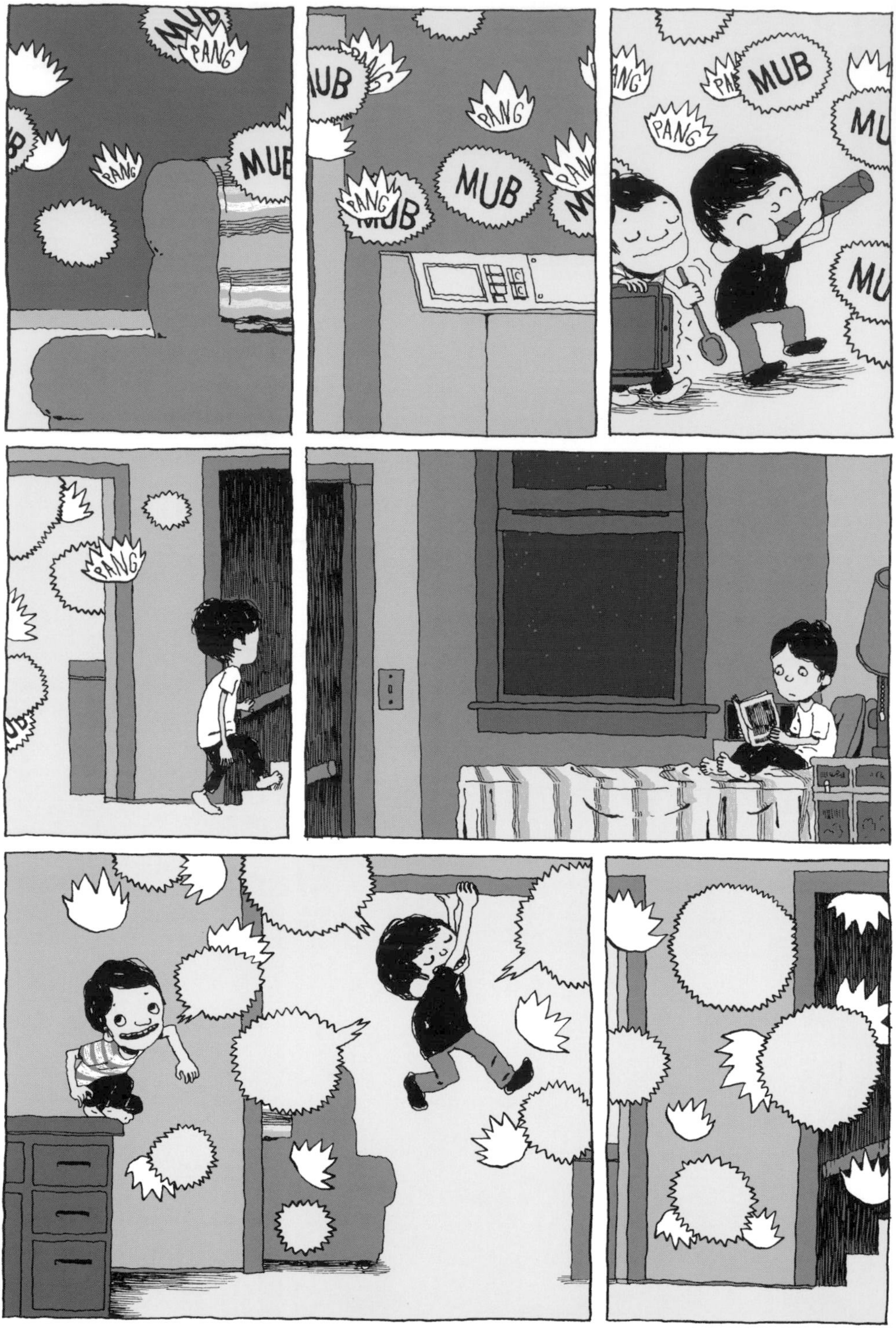
MUB
PANG
PANG
MUB
PANG
MUB
PANG
MUB
PANG
PANG
PANG

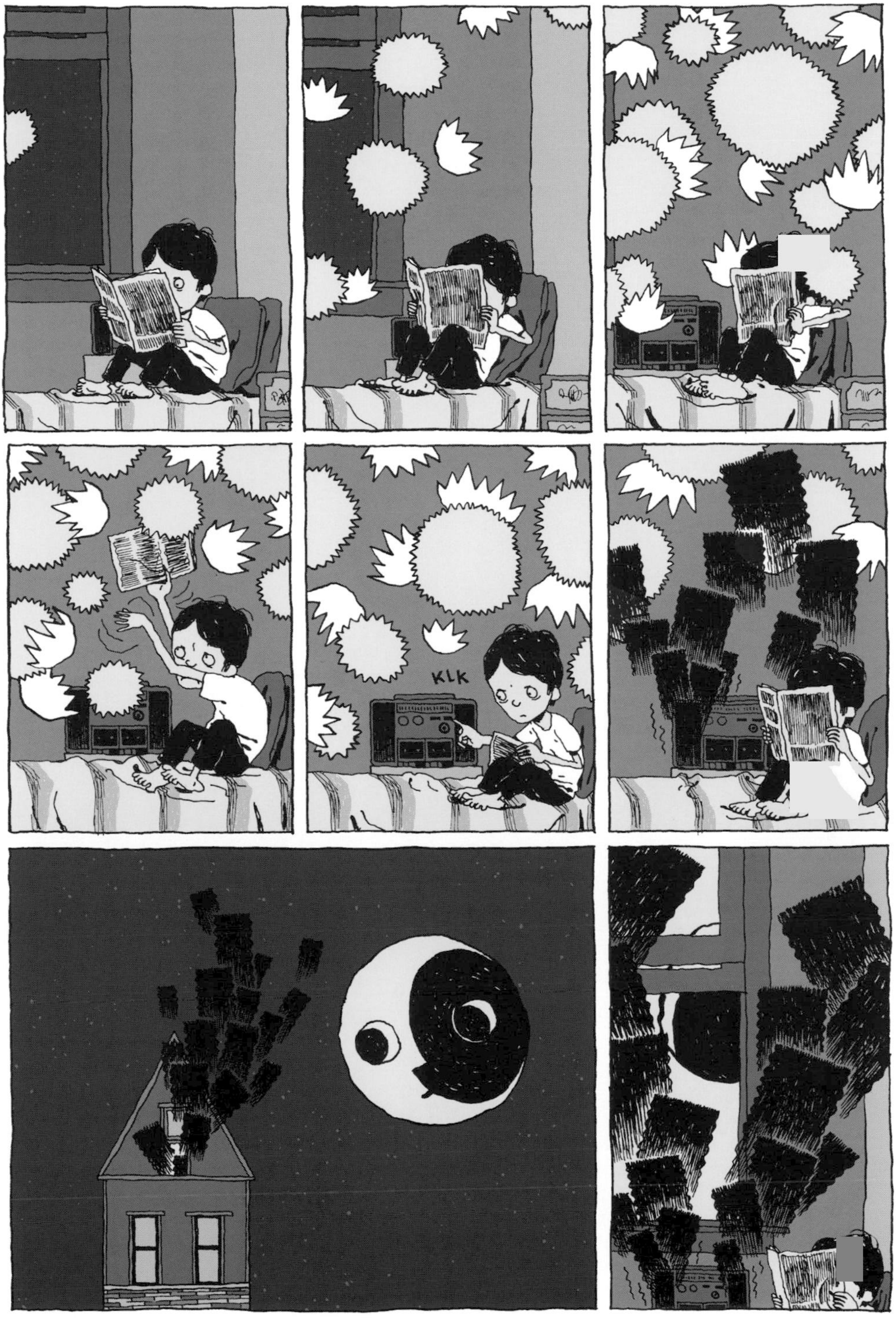
KLK

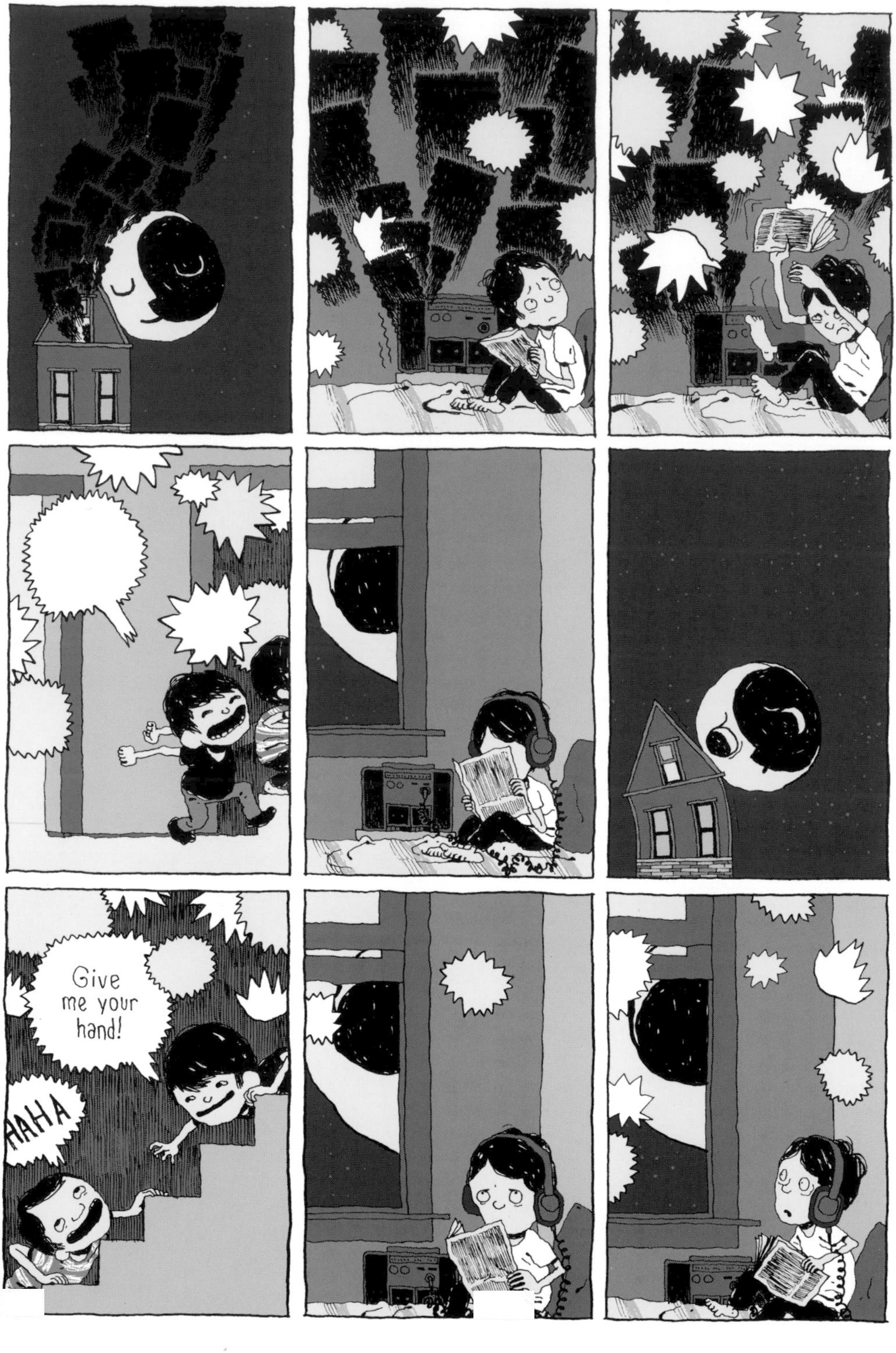
Give me your hand!
HAHA

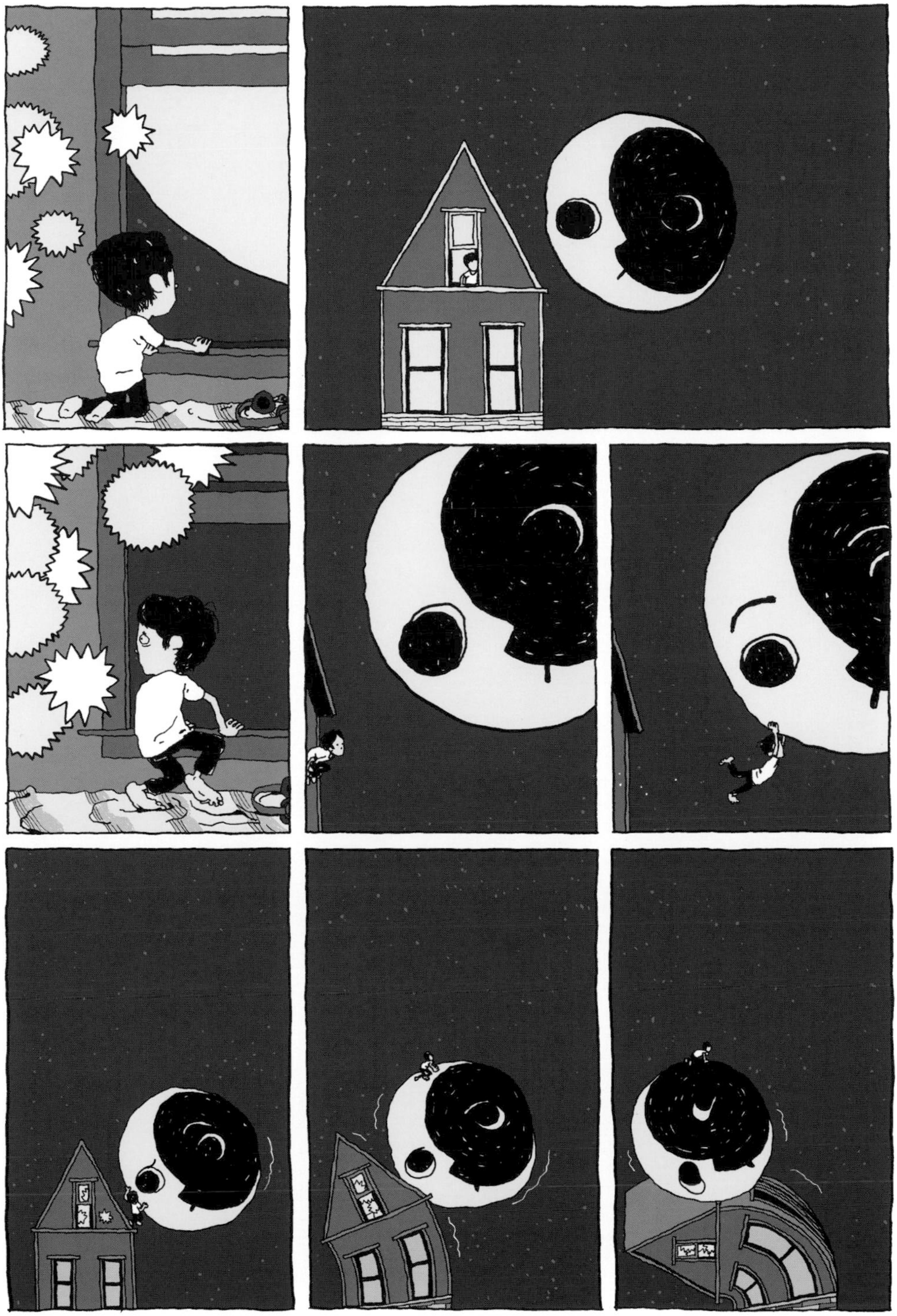

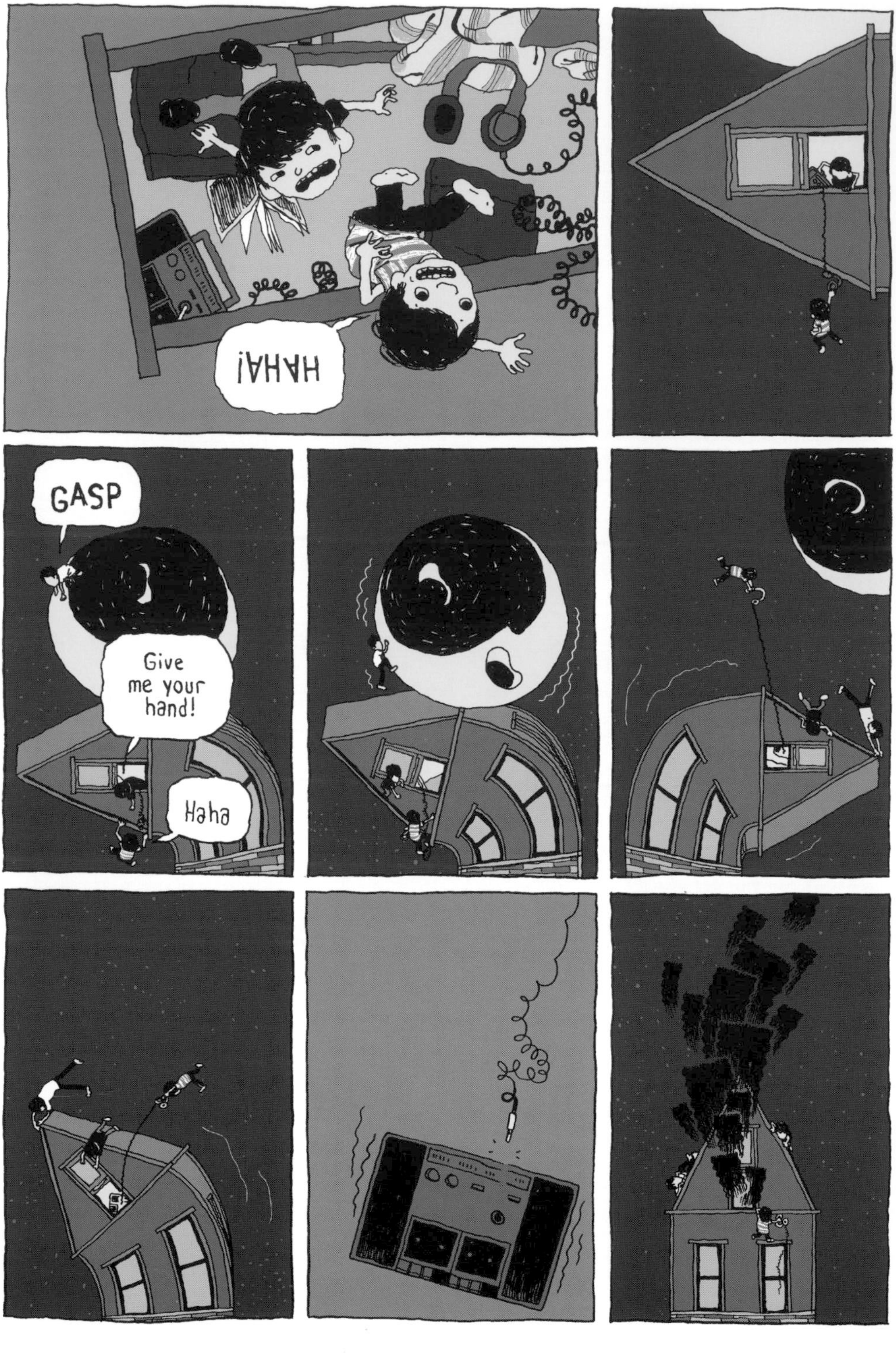
HAHA!
GASP
Give me your hand!
Haha

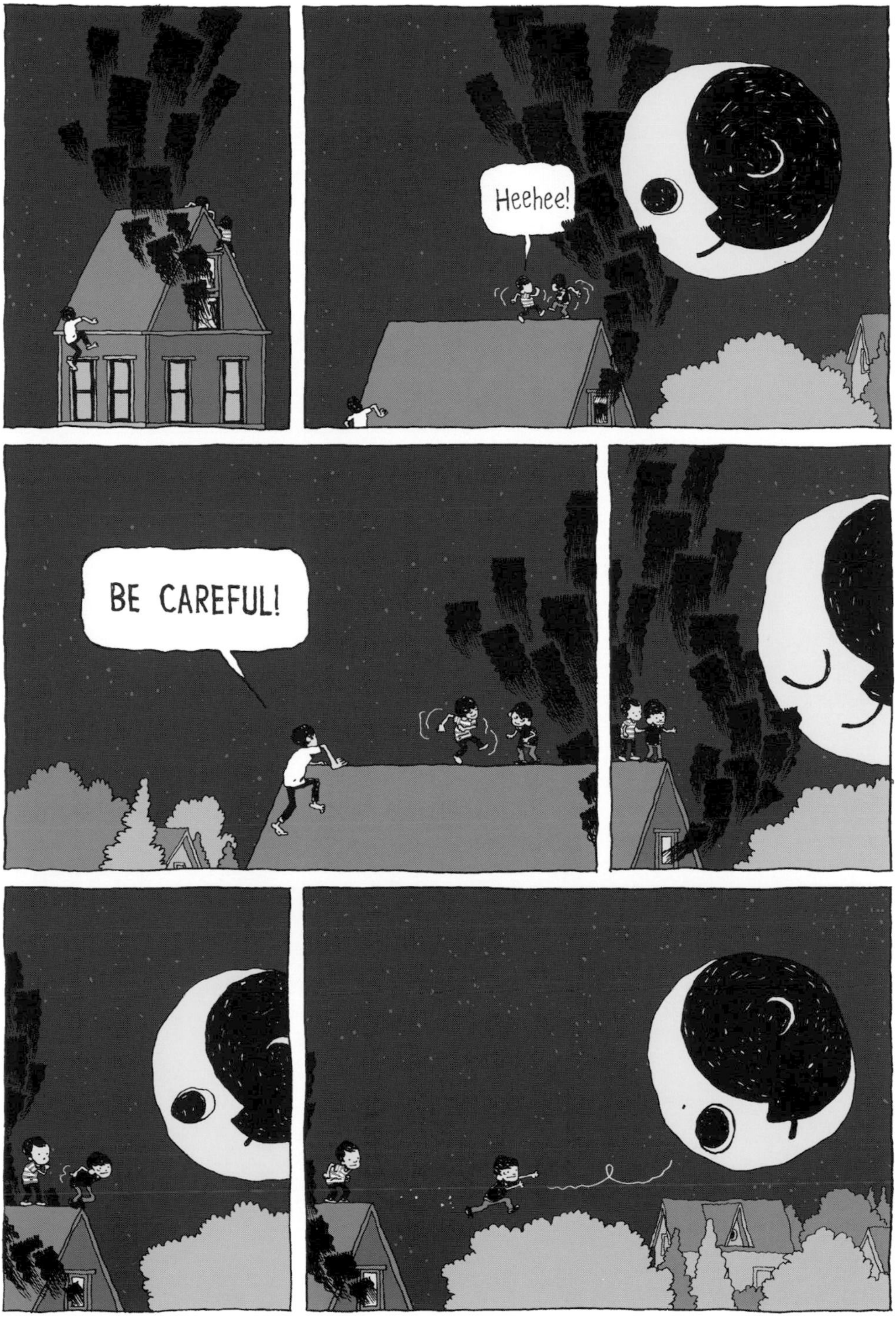
Heehee!
BE CAREFUL!

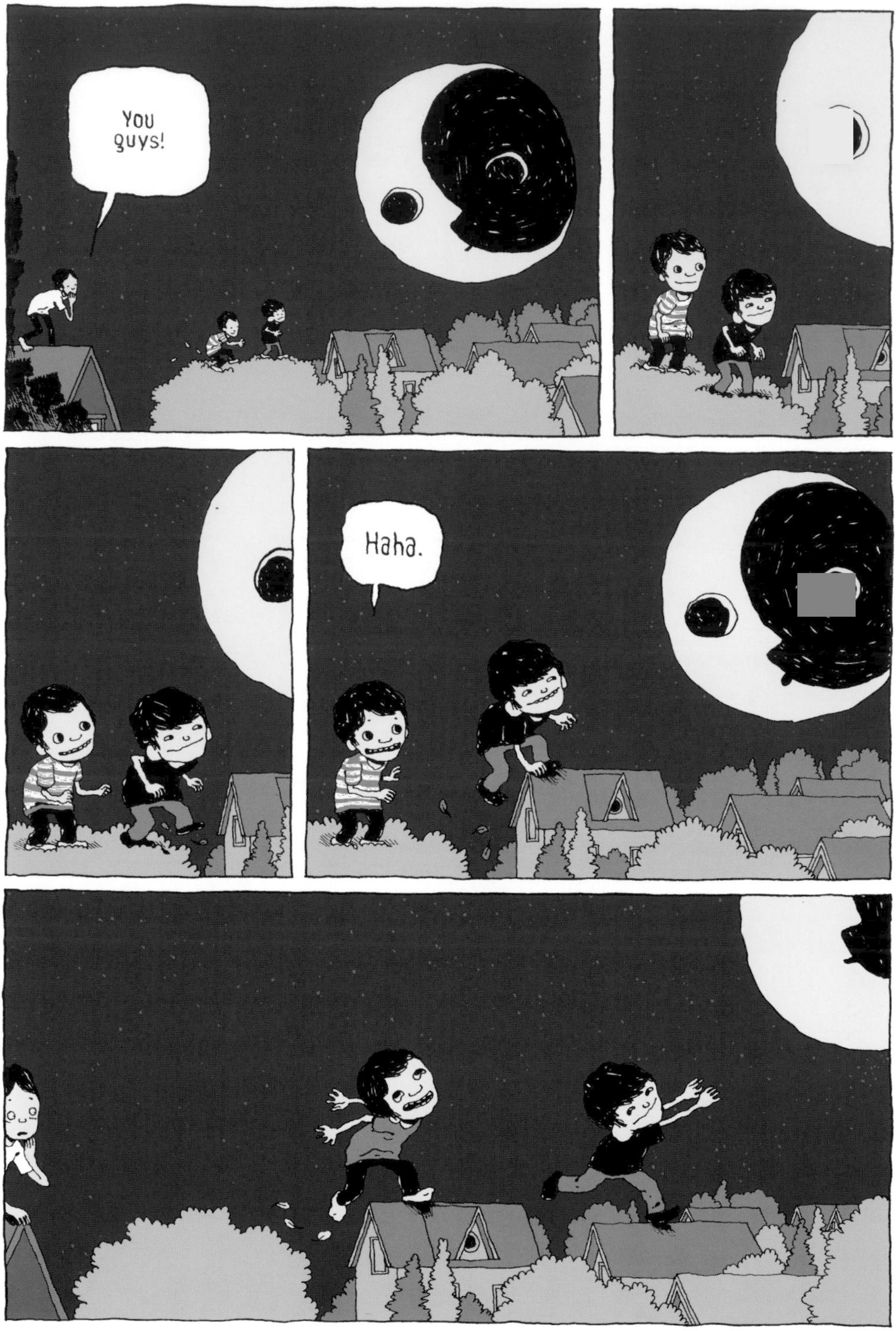
You guys!
Haha.

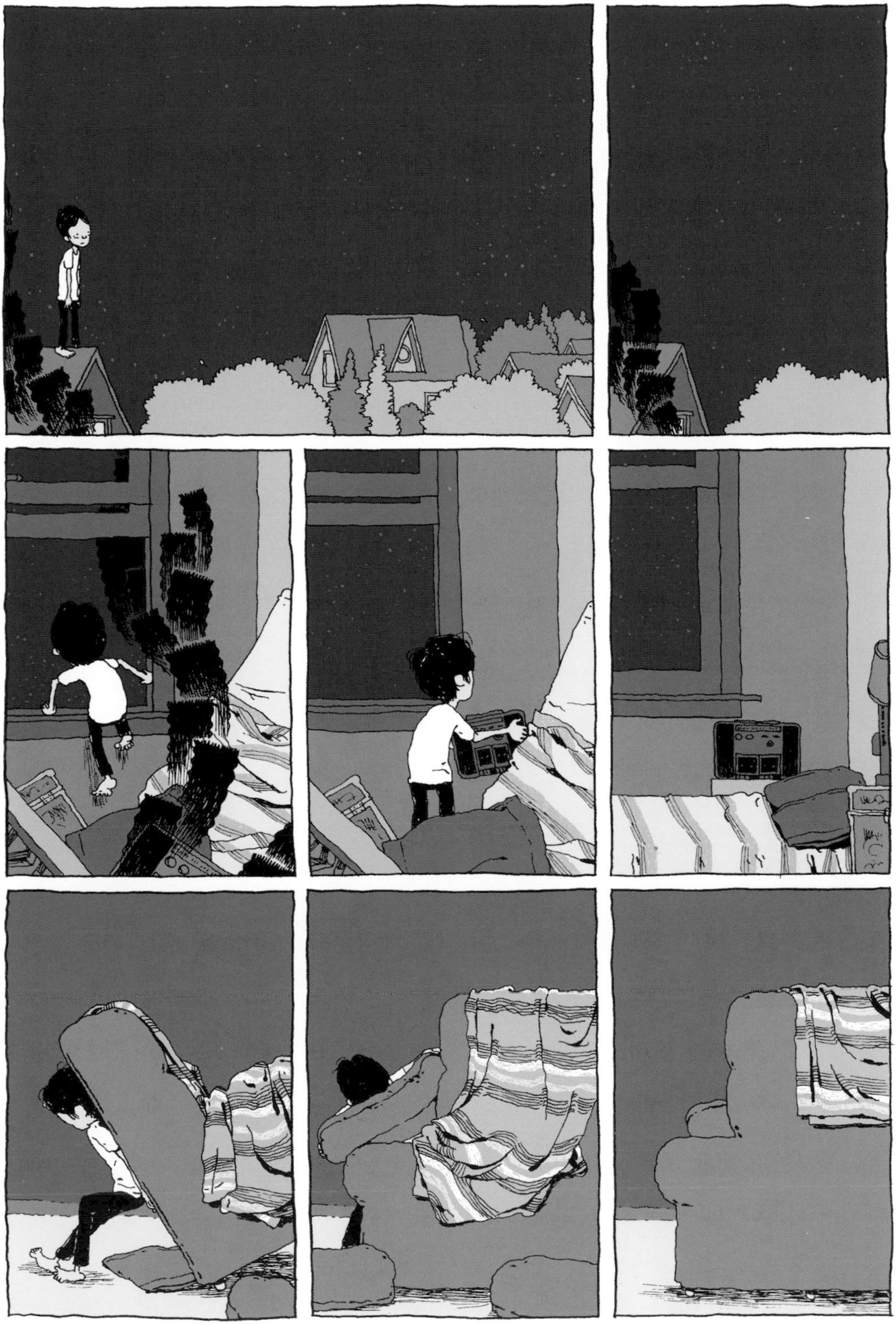

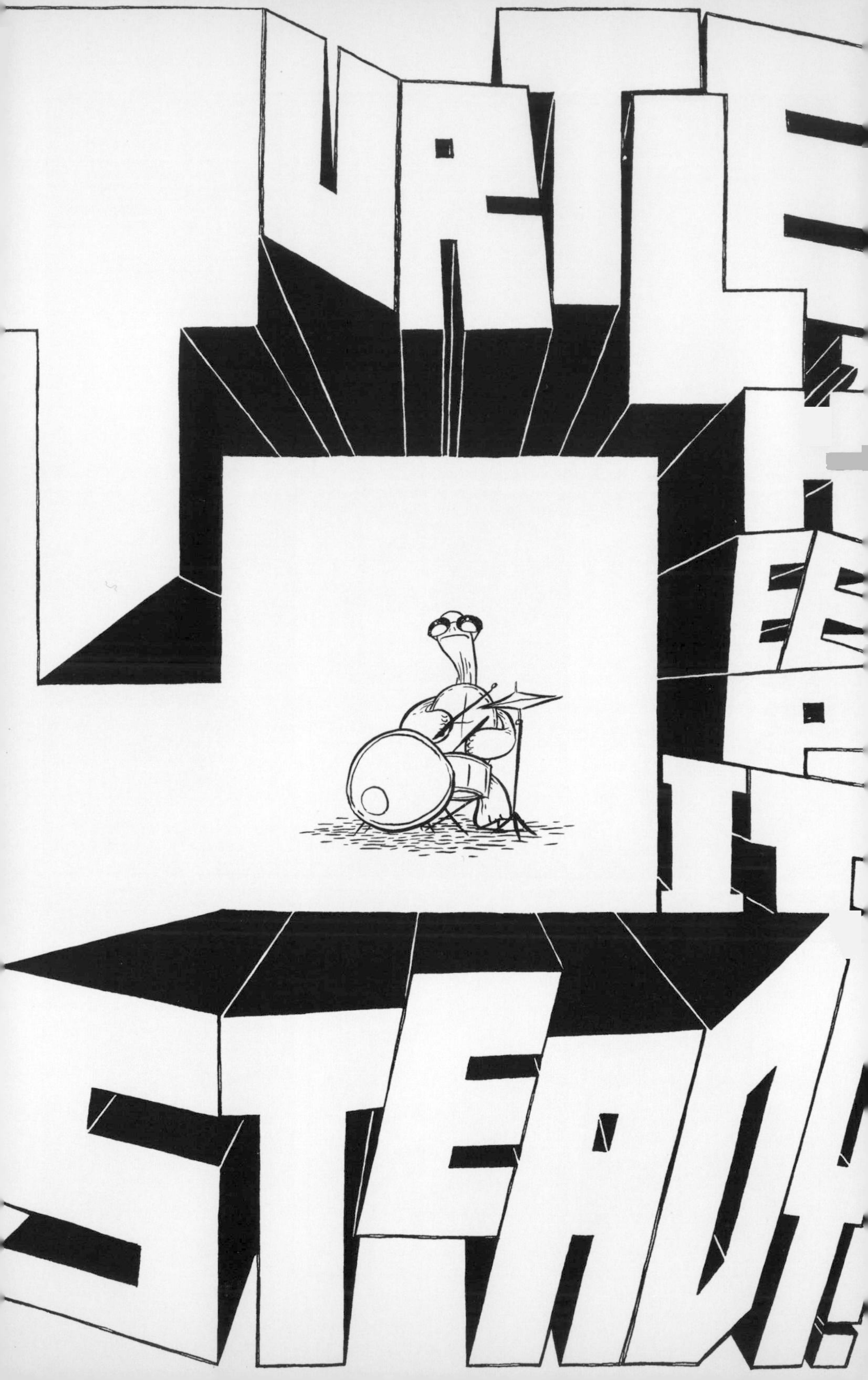

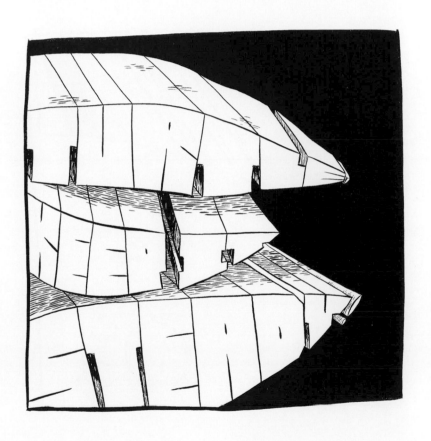

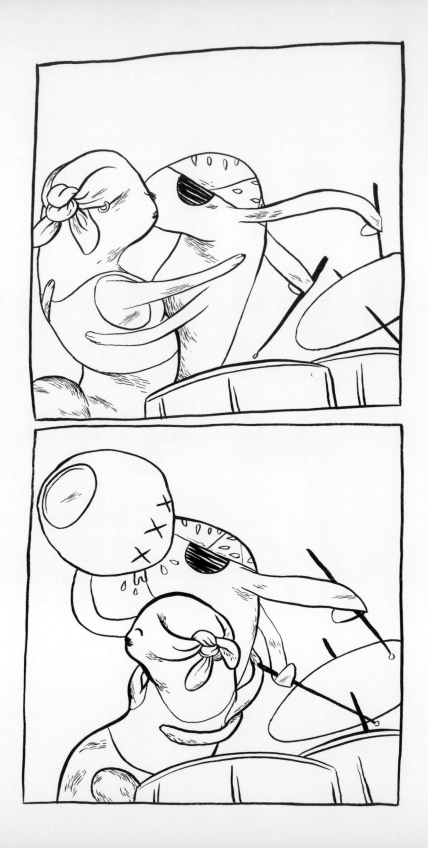

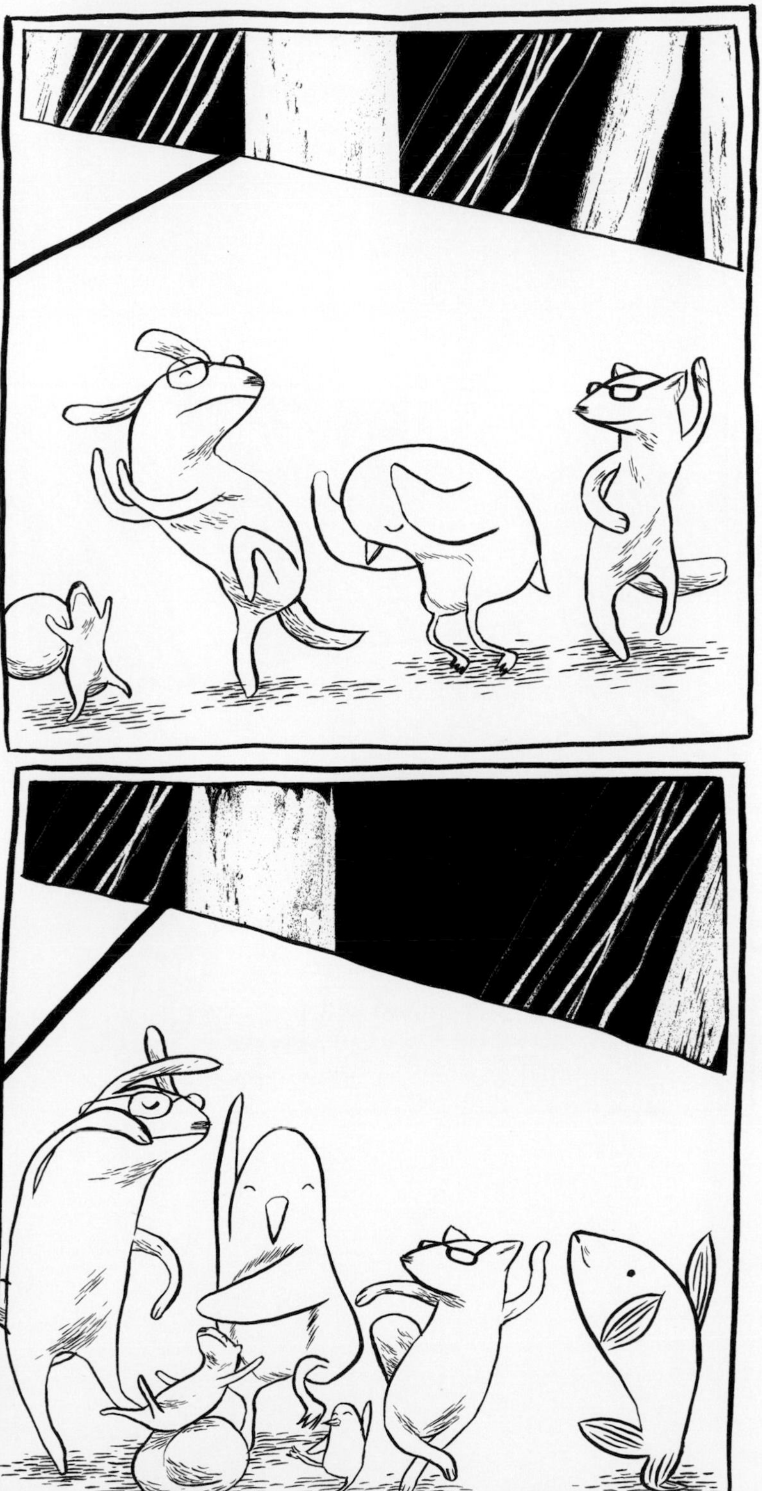

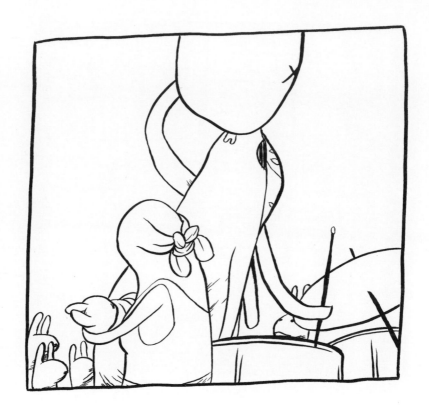

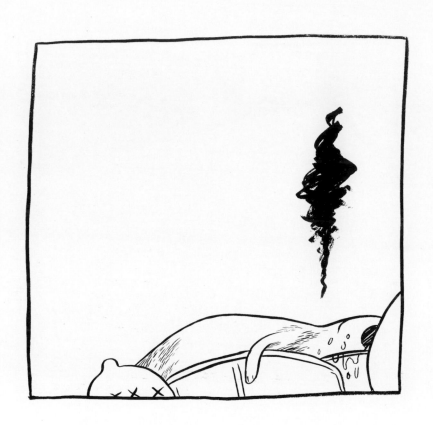

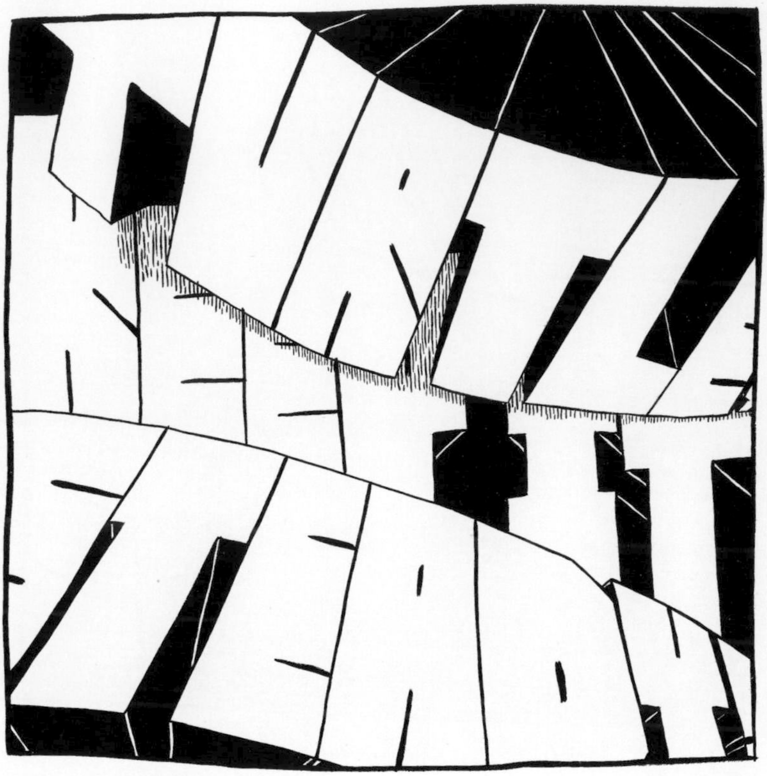
TURTLE
STEADY

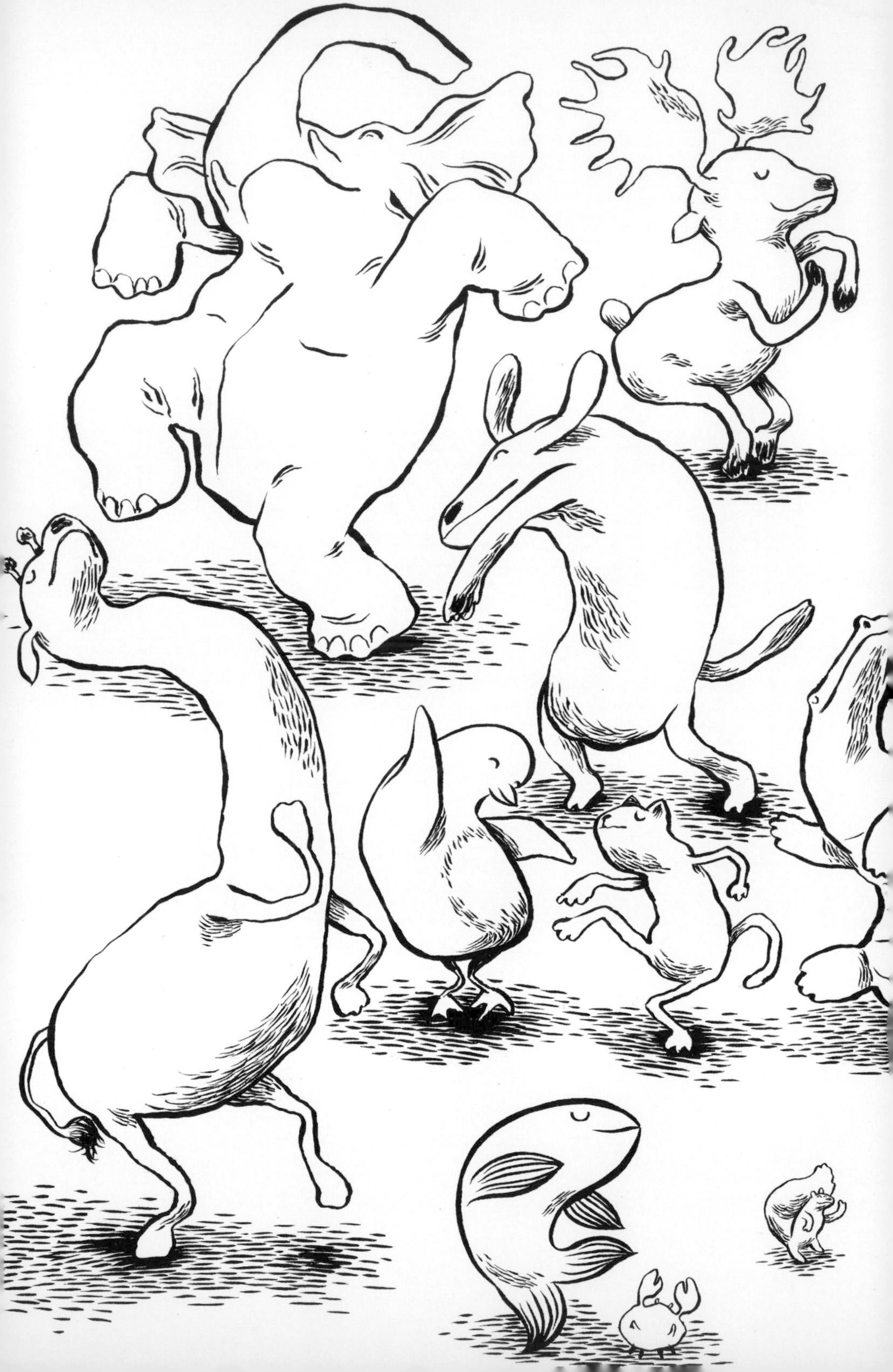

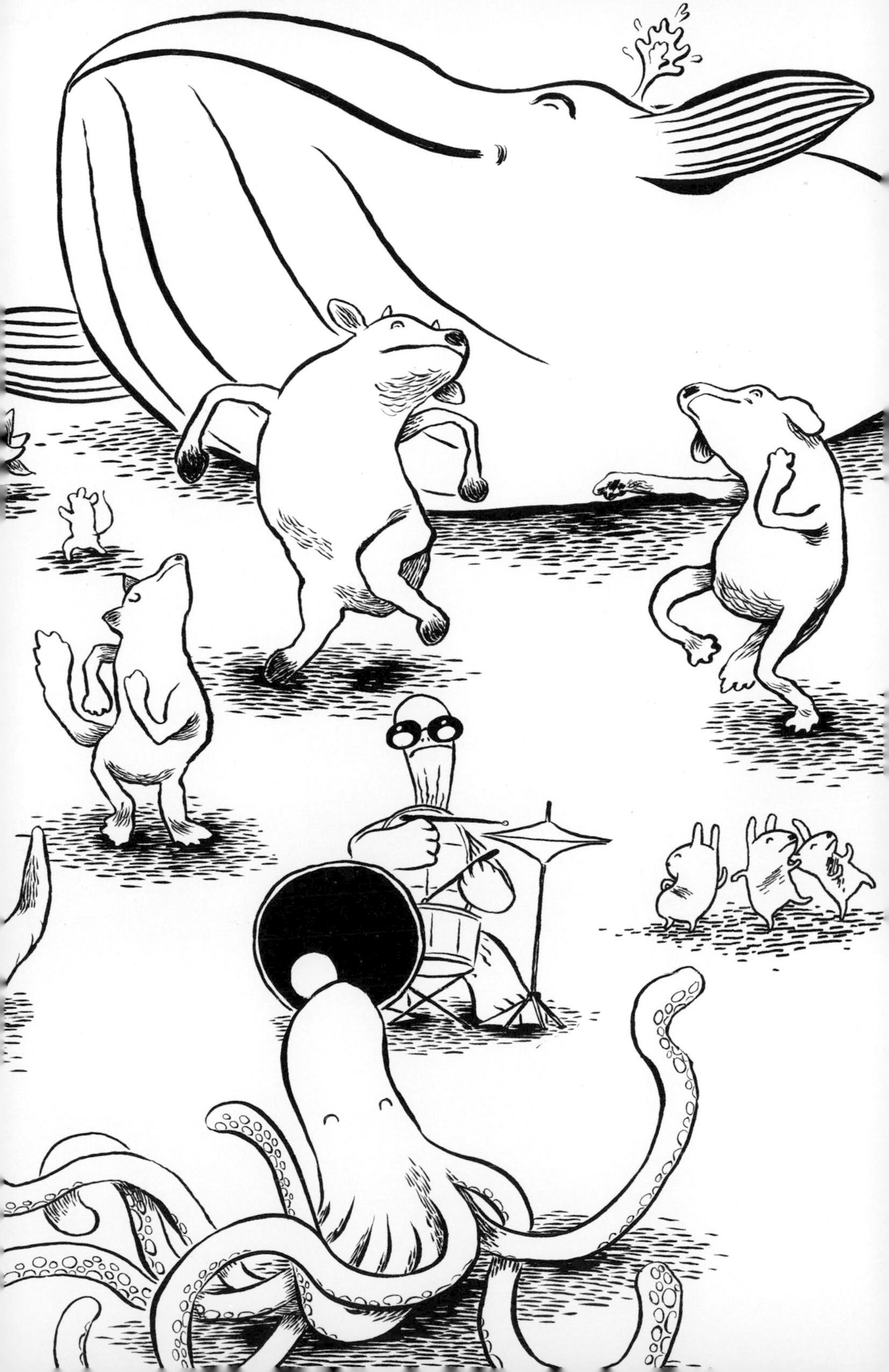

PSR

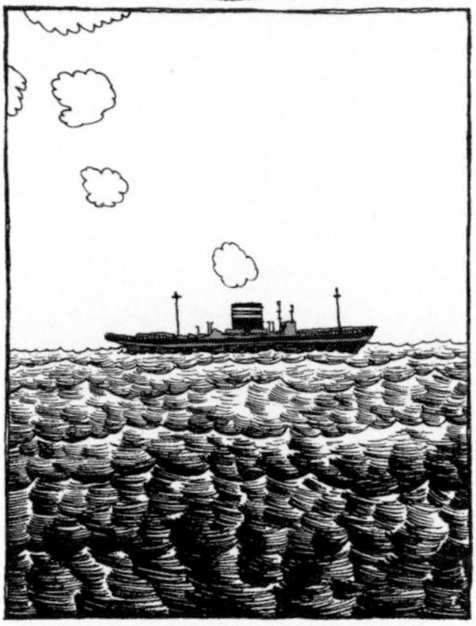

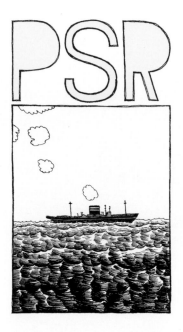

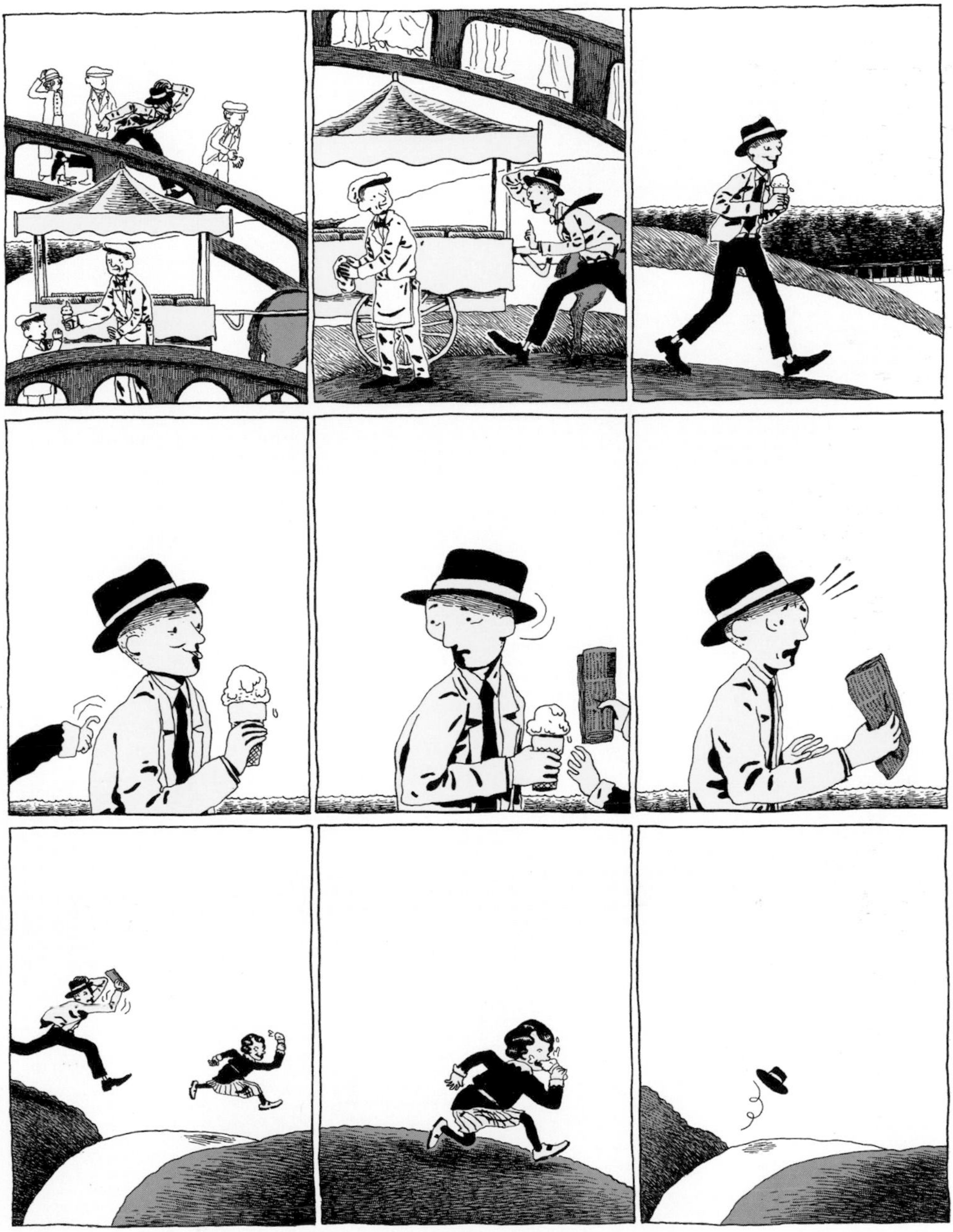

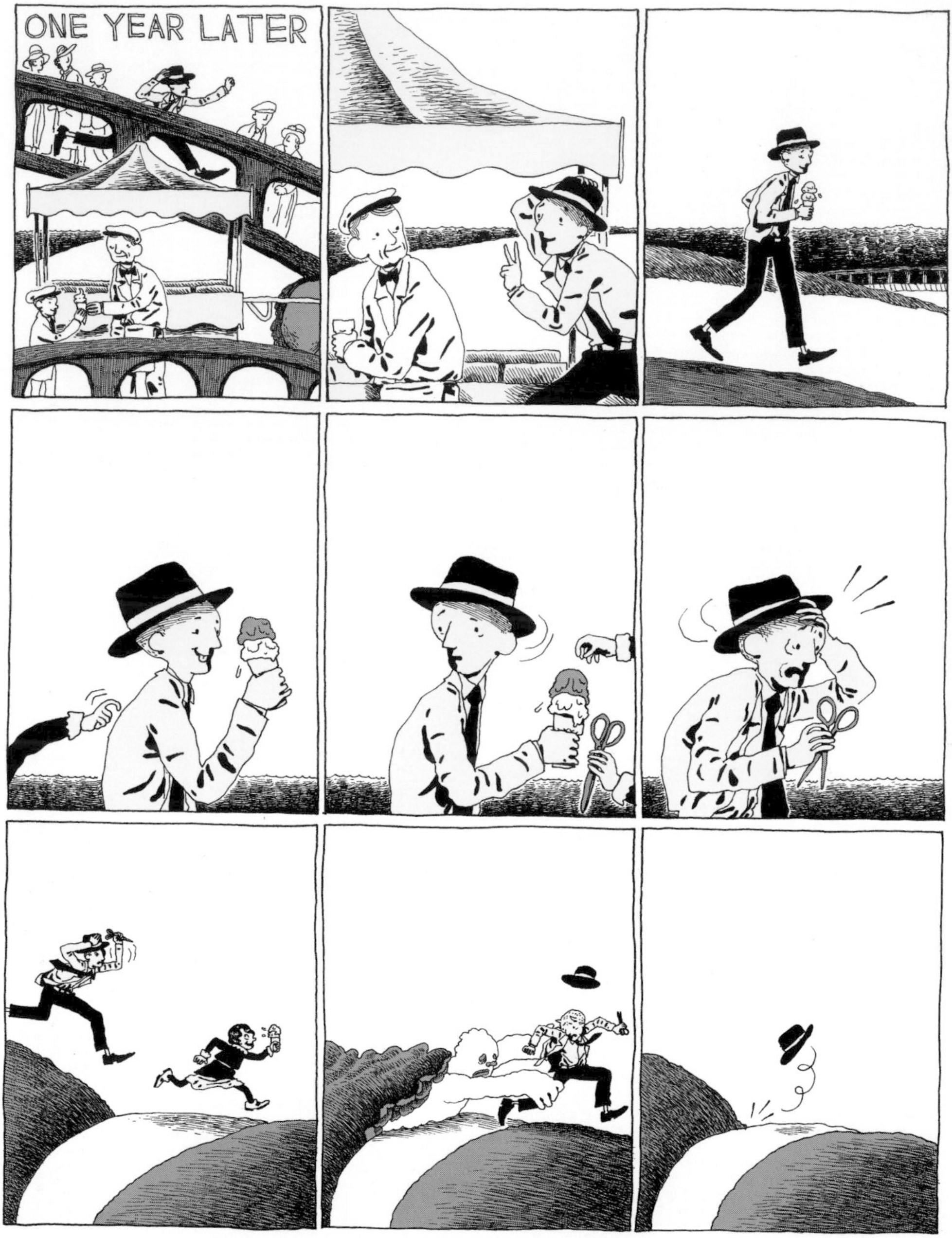
ONE YEAR LATER

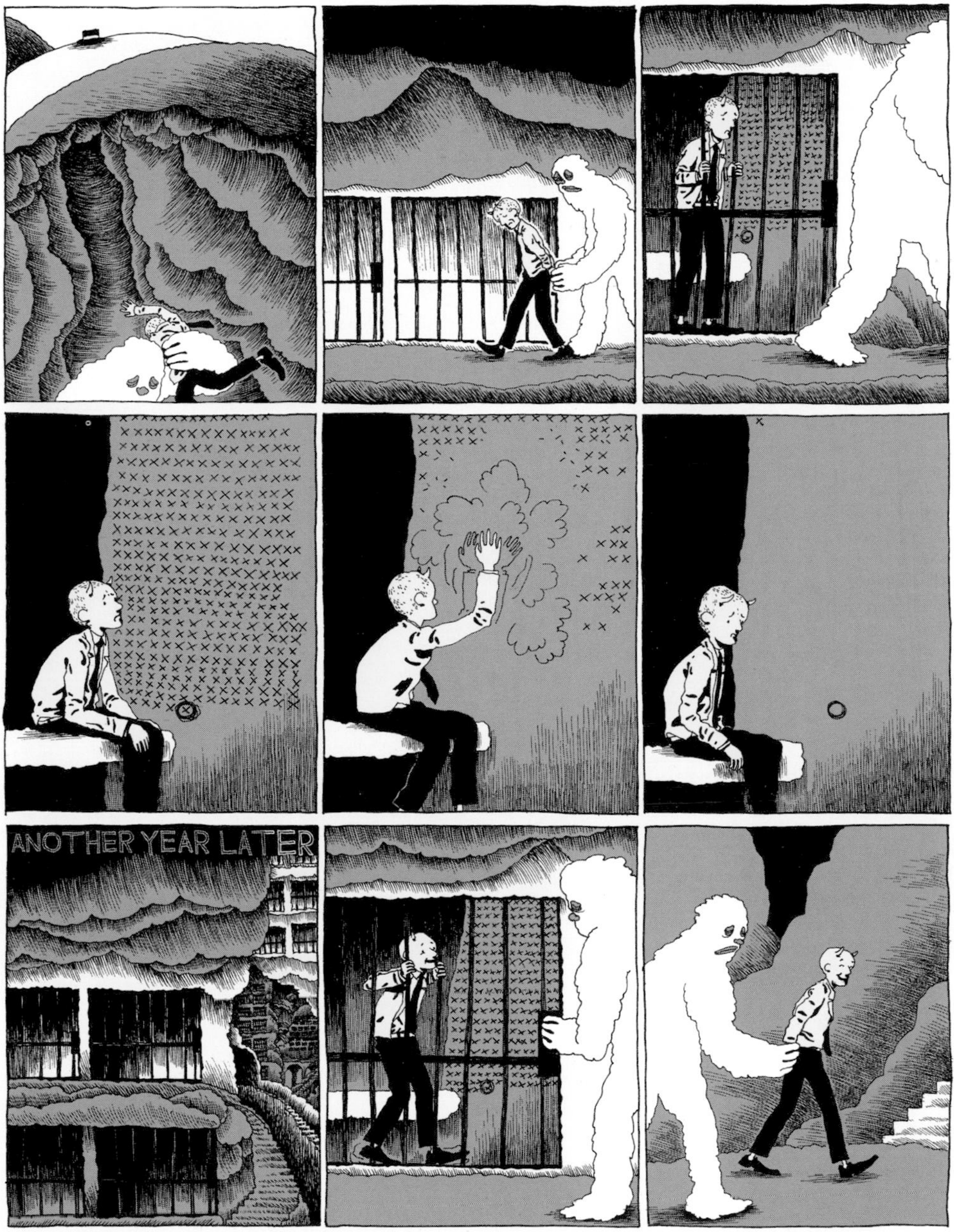
ANOTHER YEAR LATER

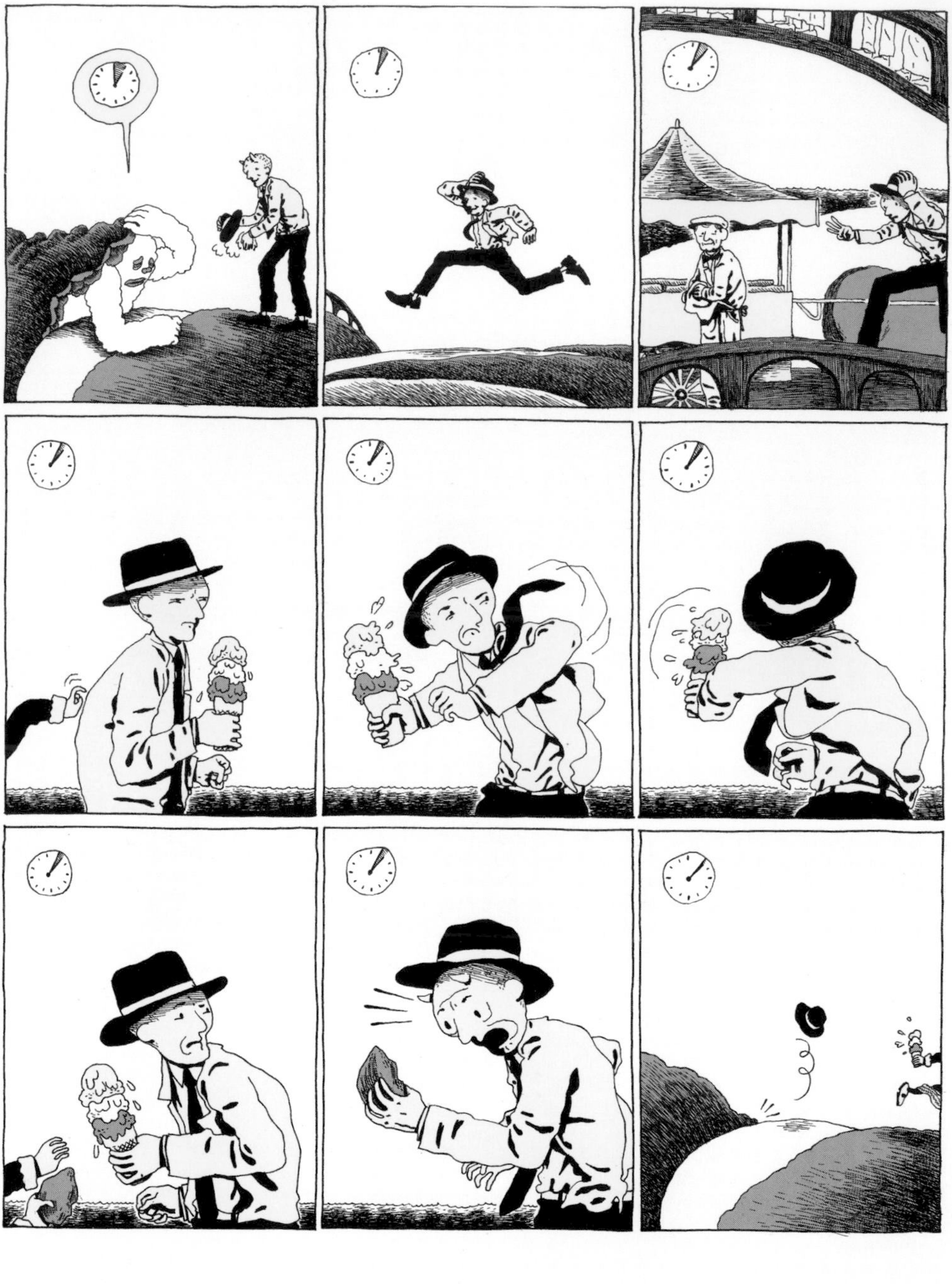

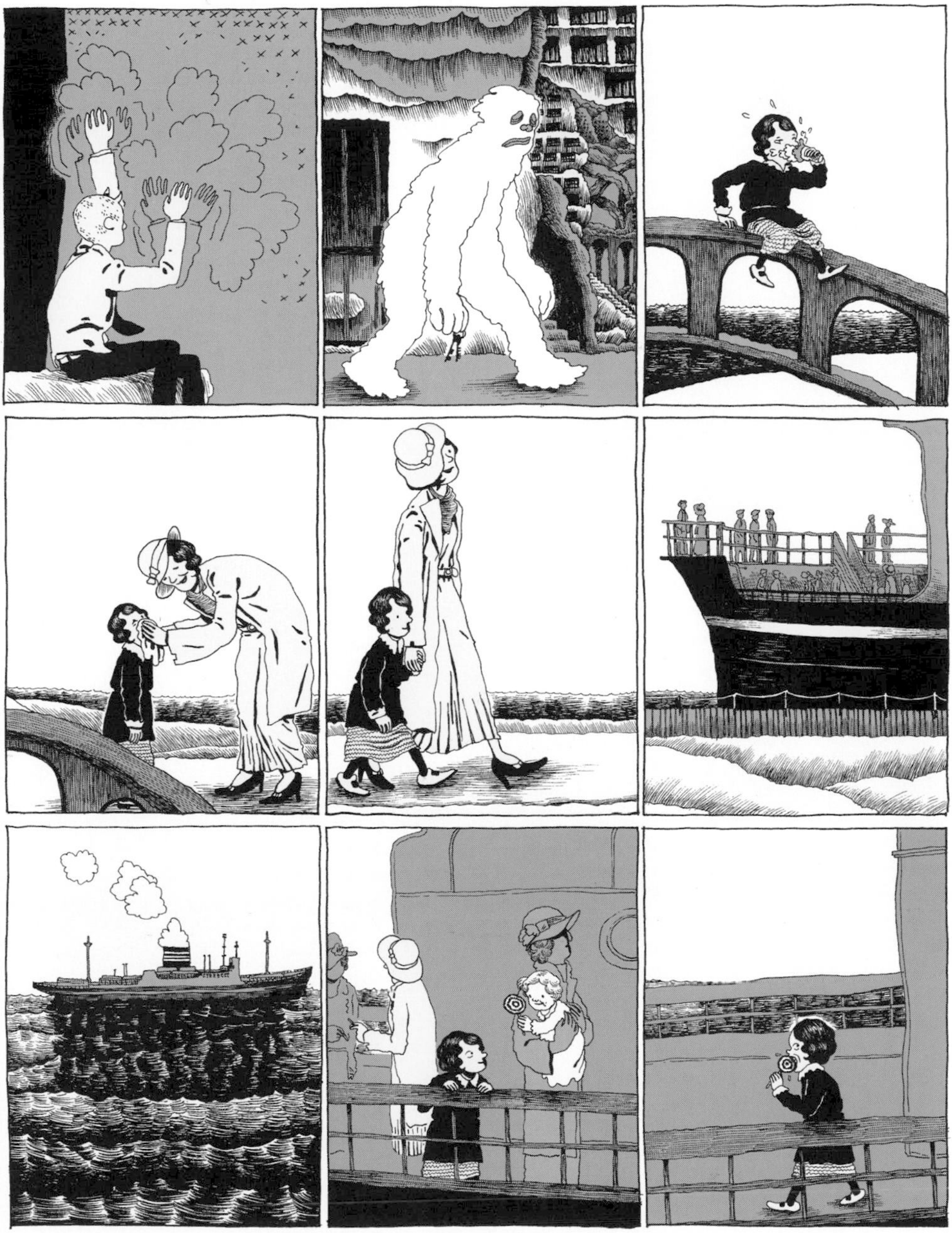

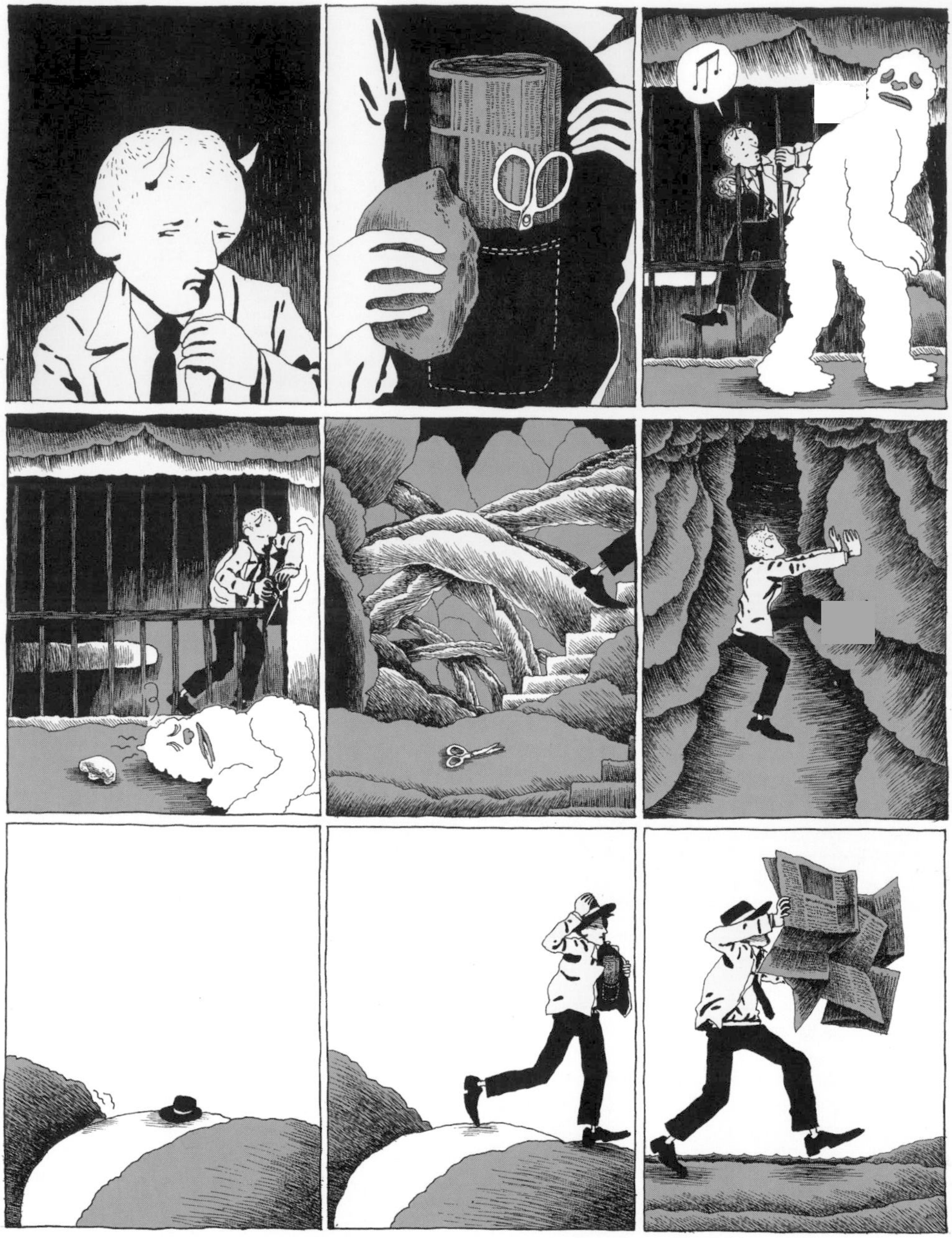

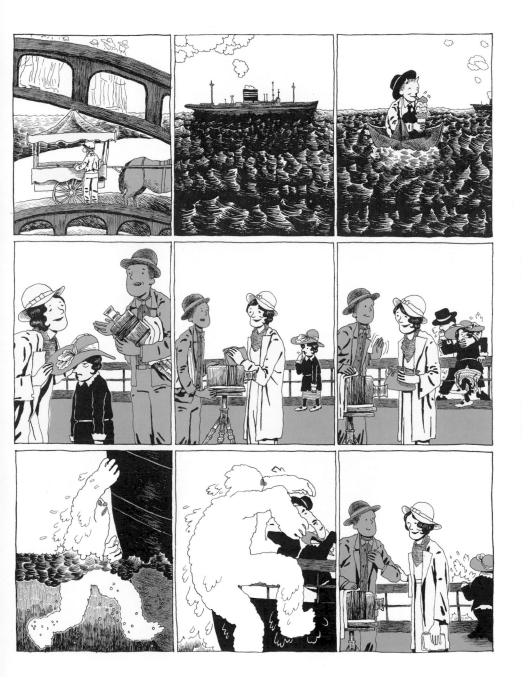

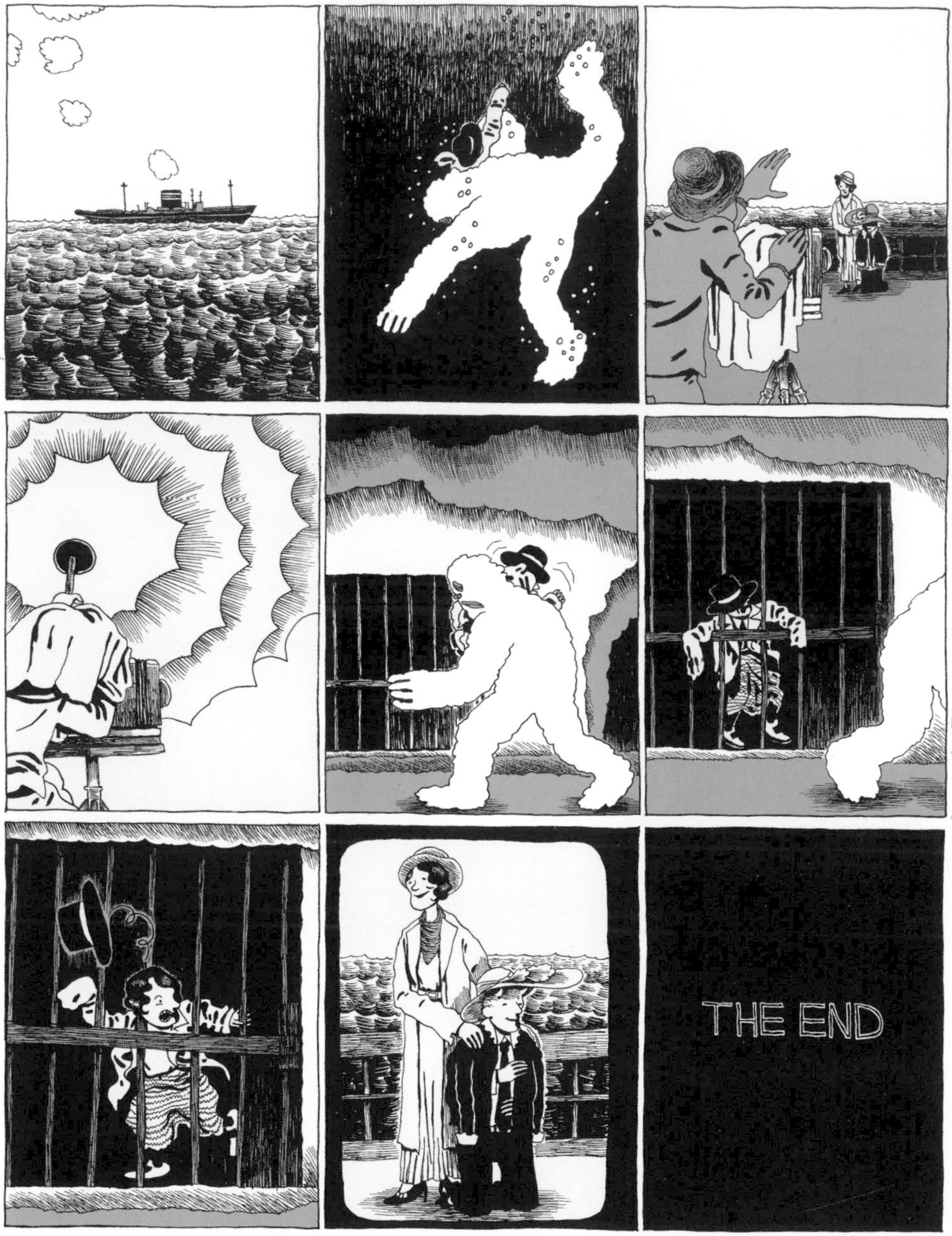
THE END

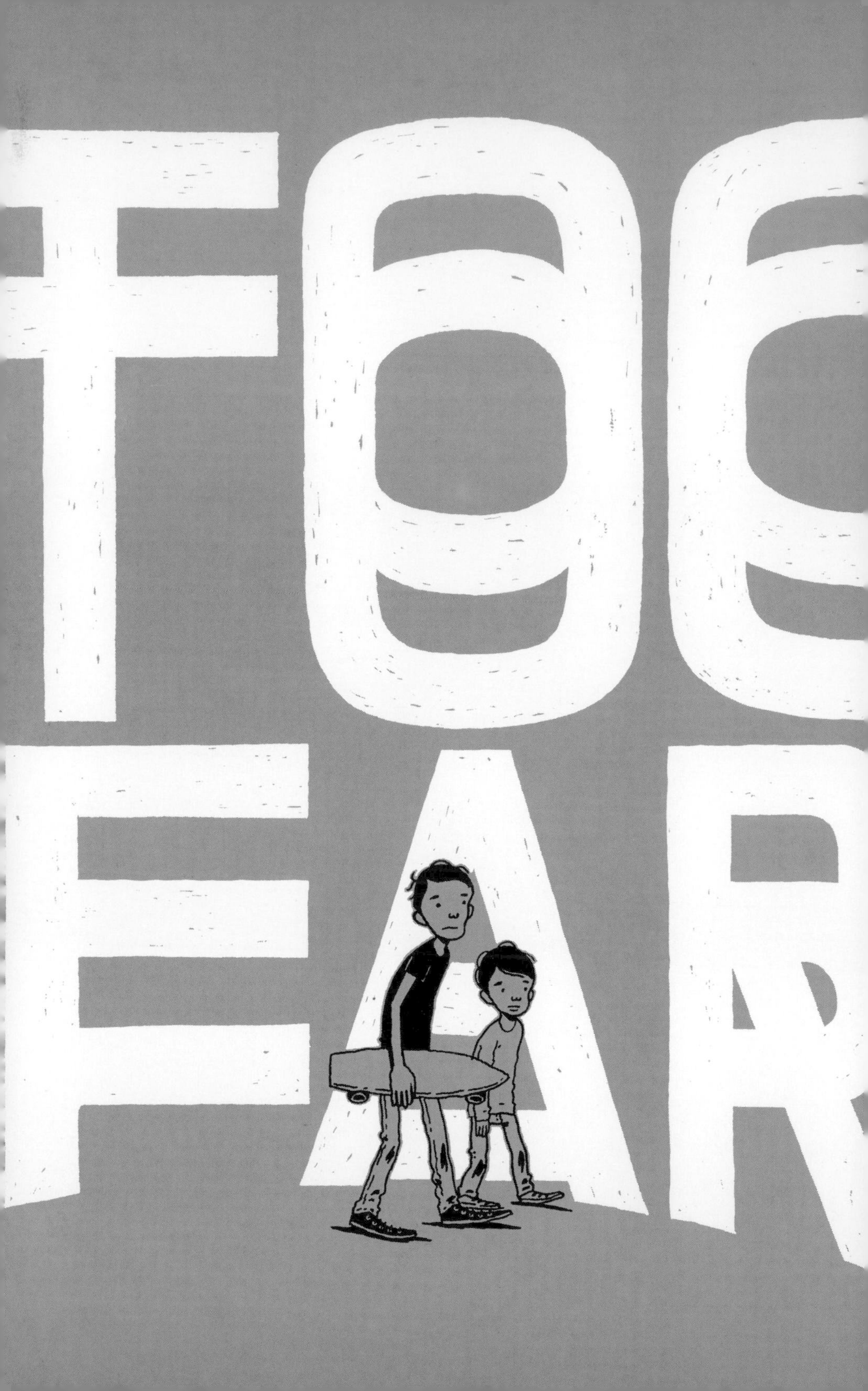
TOO
FAR

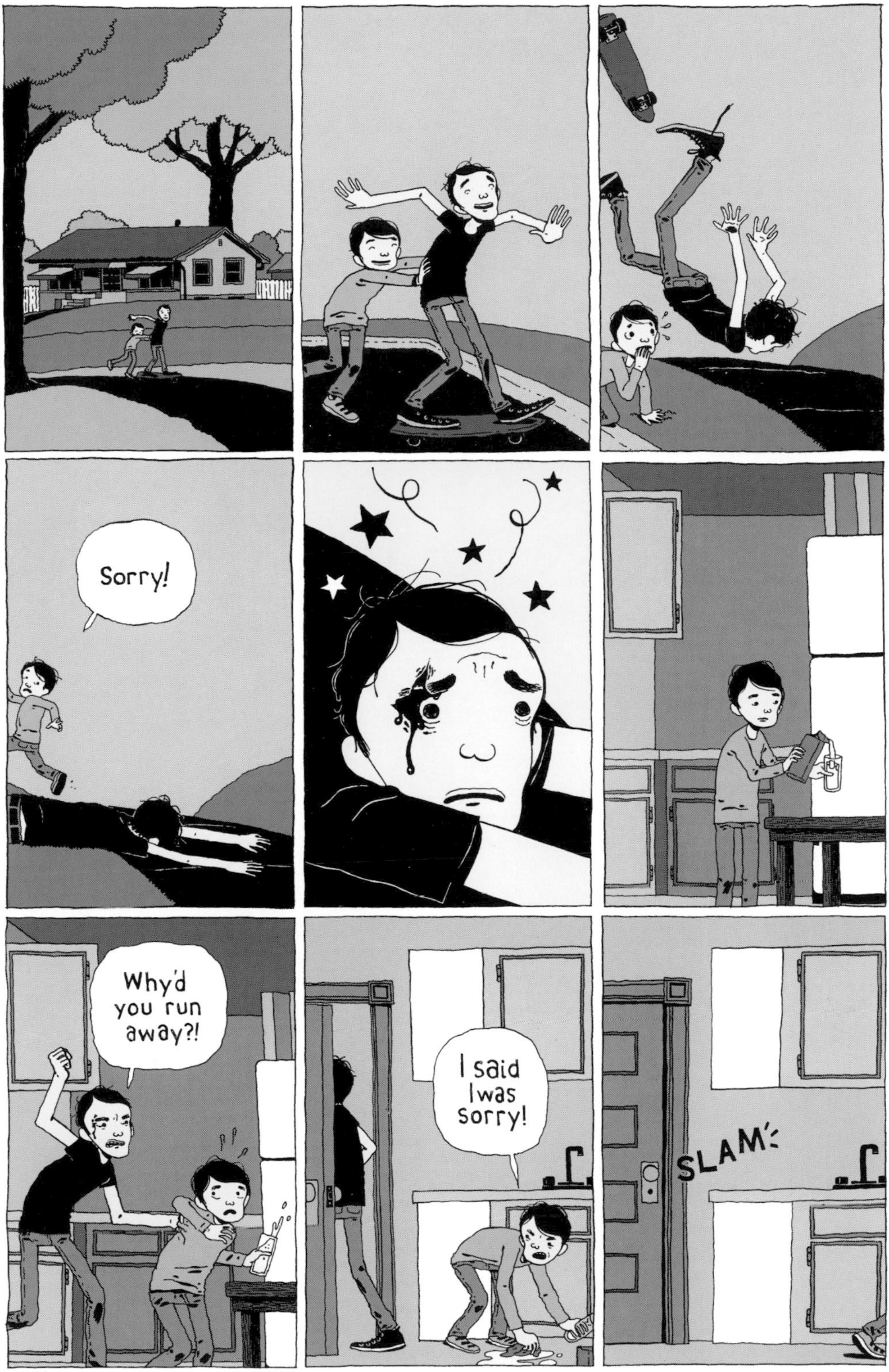

Sorry!
Why'd you run away?!
I said I was sorry!
SLAM

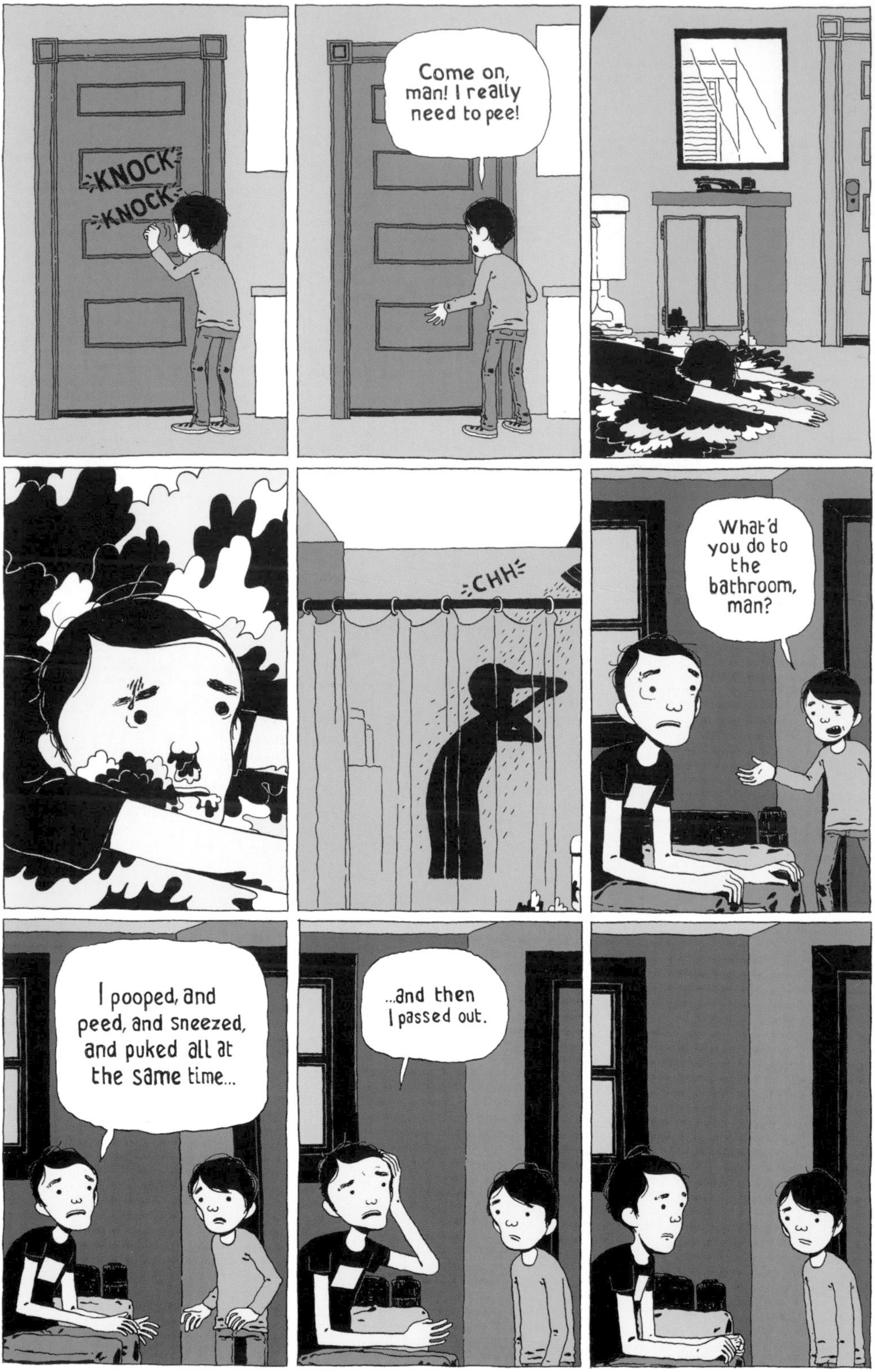
KNOCK
KNOCK
Come on, man! I really need to pee!
CHH
What'd you do to the bathroom, man?
I pooped, and peed, and sneezed, and puked all at the same time...
...and then I passed out.

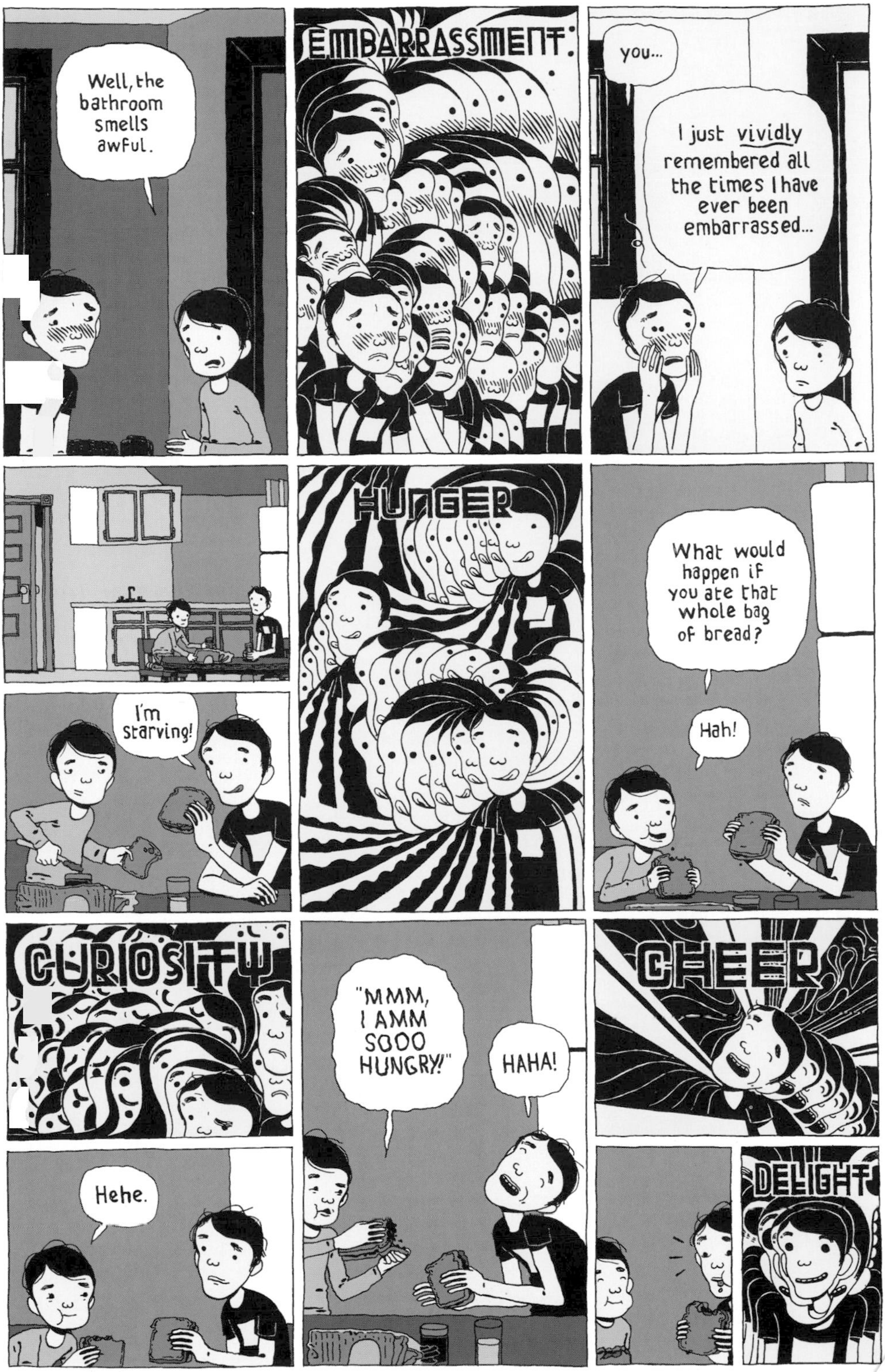
Well, the bathroom smells awful.
EMBARRASSMENT
you...
I just vividly remembered all the times I have ever been embarrassed...
HUNGER
I'm starving!
What would happen if you ate that whole bag of bread?
Hah!
CURIOSITY
"MMM, I AMM SOOO HUNGRY!"
HAHA!
CHEER
Hehe.
DELIGHT

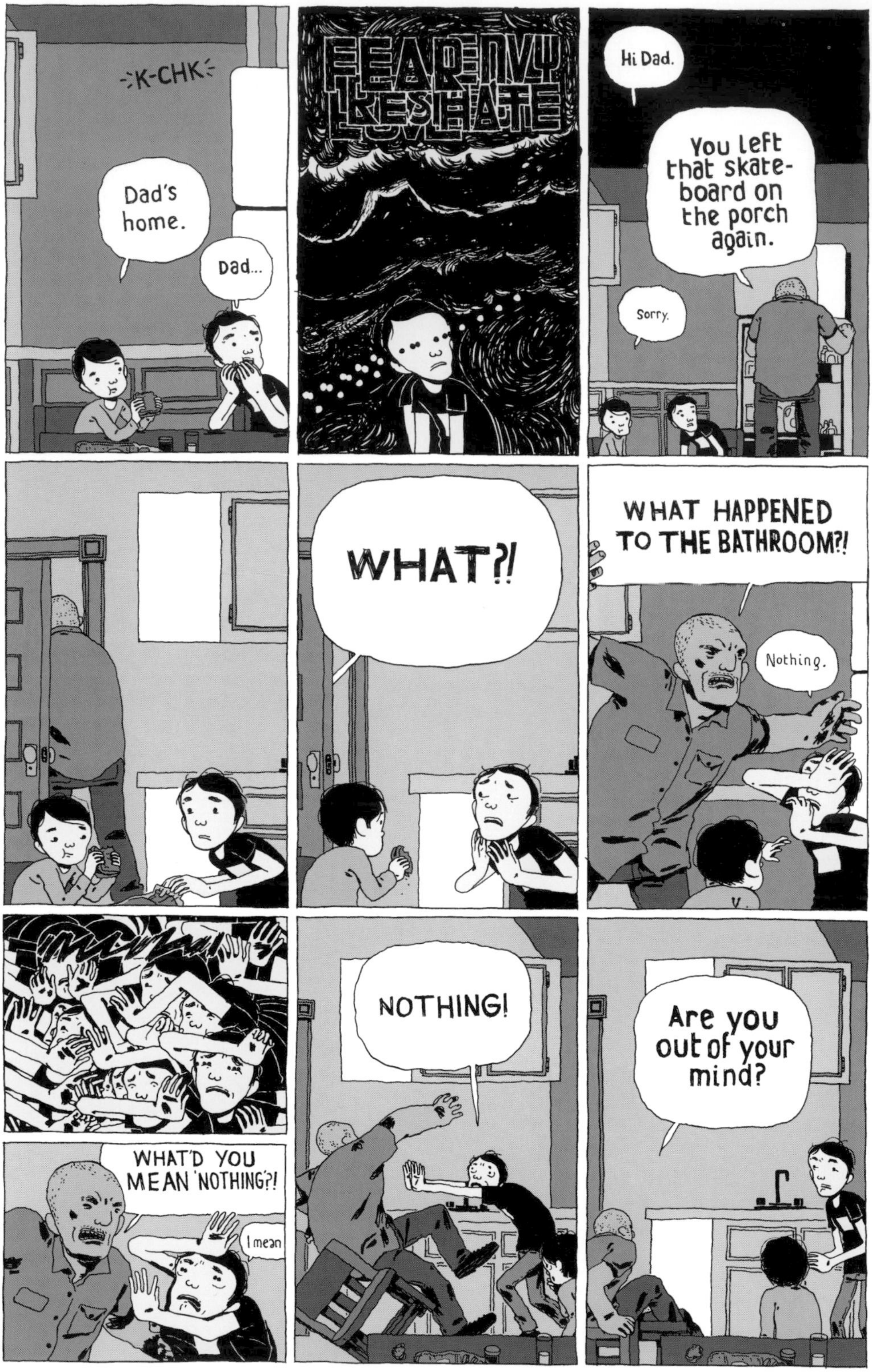
K-CHK
Dad's home.
Dad...
FEAR
ENVY
LOVE
HATE
Hi Dad.
You left that skate-board on the porch again.
Sorry.
WHAT?!
WHAT HAPPENED TO THE BATHROOM?!
Nothing.
WHAT'D YOU MEAN 'NOTHING'?!
I mean
NOTHING!
Are you out of your mind?

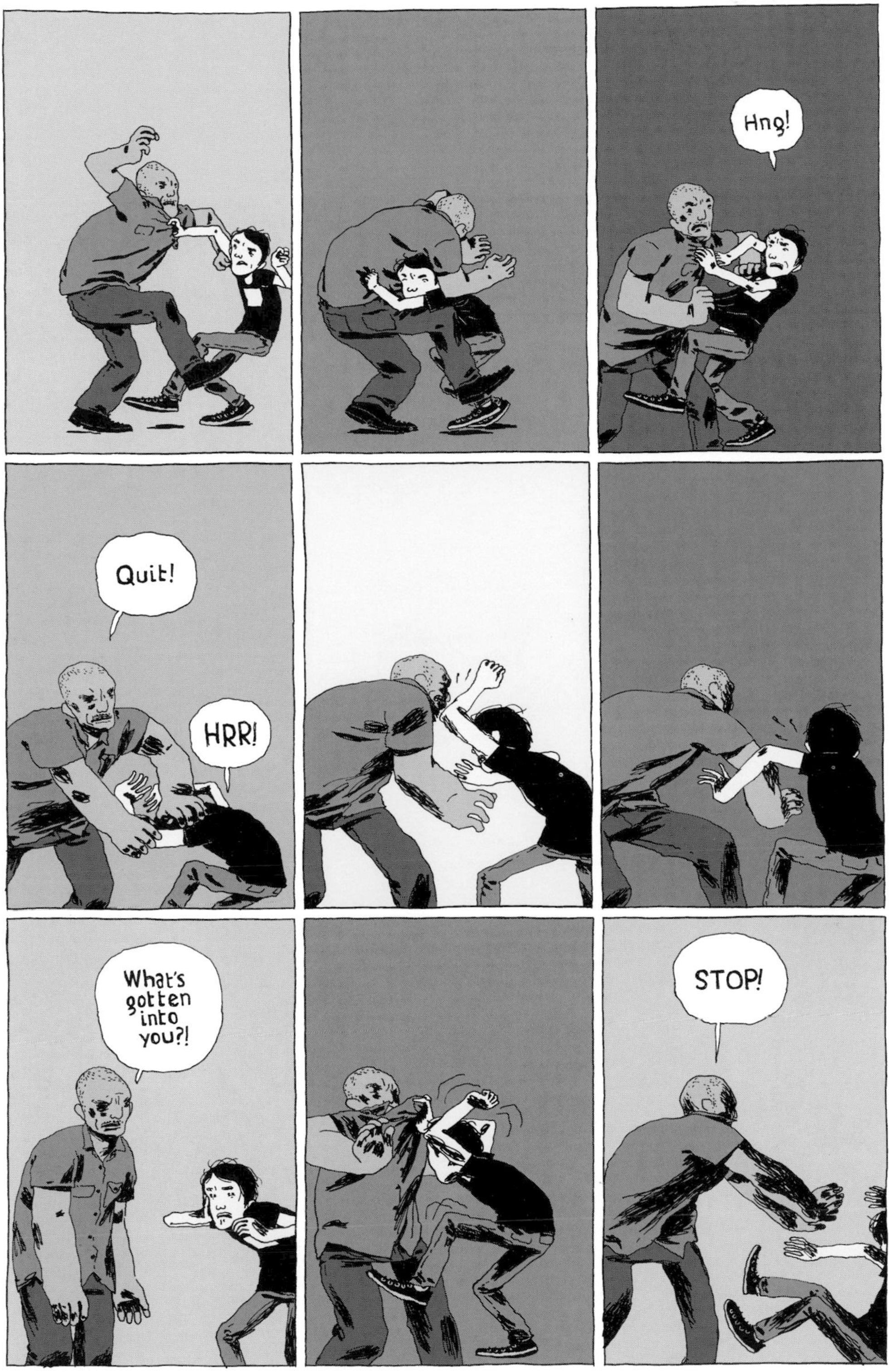
Hng!
Quit!
HRR!
What's gotten into you?!
STOP!

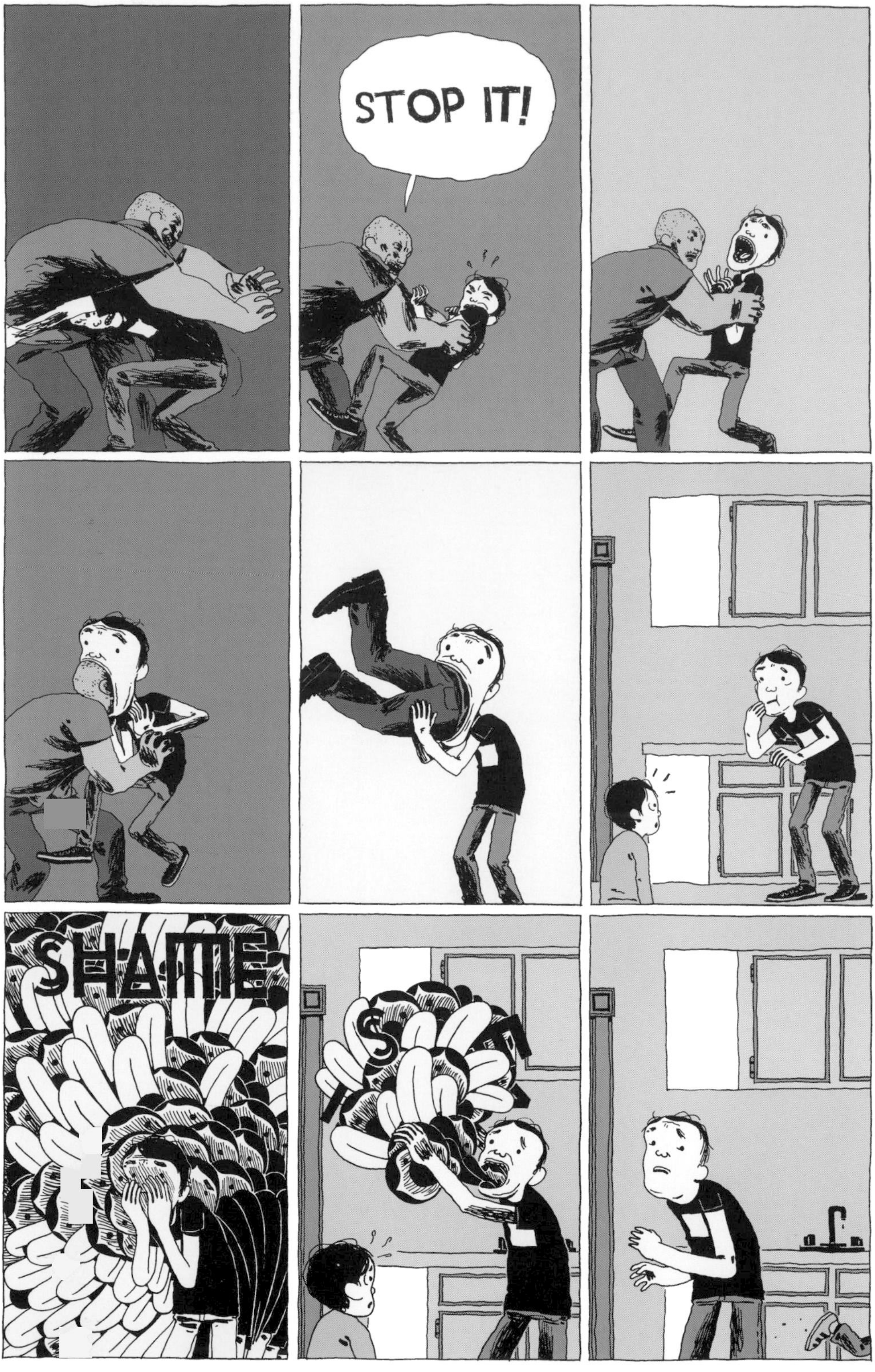
STOP IT!
SHAME

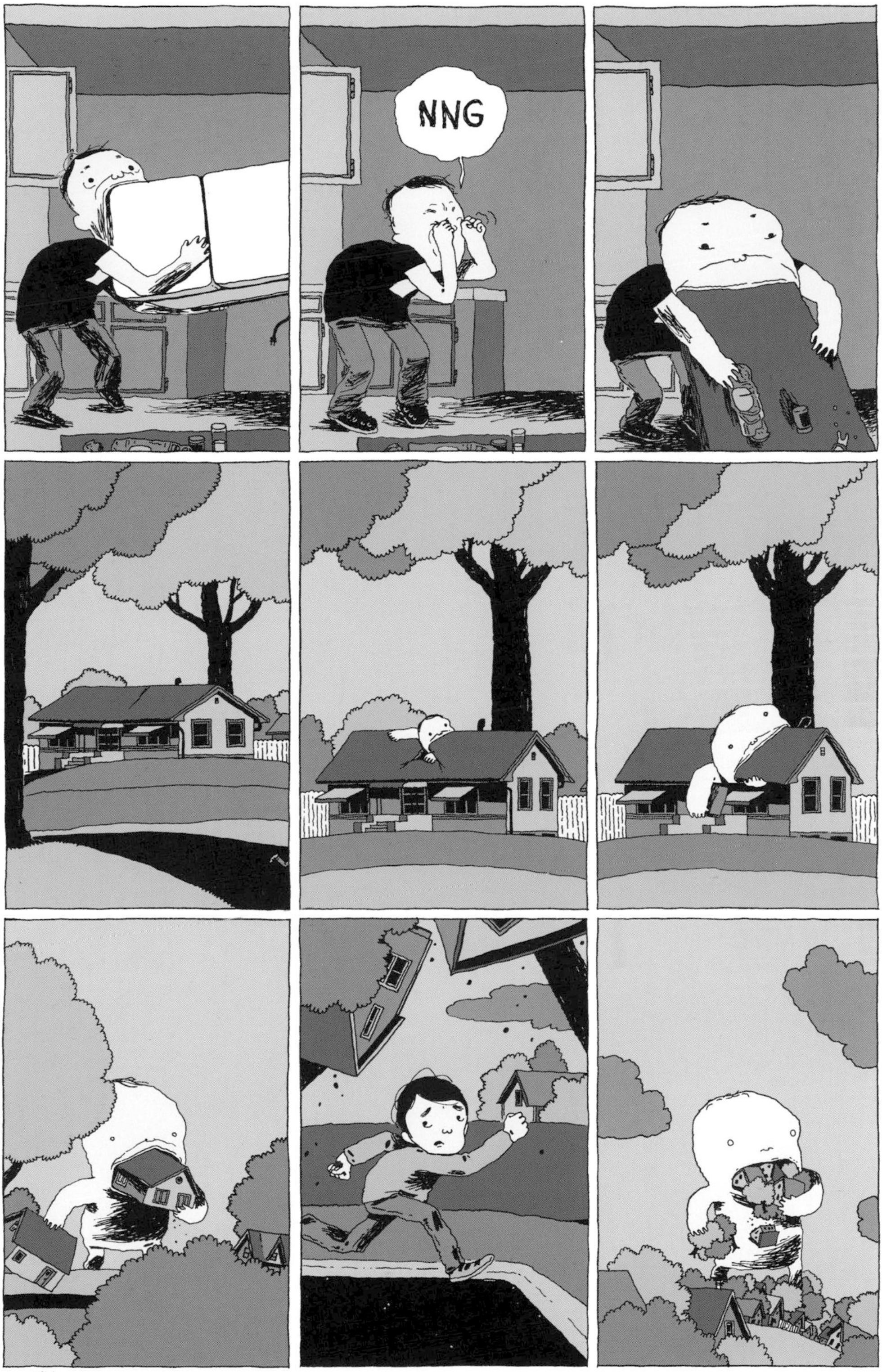
NNG

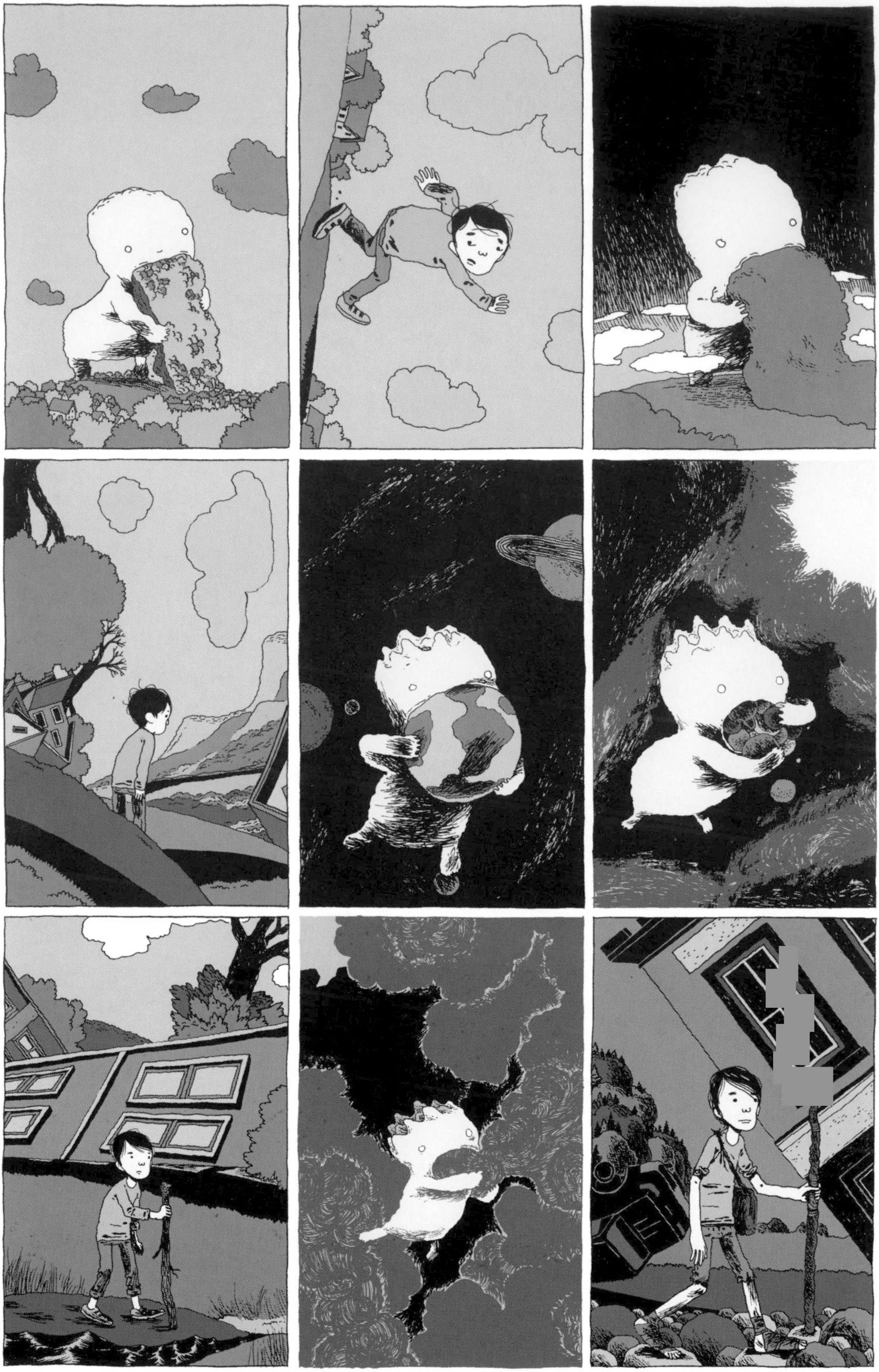

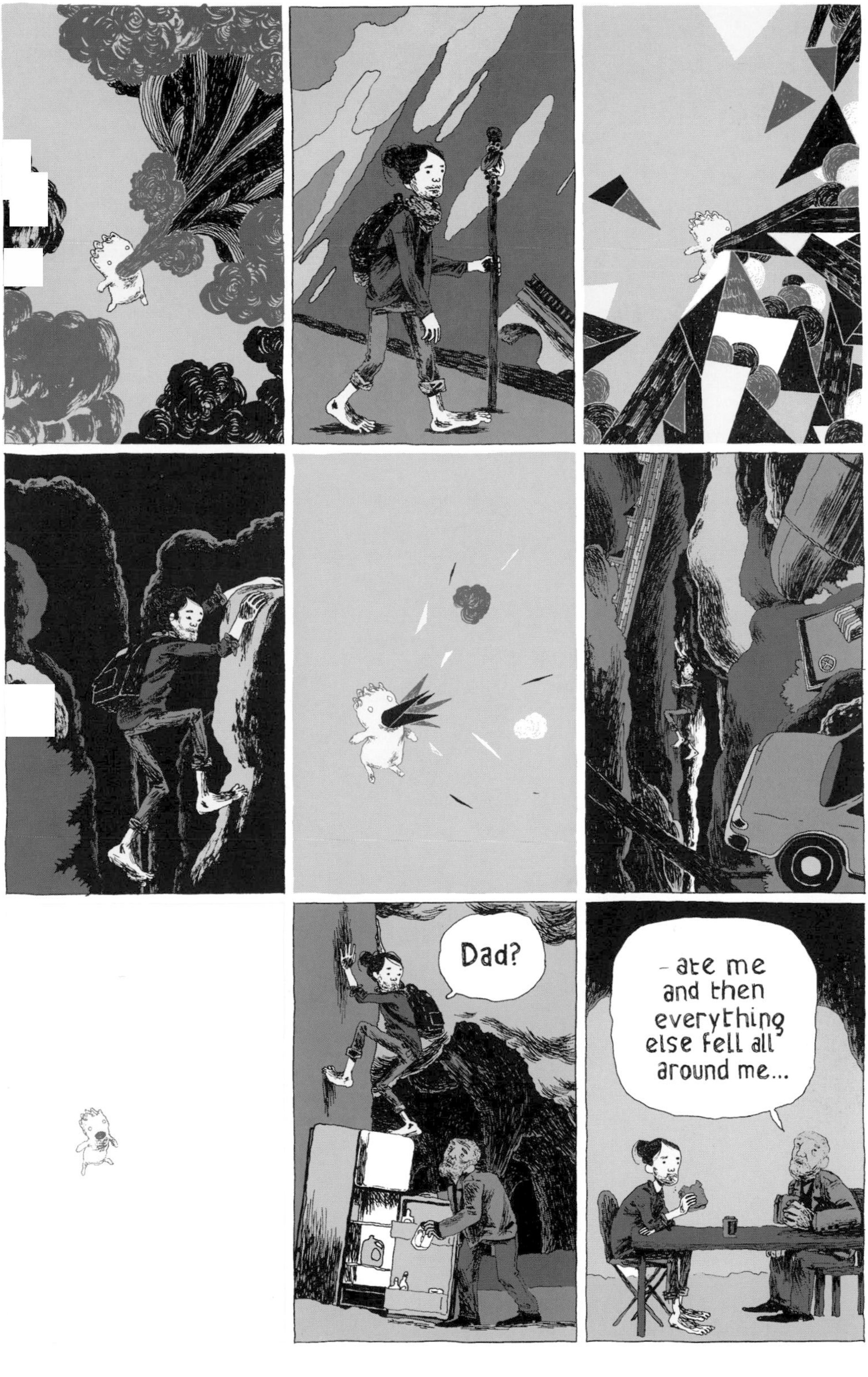
Dad?
– ate me and then everything else fell all around me...

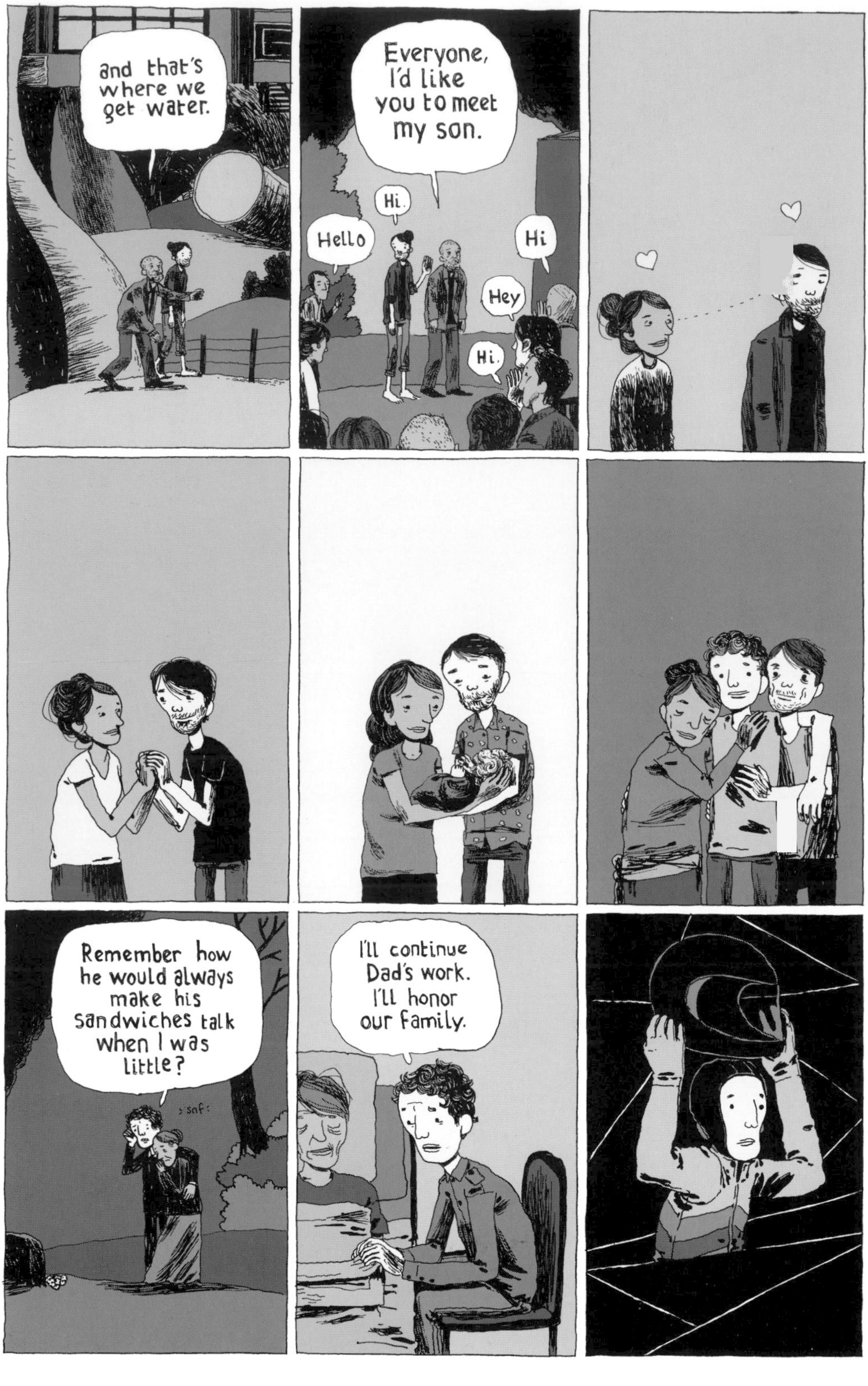
and that's where we get water.
Everyone, I'd like you to meet my son.
Hi.
Hello
Hi
Hey
Hi.
Remember how he would always make his sandwiches talk when I was little?
>snf<
I'll continue Dad's work. I'll honor our family.

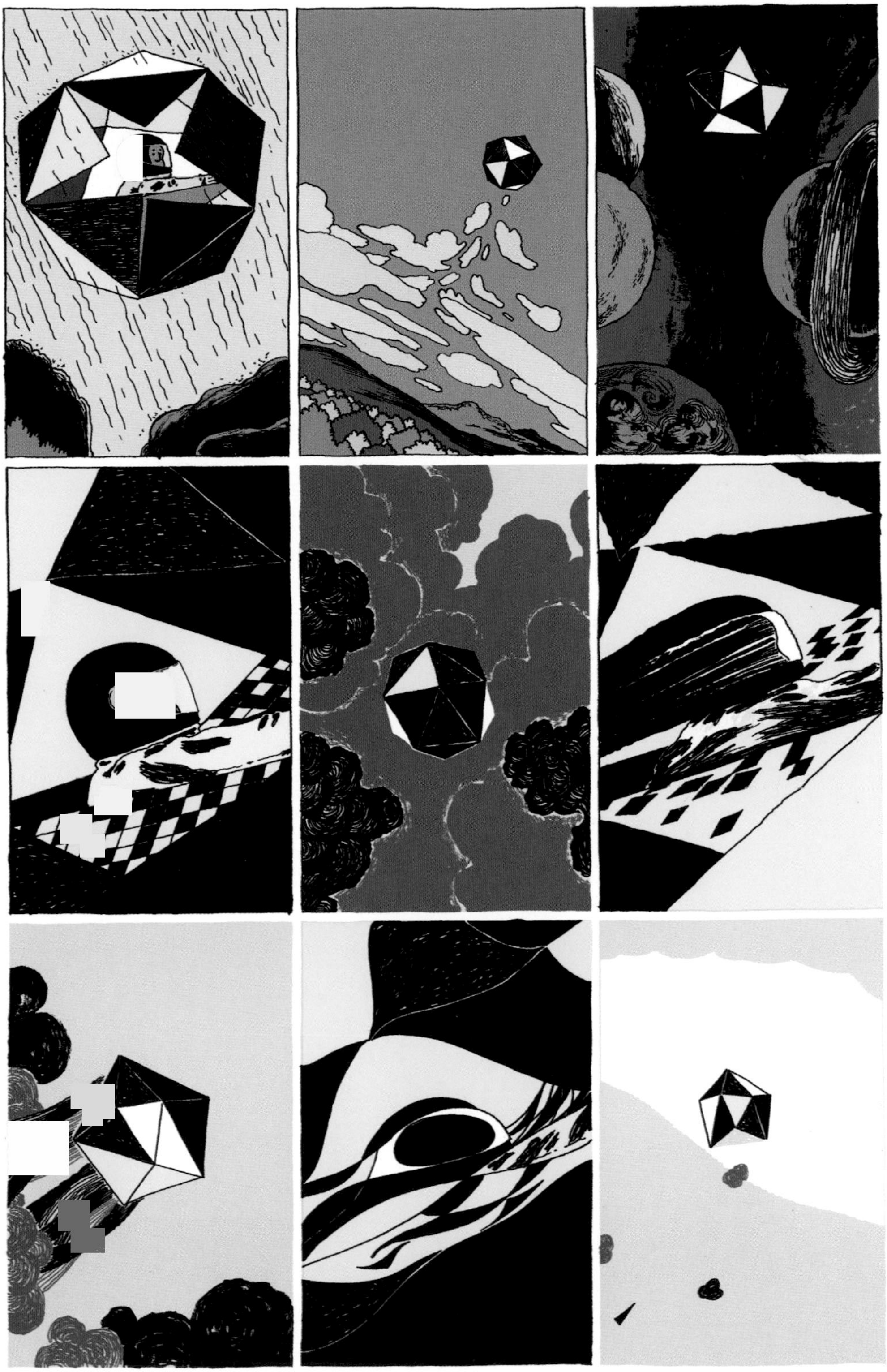

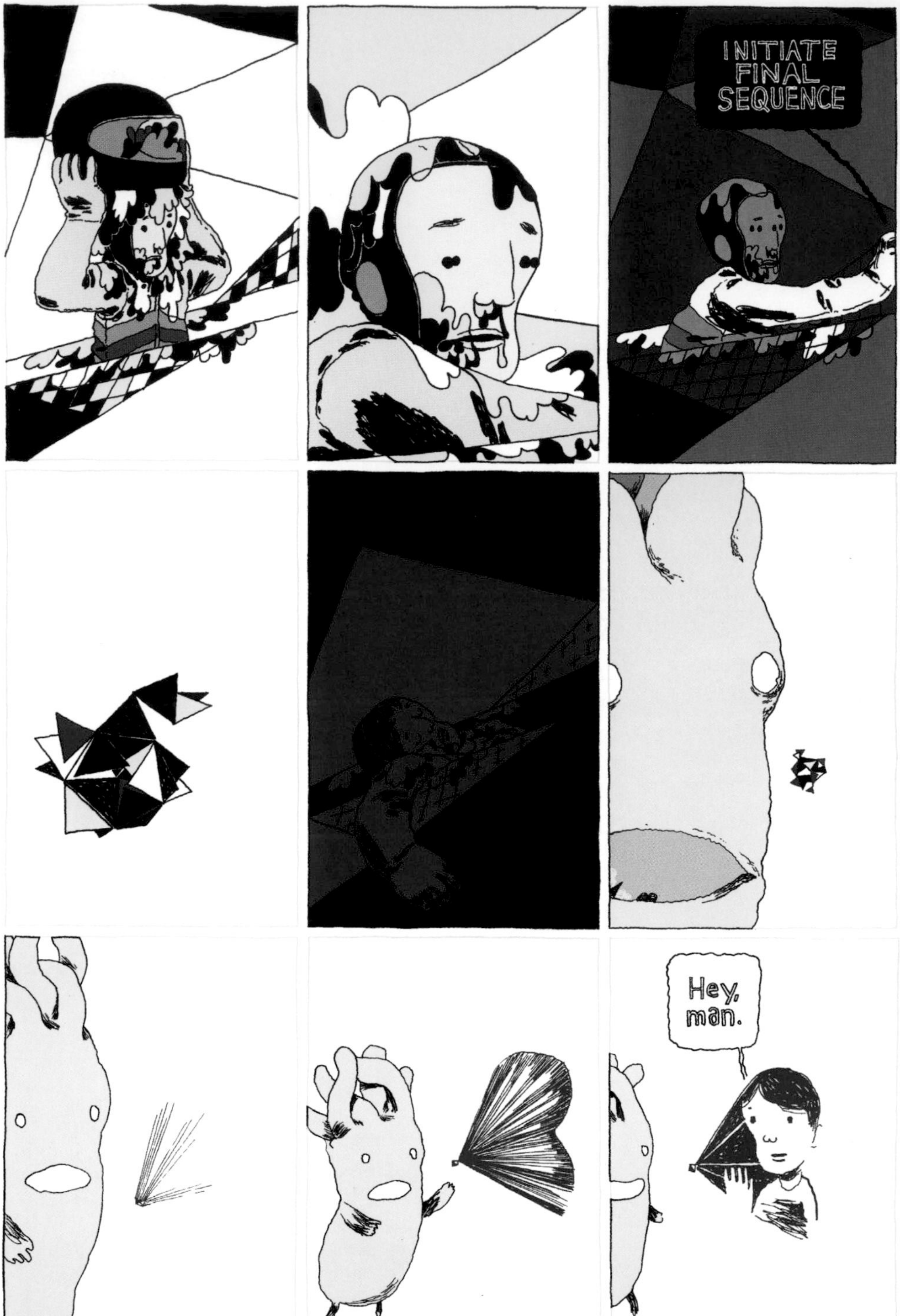
INITIATE FINAL SEQUENCE
Hey, man.

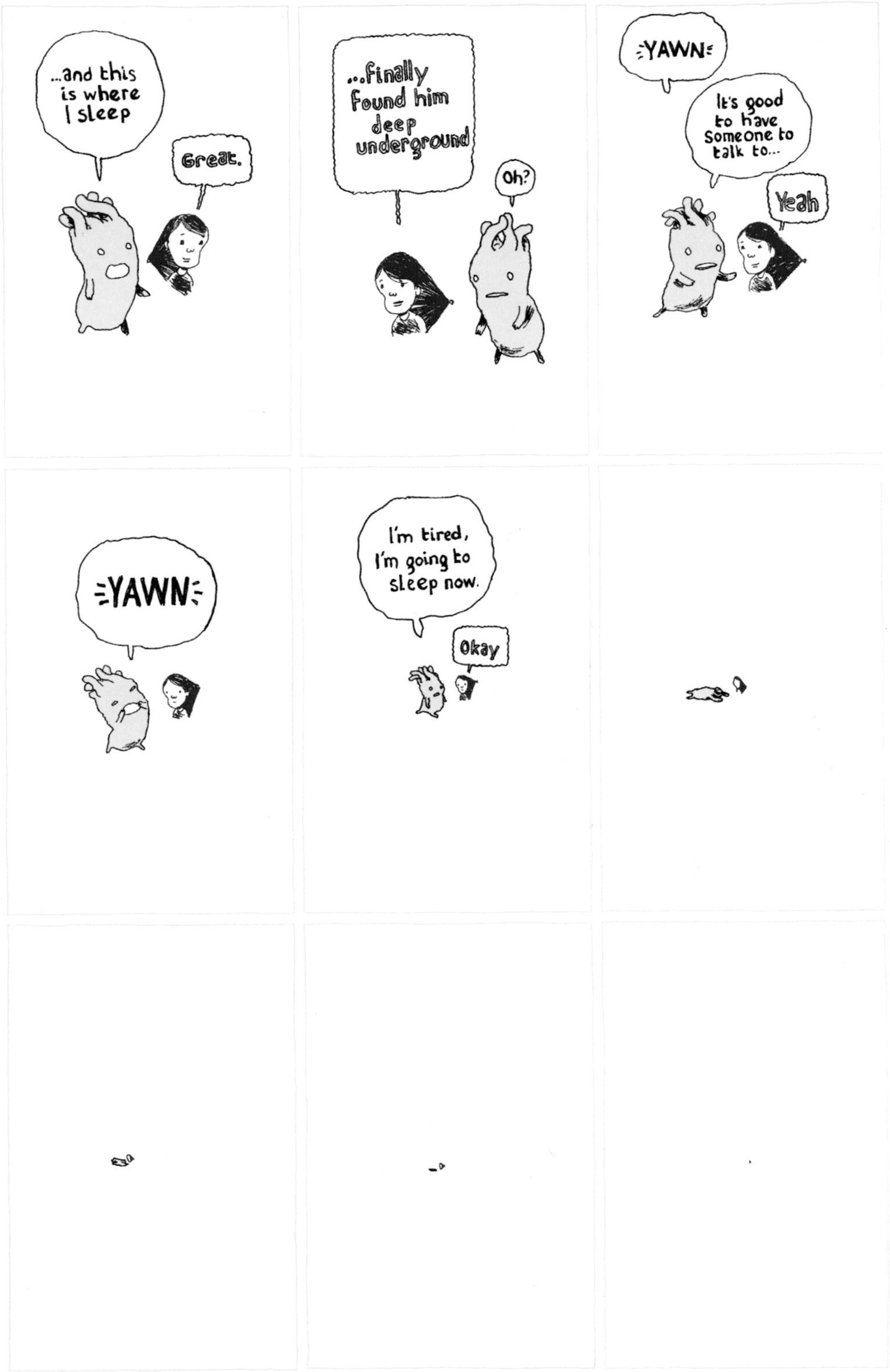
...and this is where I sleep
Great.
...finally found him deep underground
Oh?
YAWN
It's good to have someone to talk to...
Yeah
YAWN
I'm tired, I'm going to sleep now.
Okay

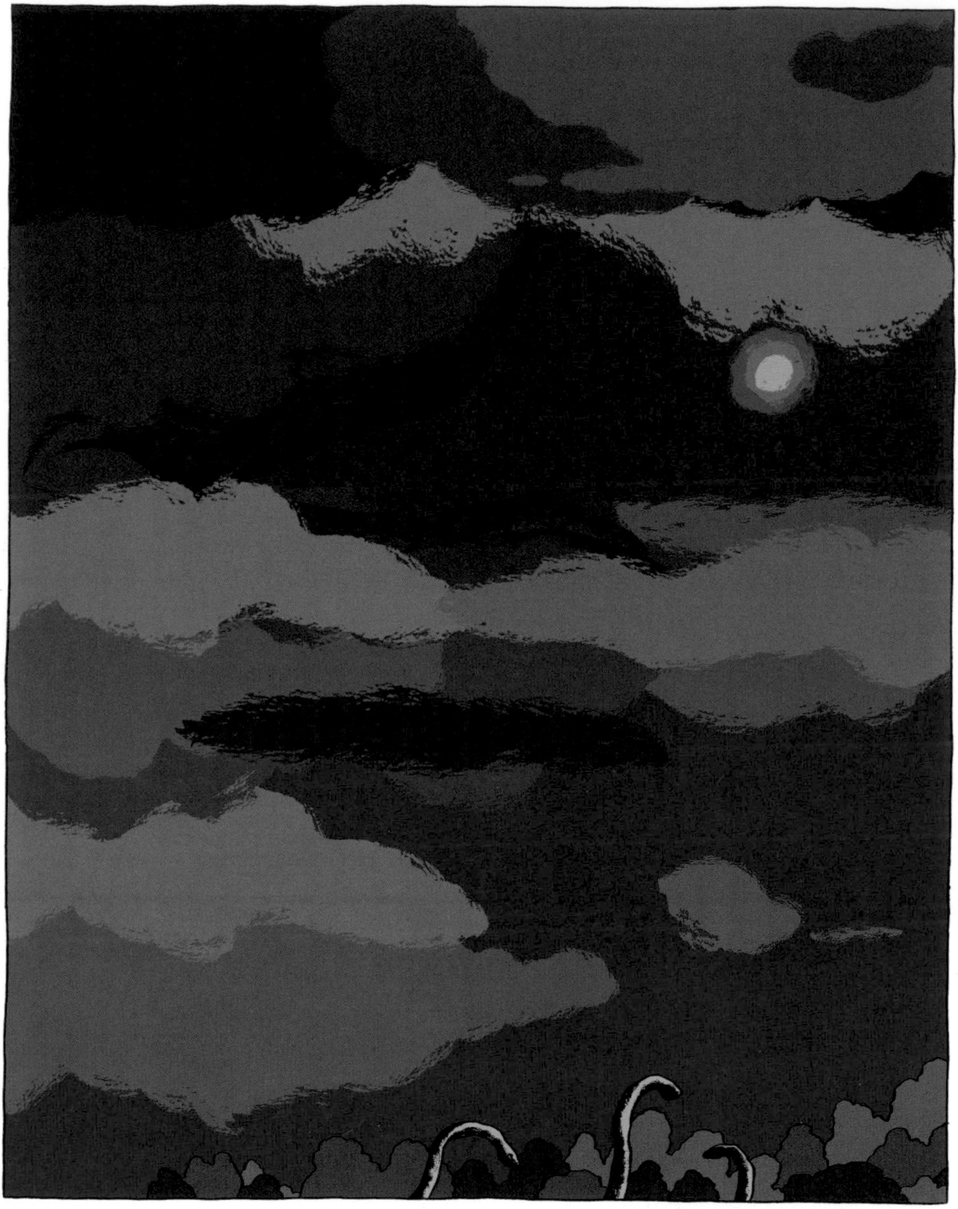

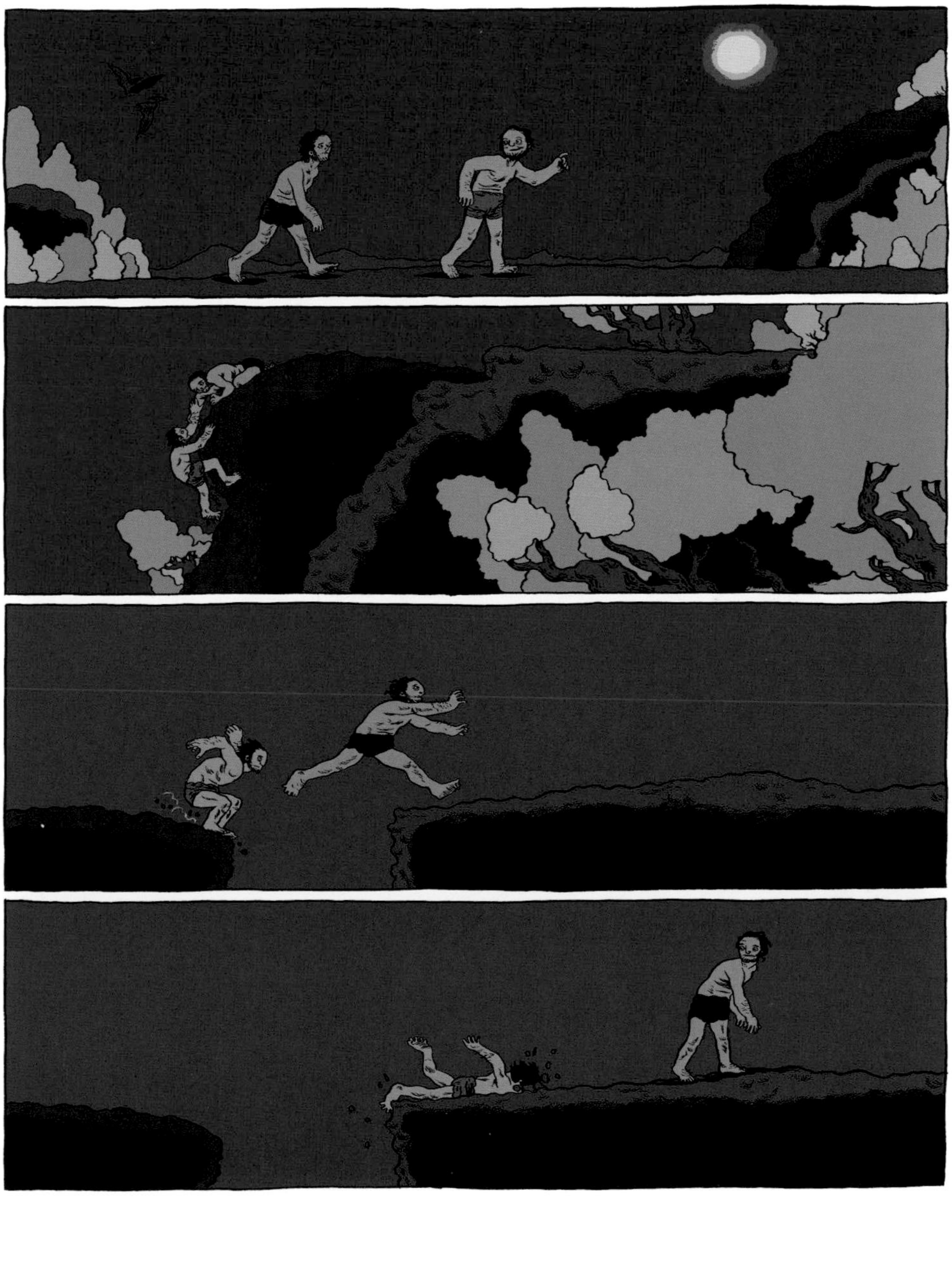

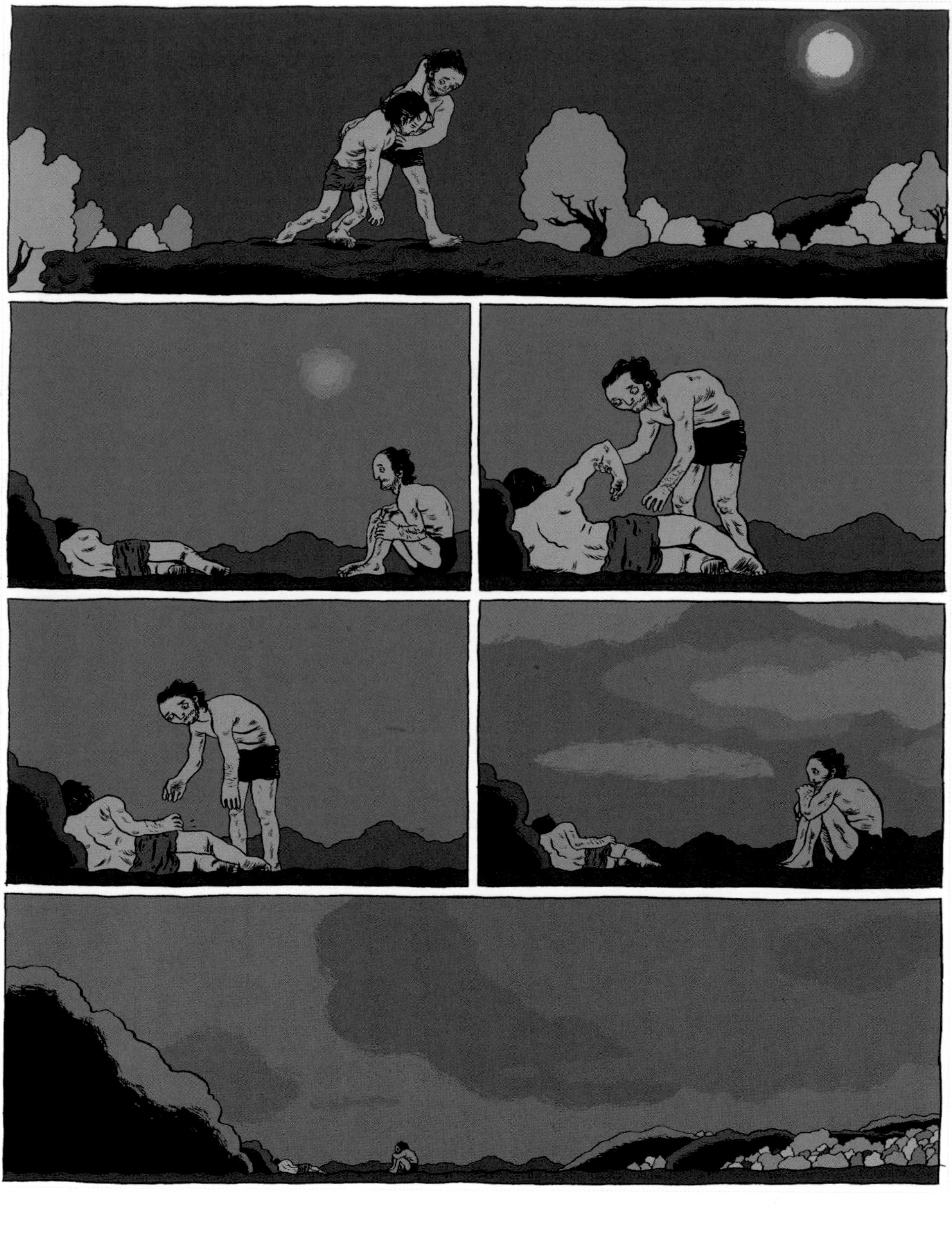

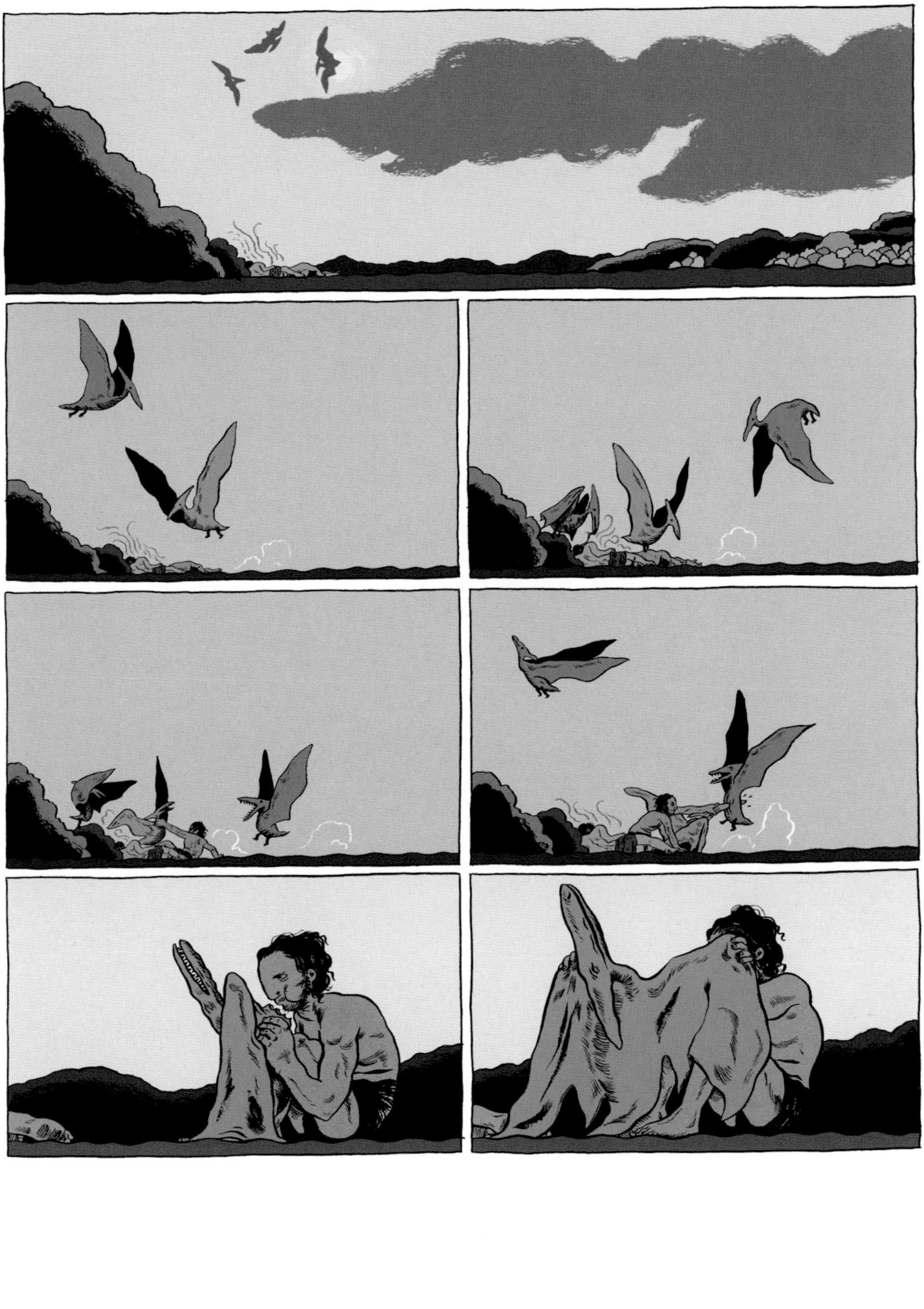

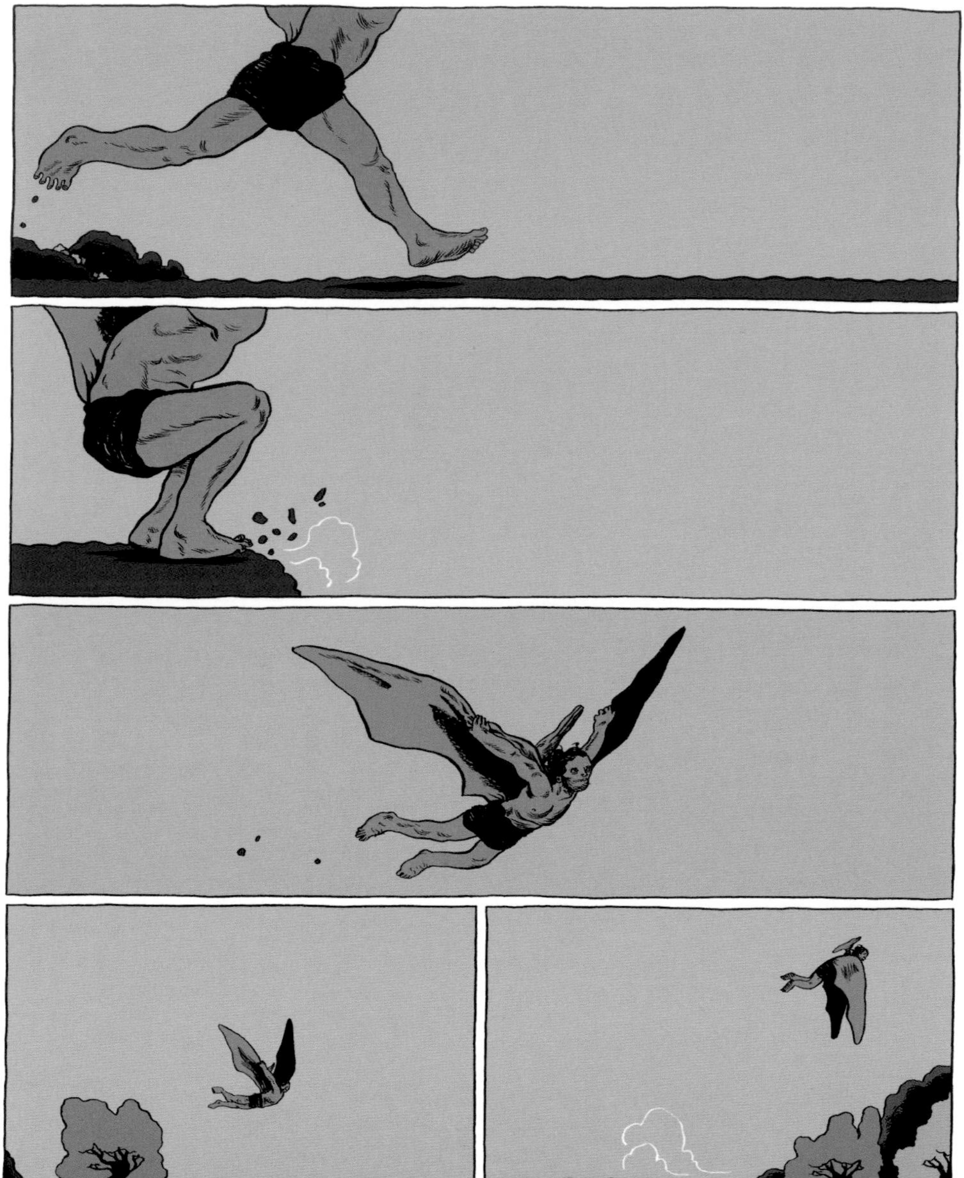

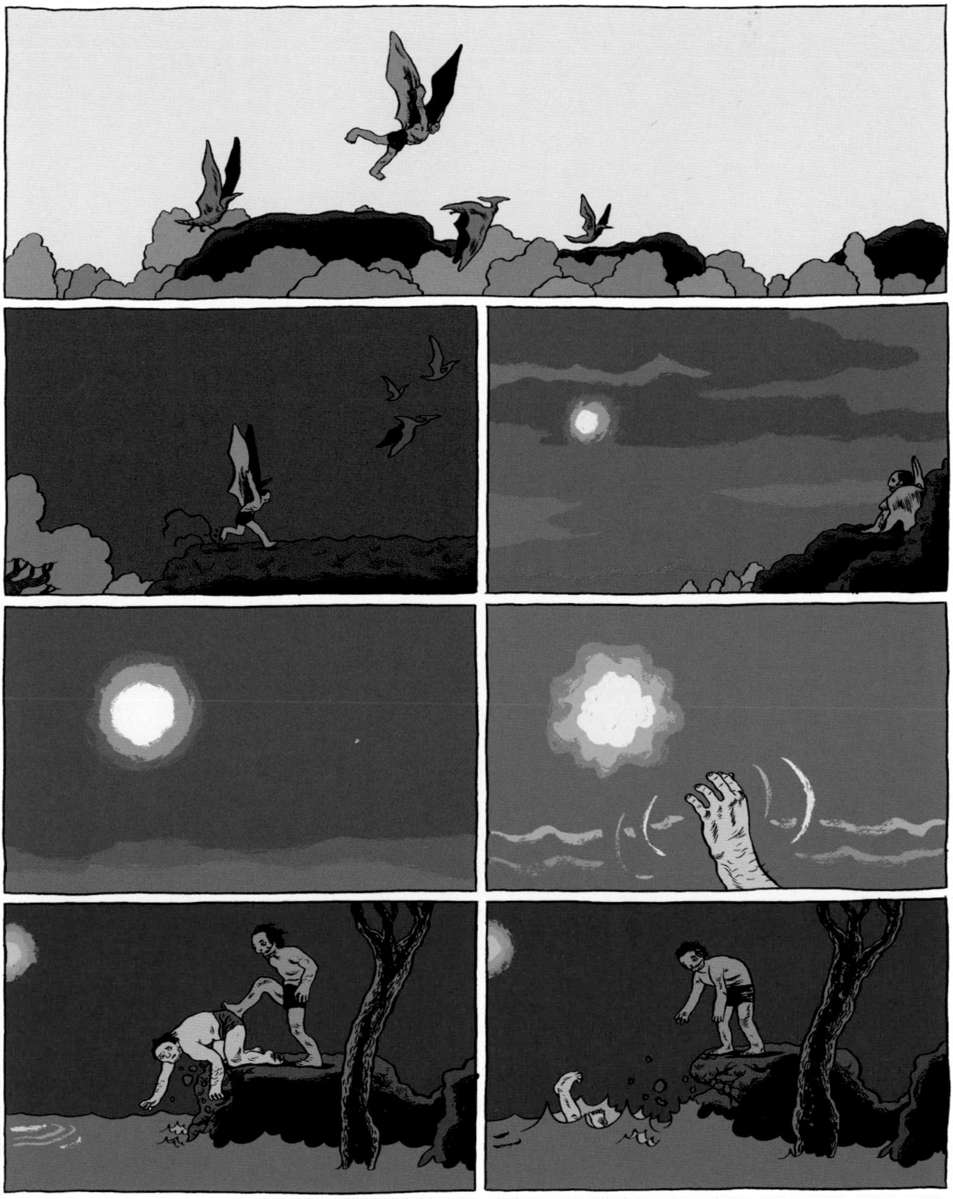

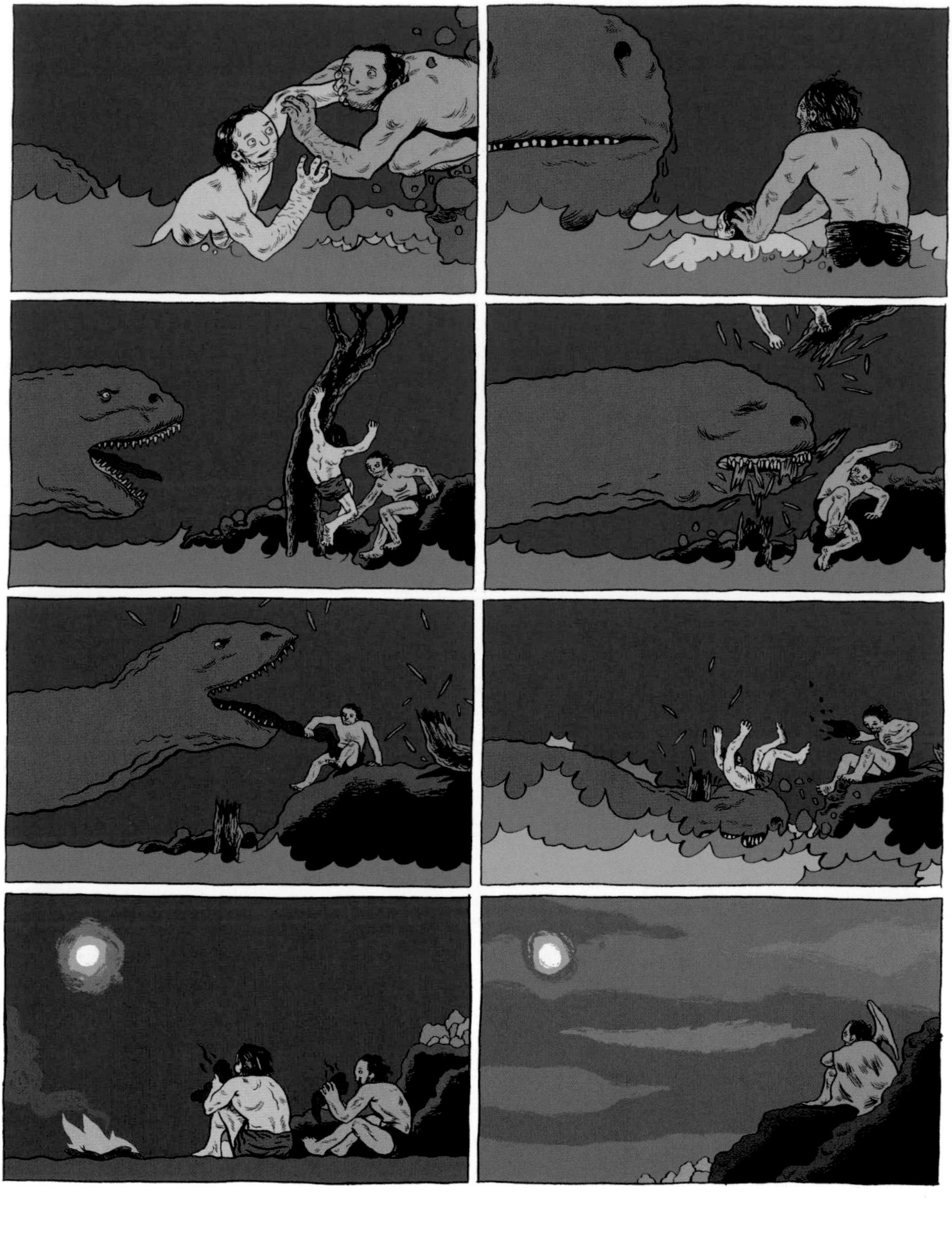

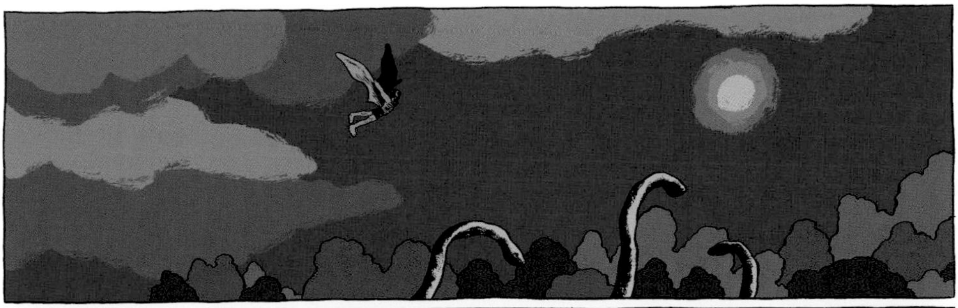
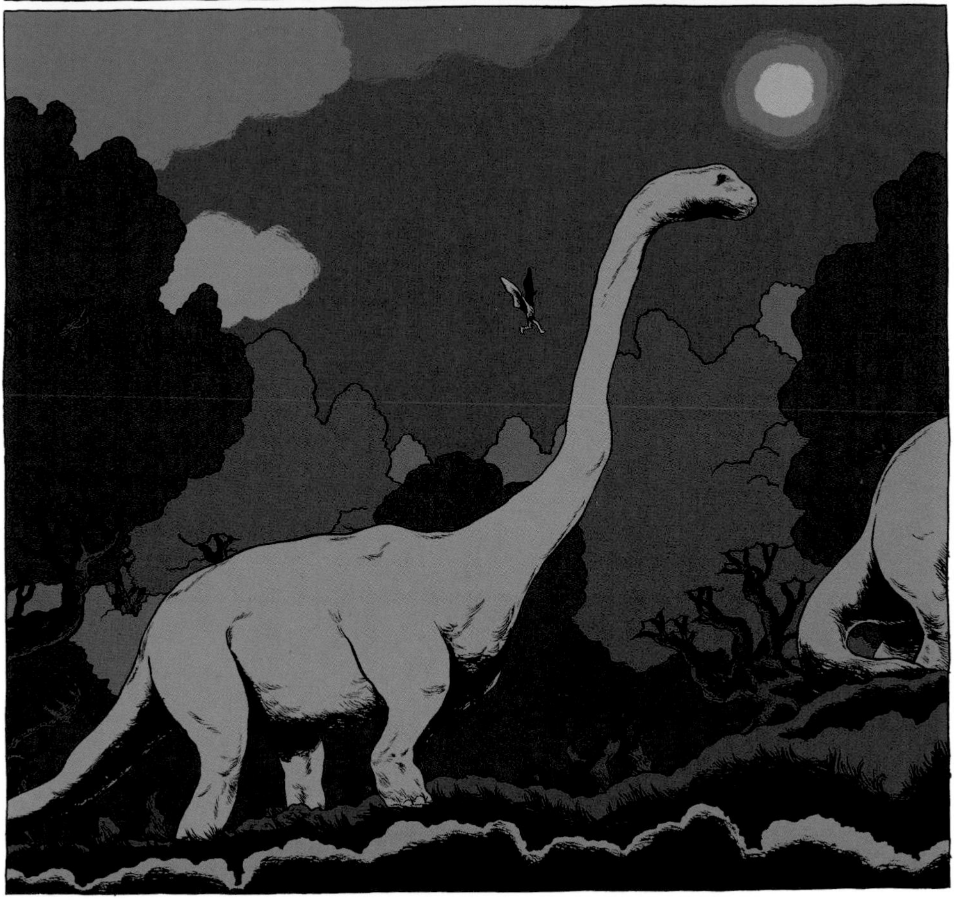

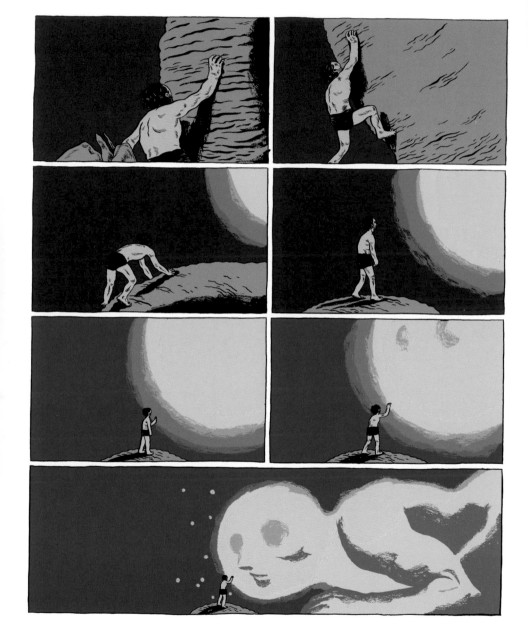

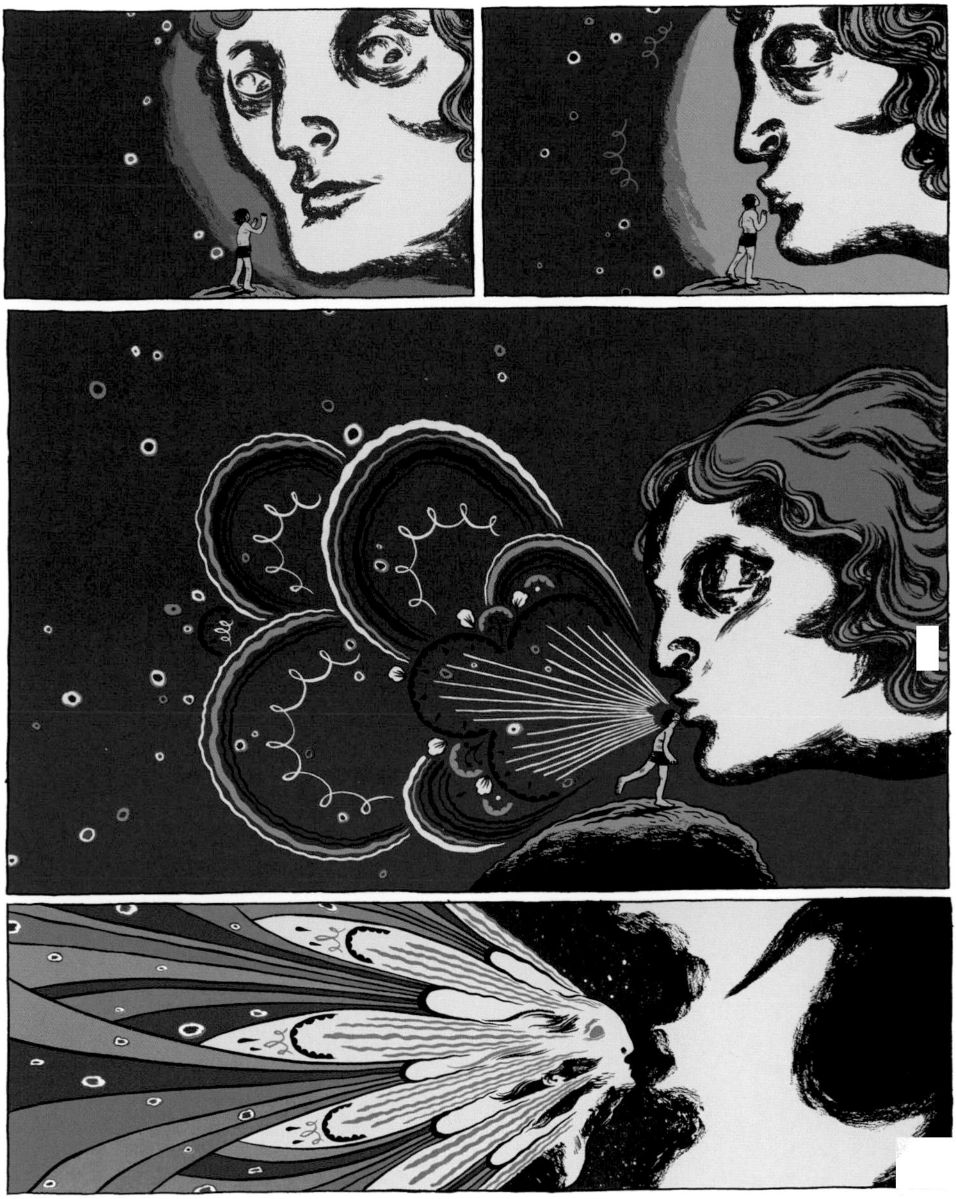

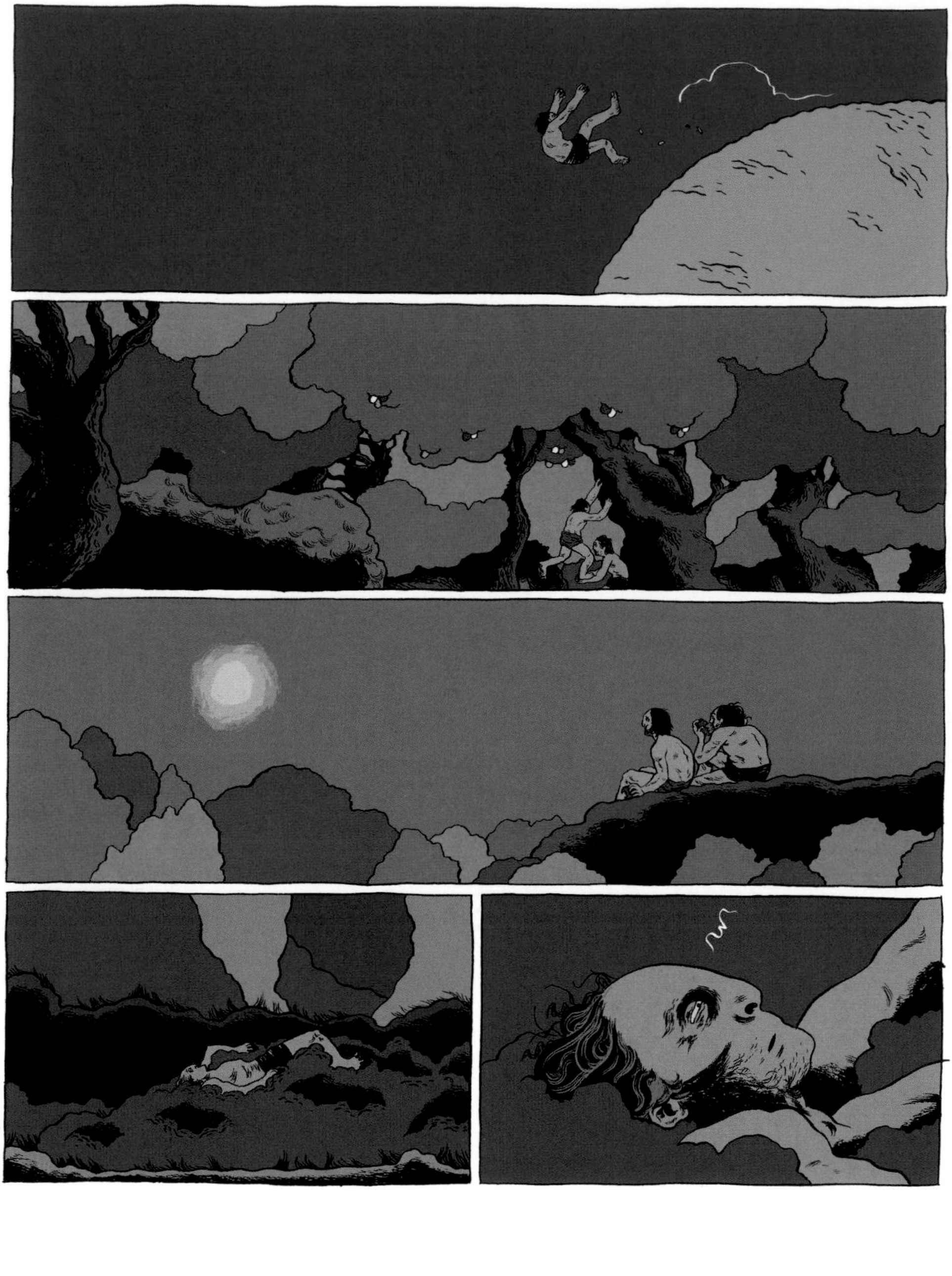

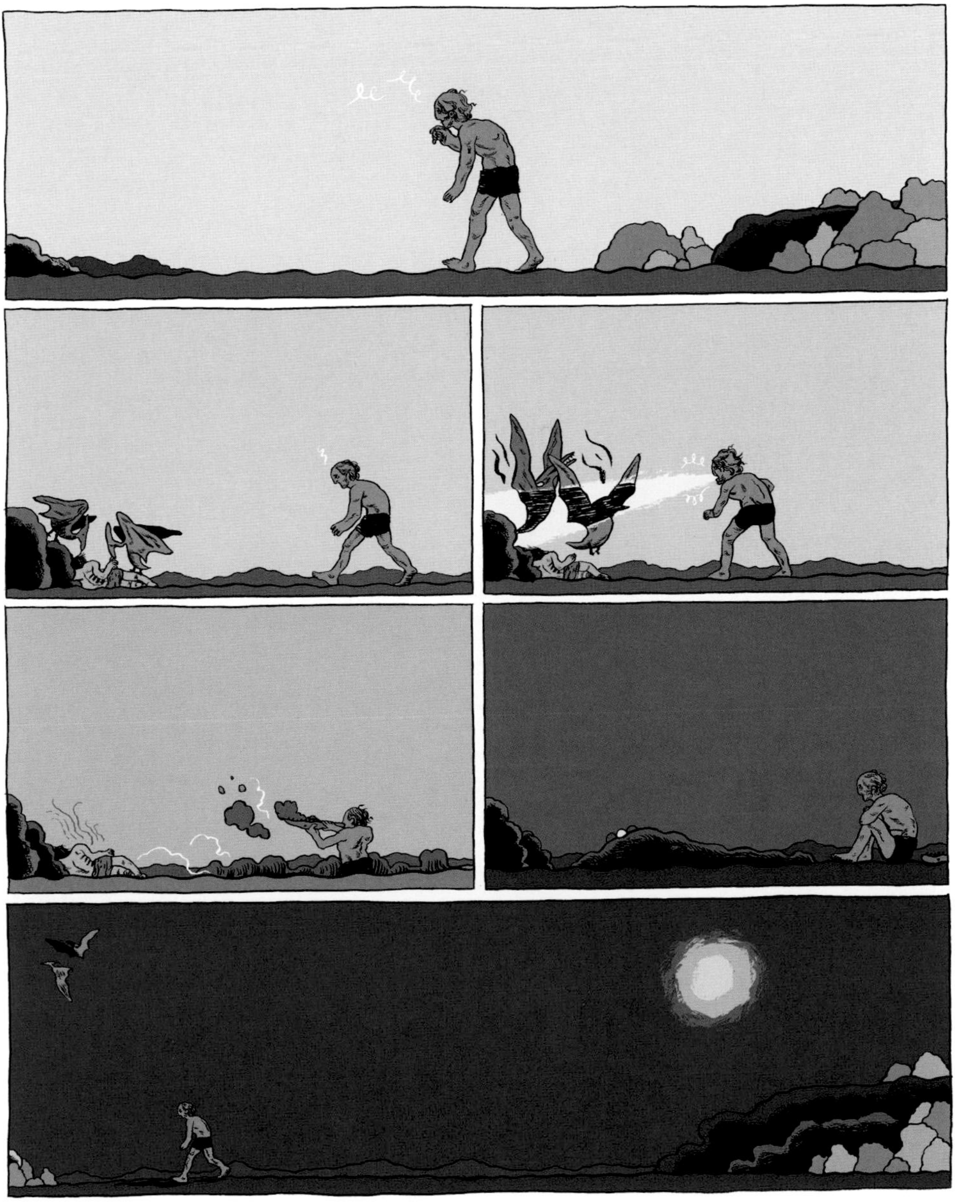

EVERYDAY

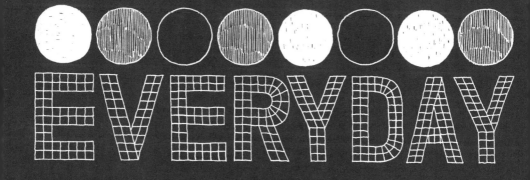

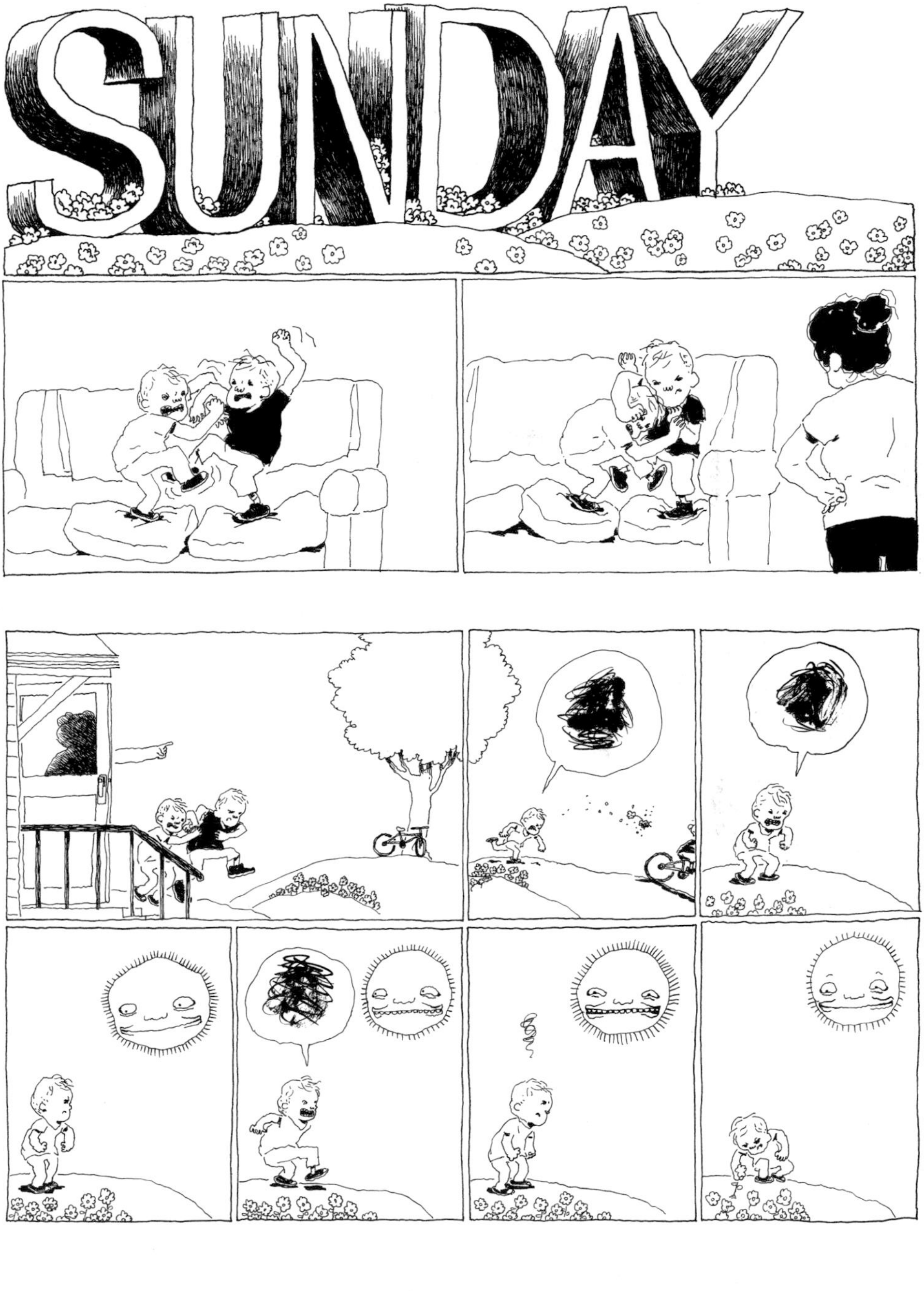
SUNDAY

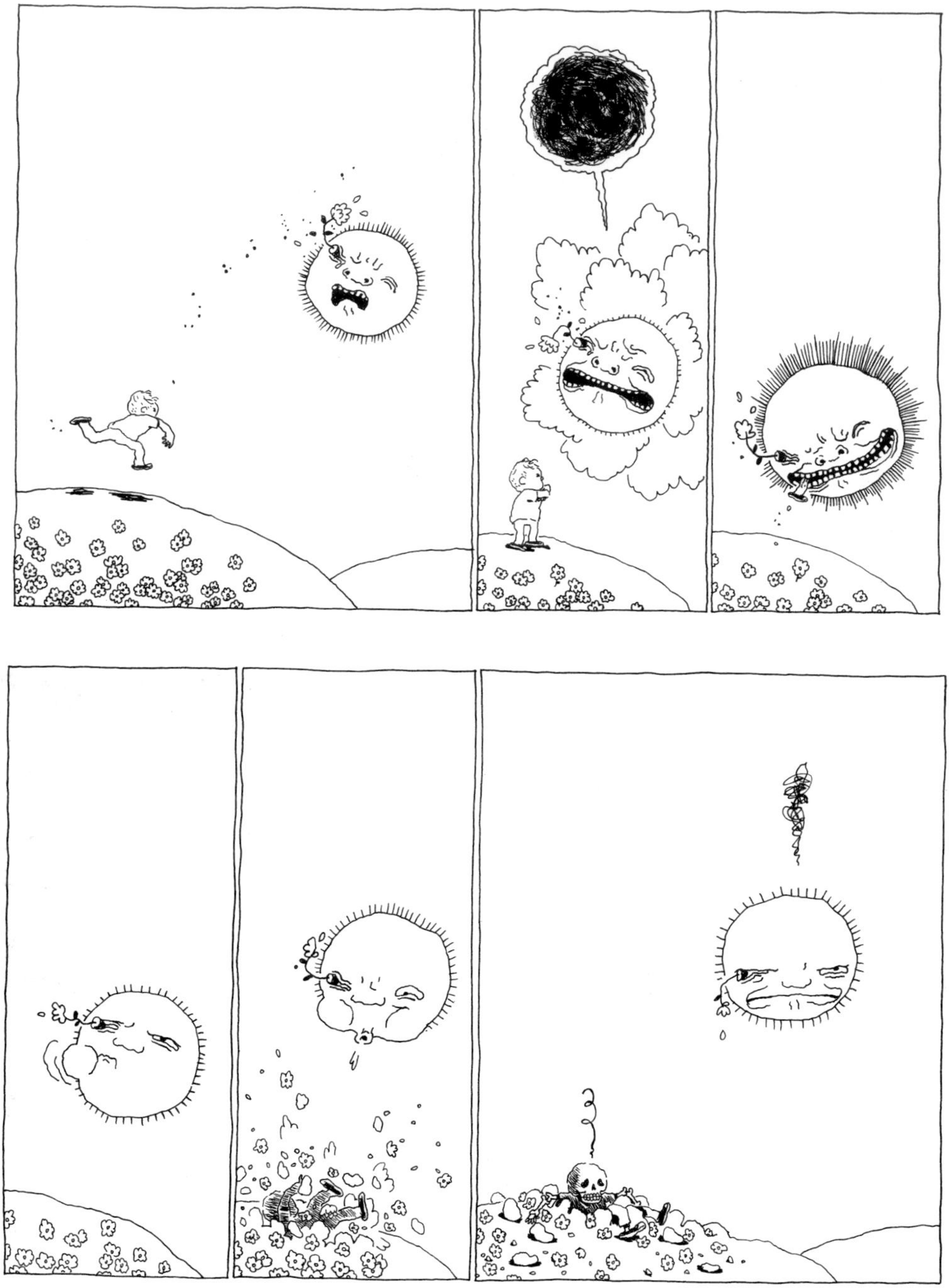

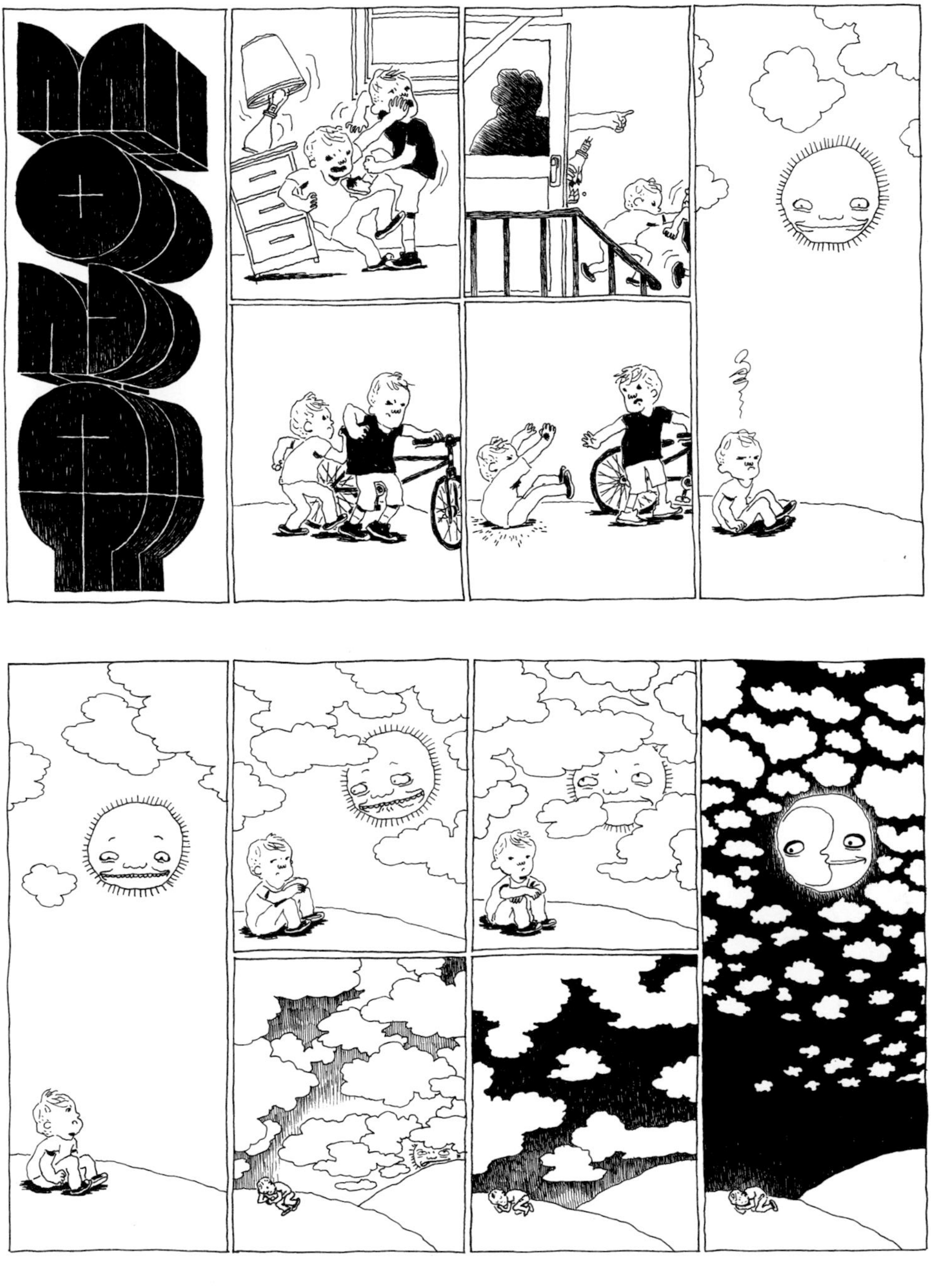

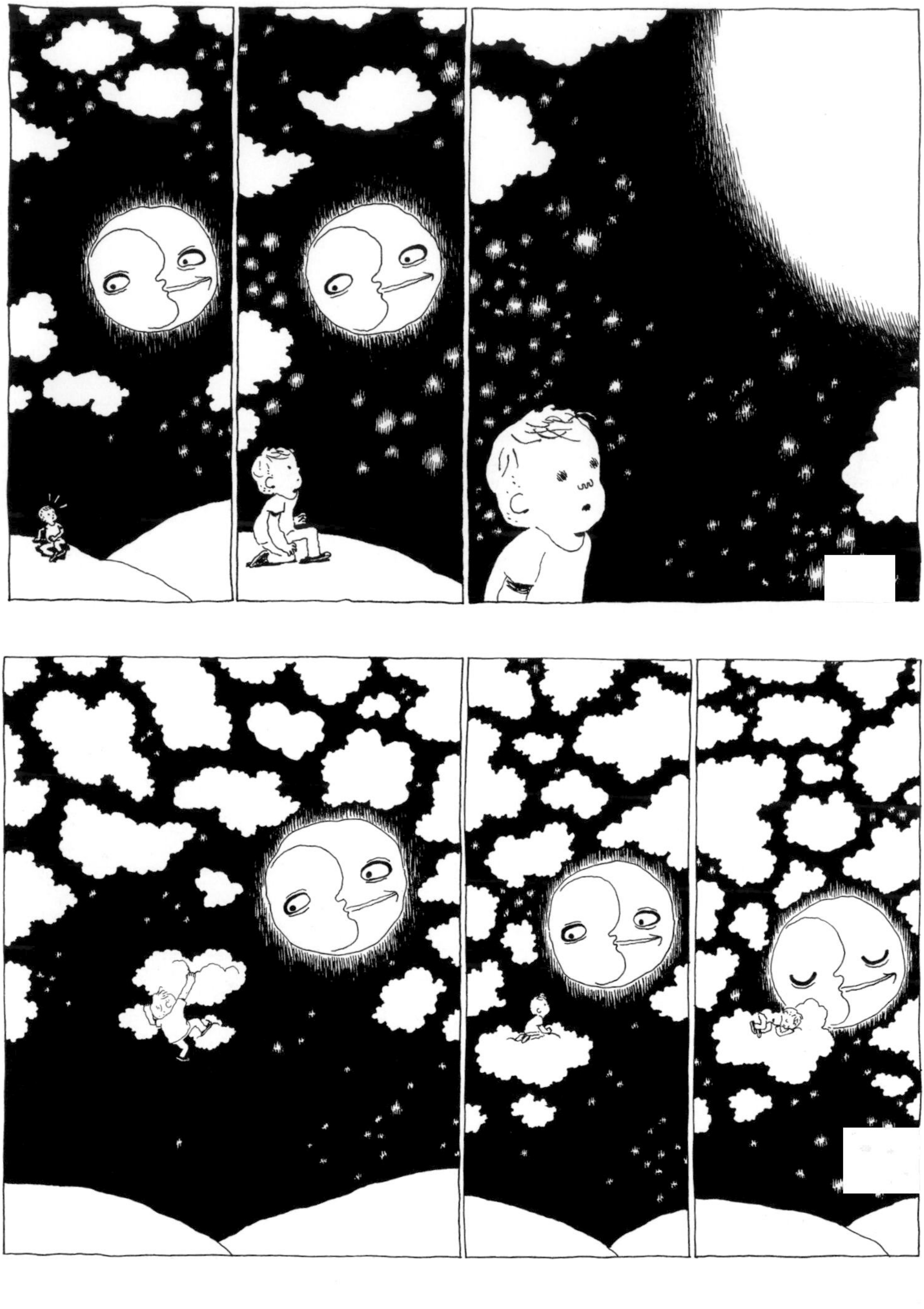

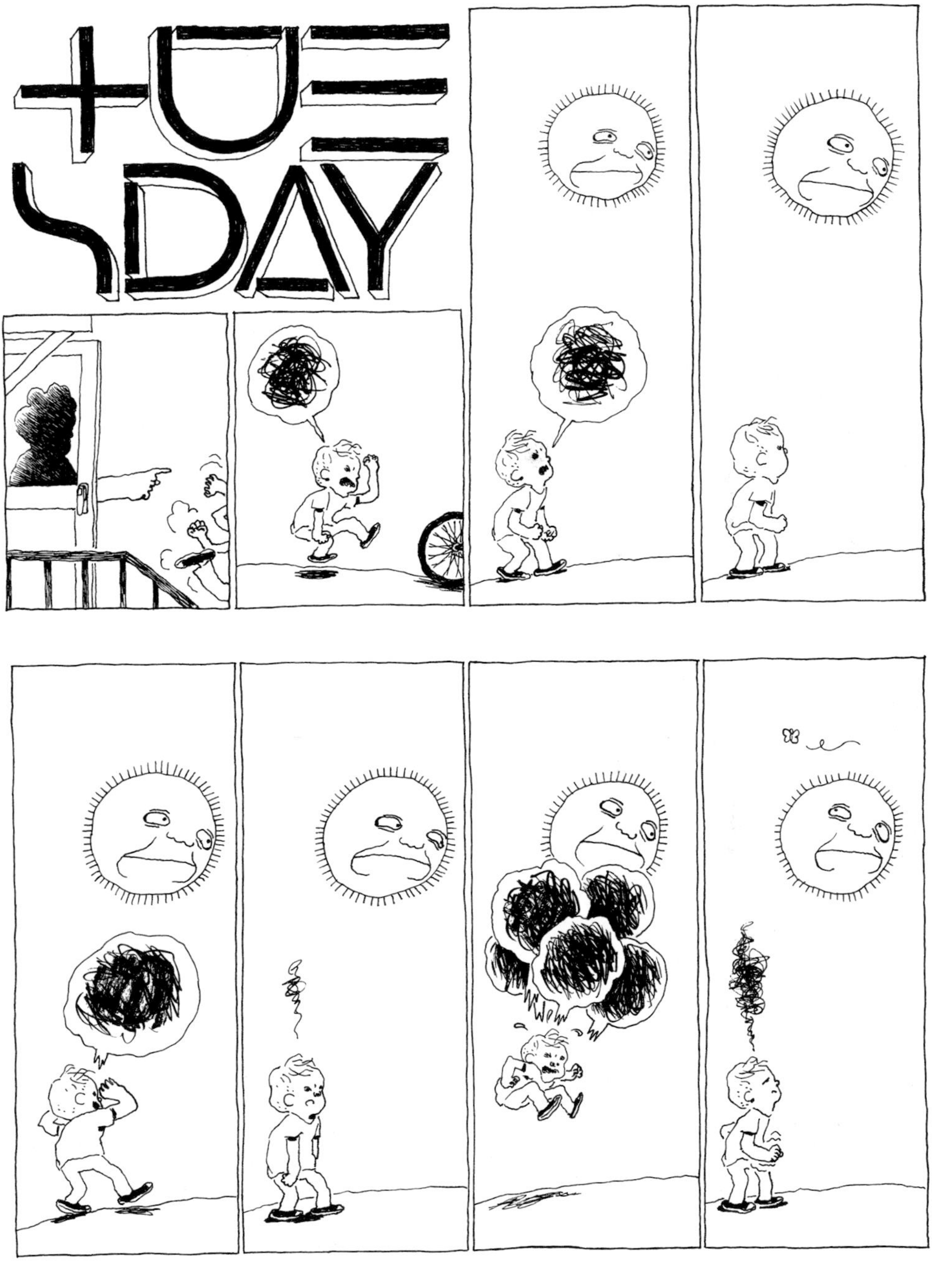
TUESDAY

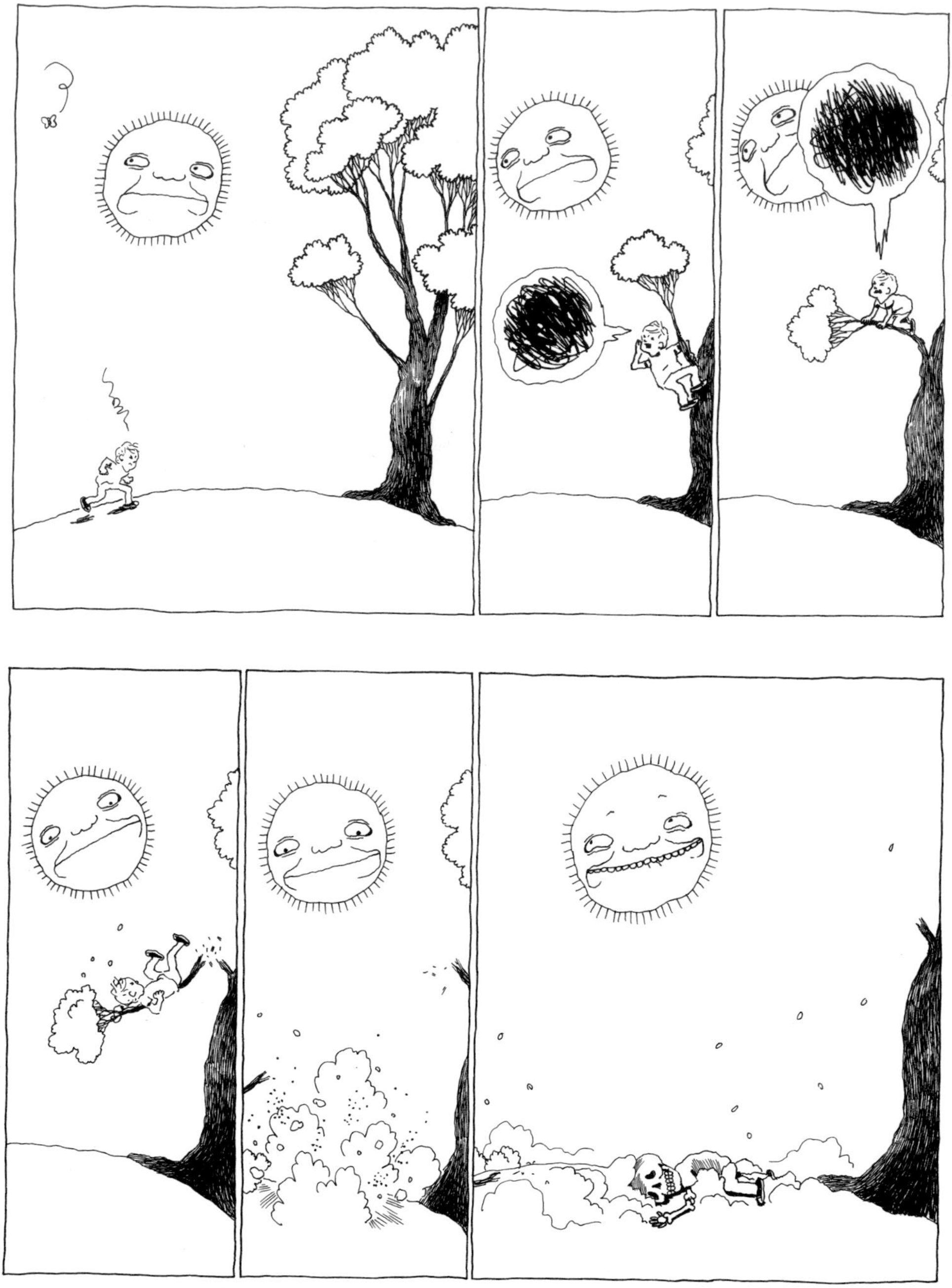

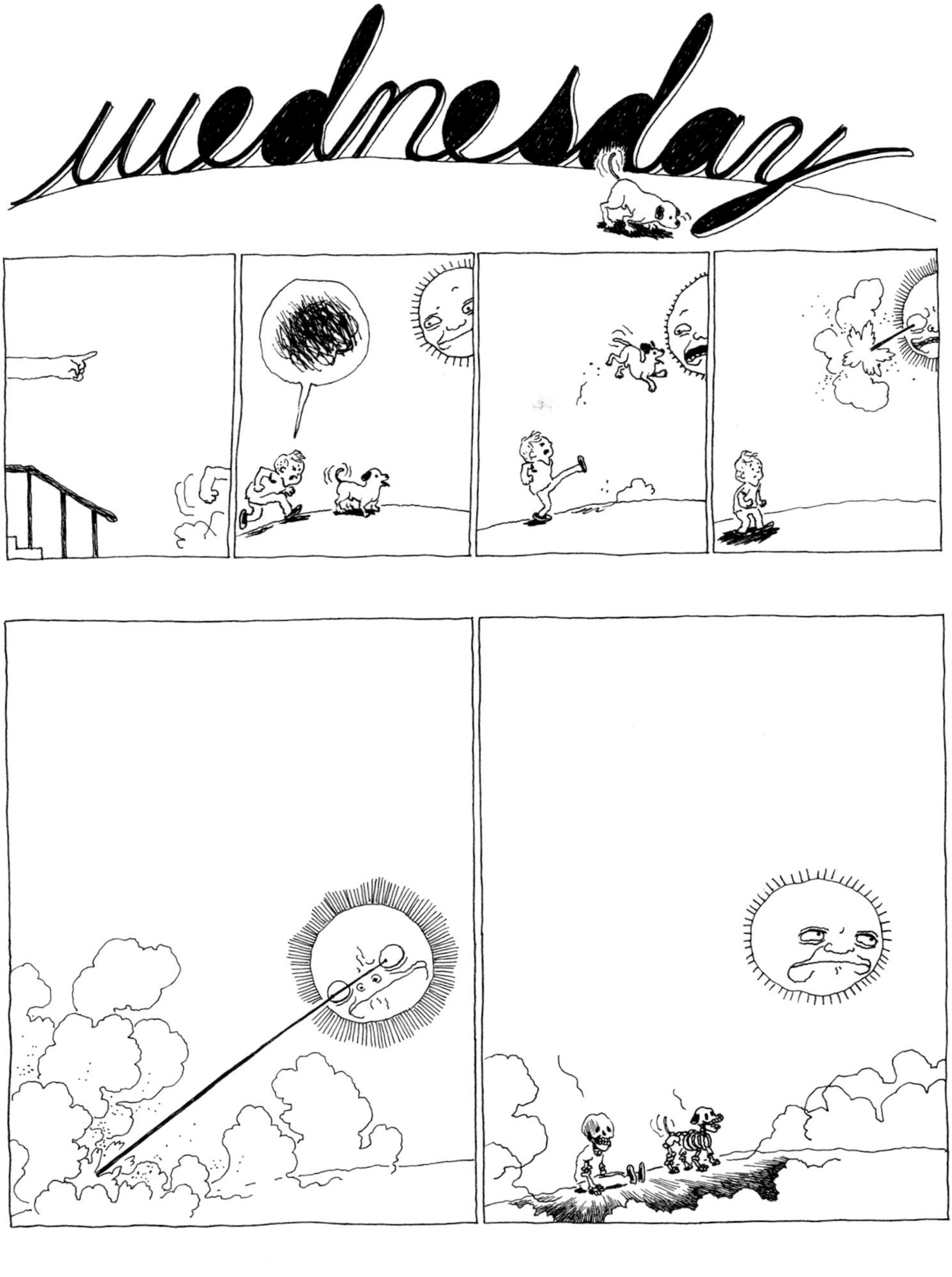
wednesday

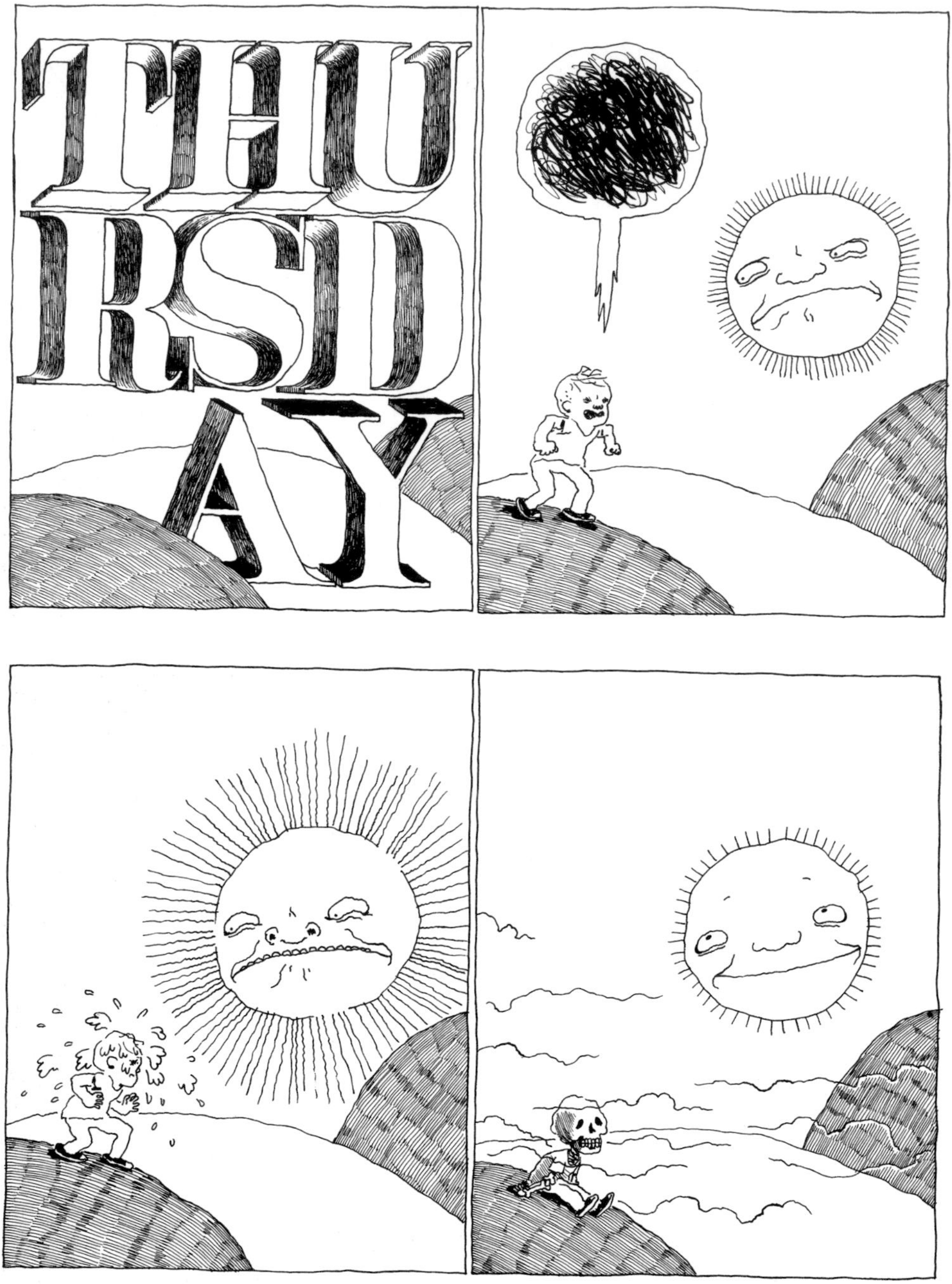
THU
RSD
AY

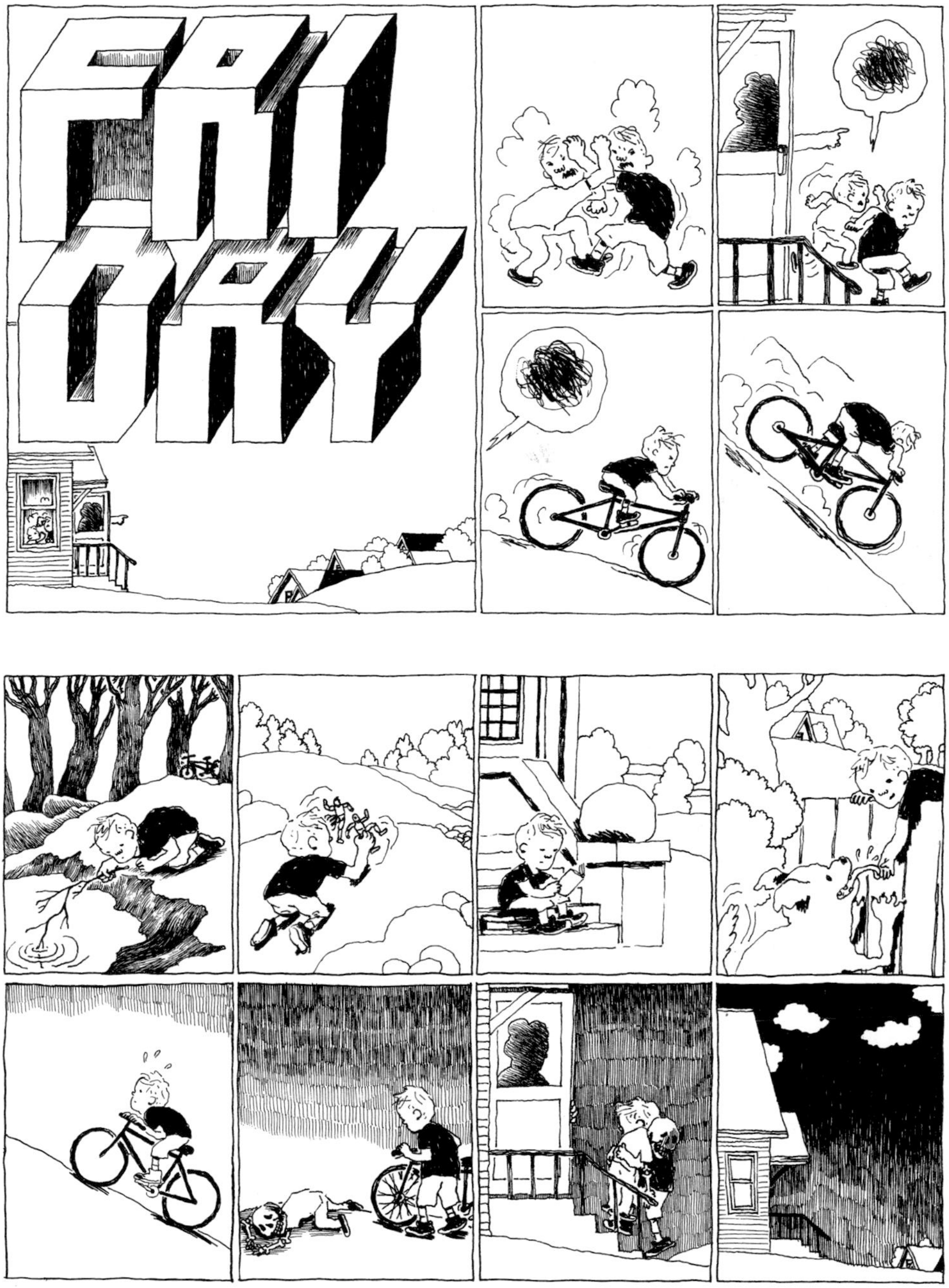

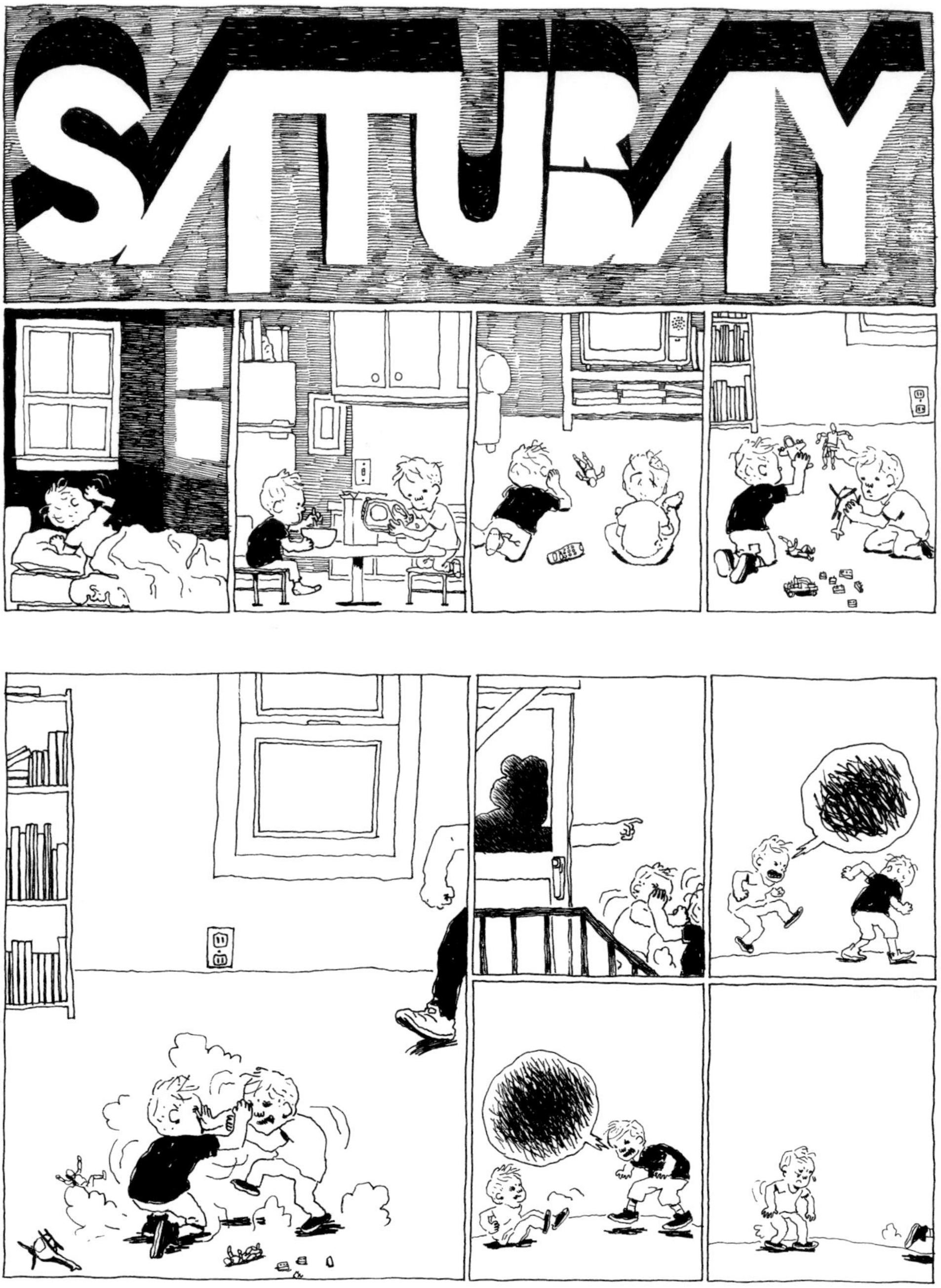
SATURDAY

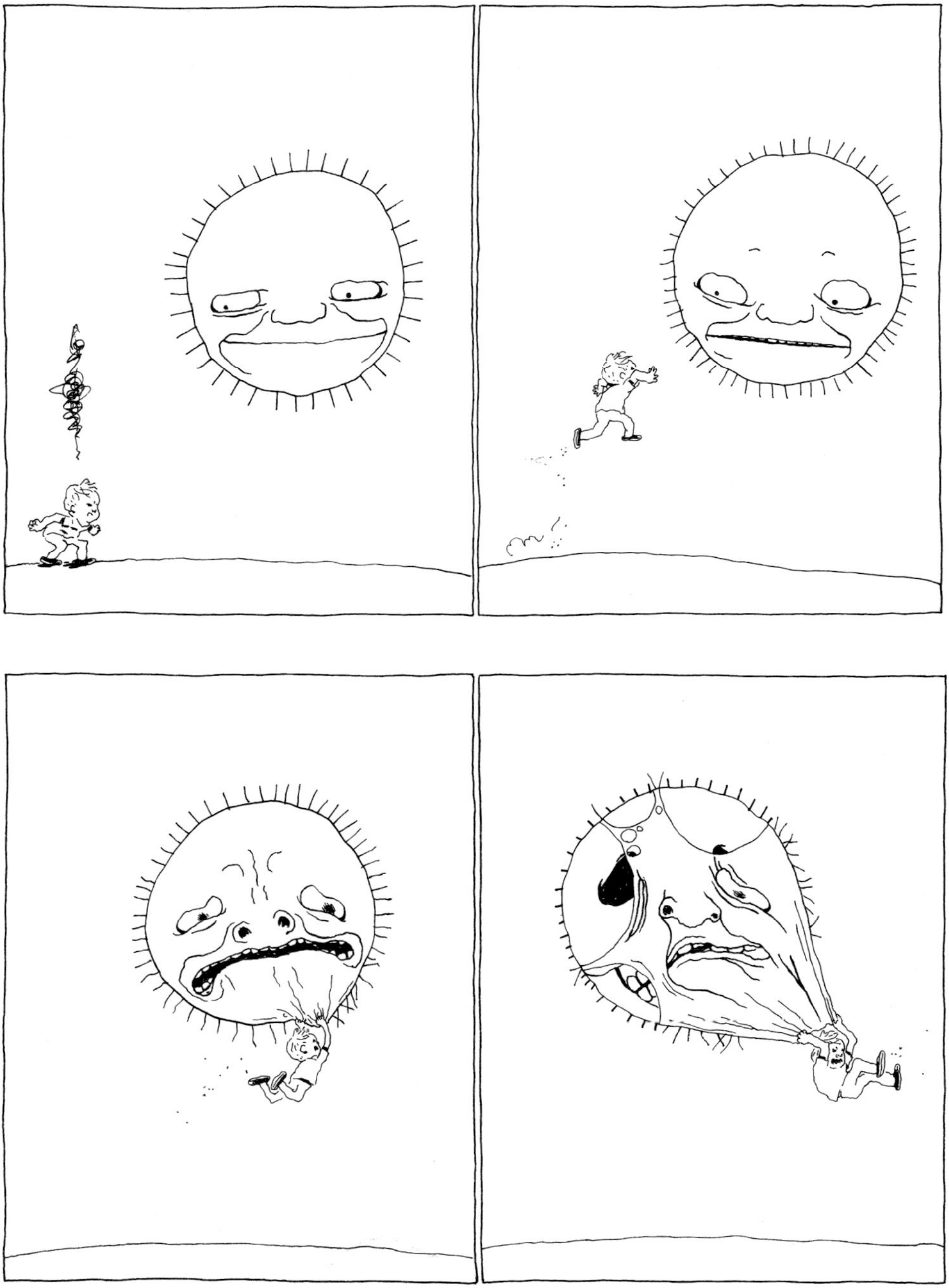

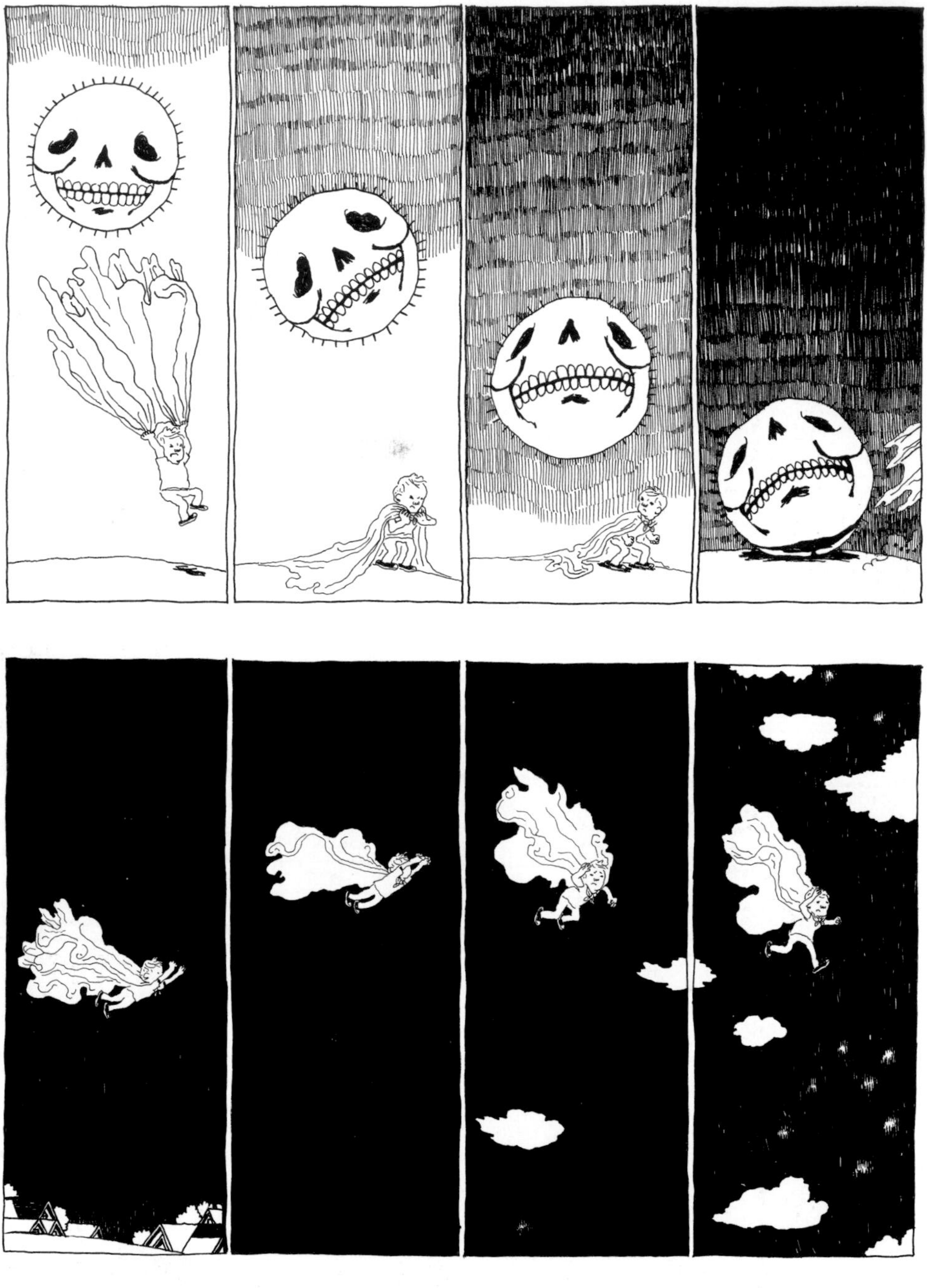

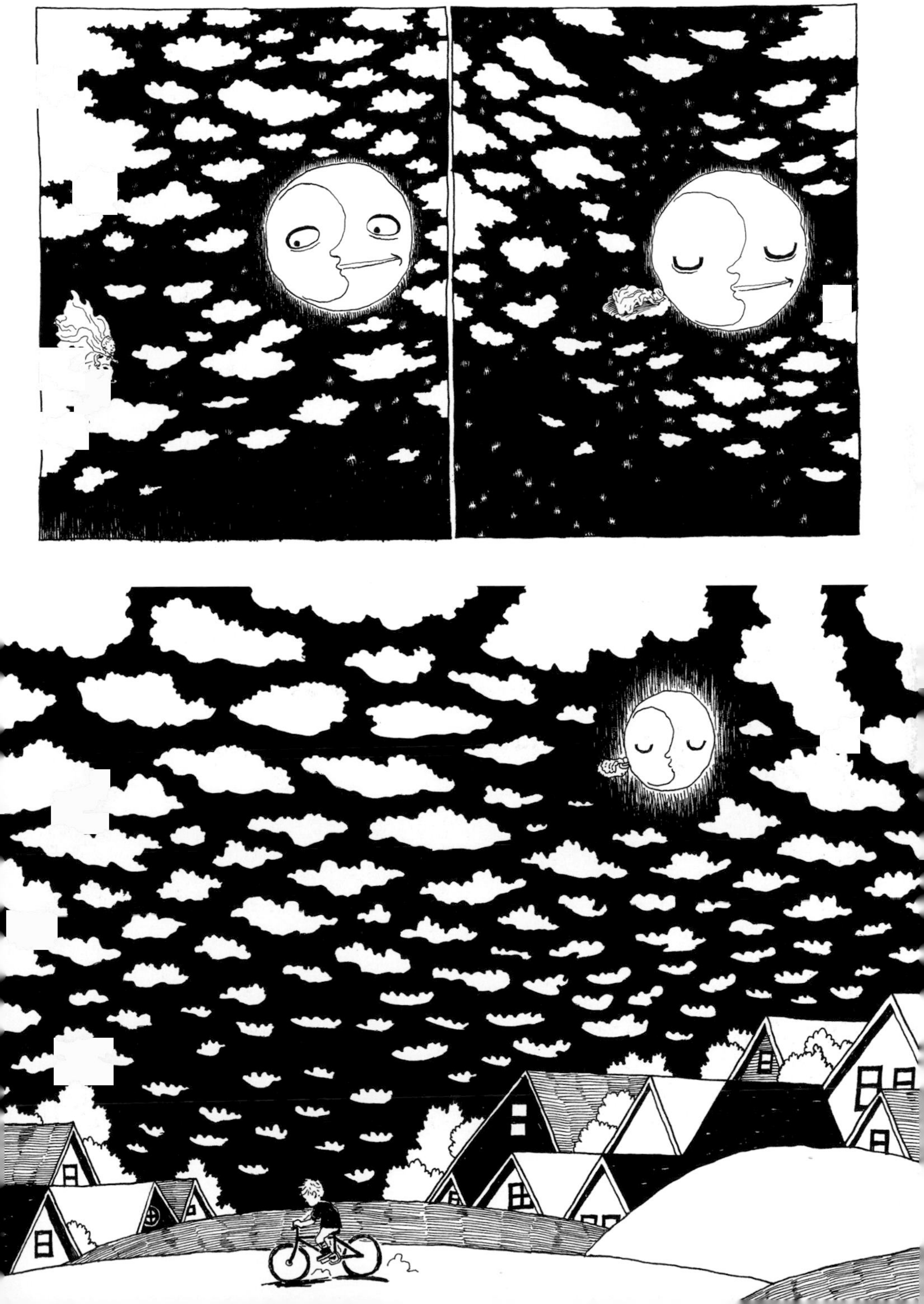

thanks for reading

Published by Secret Acres
75-22 37th Avenue, #452
Jackson Heights, NY
11372
Designed by Joseph Lambert | Printed in China
Library of Congress Control# 2009921274
ISBN 13: 978-0-9799609-5-9 | ISBN 10: 0-9799609-5-9

I-WILL-BITE-YOU!

as my
rst mini-comic,
elf-published in '06
rawn with Pigma Micron Pens on bristol board

AFTER SCHOOL SNACKS

Drawn on bristol board with a Pentel Pocket Brush, but instead of using its replaceable ink cartridges I dipped it in india ink like a regular brush. The story was rewritten/redrawn for this book. The original version appeared in the 2007 Fluke Anthology, edited by Drew Weing.

MOM SAID

rawn with Pigma Micron Pens on bristol board.
his is an original story created for this book.

TURTLE, KEEP IT STEADY!

Draw with a #3 nylon brush & india ink on copy paper
This story is the result of an assignment from
James Sturm's Cartoon-Studio class at The
Center for Cartoon Studies to retell
the story of The Tortoise and the Hare. I self-
published the story as a mini-comic in '07.
The story was also included in The Best American
Comics 2008, edited by Lynda Barry.

PSR

PAPERSCISSORROCK

This story originally appeared in Anchorless, an anthology I put together with artists from One Percent Press.

TOO FAR

Drawn with a G-Nib & india ink. Originally created for Too Far, an anthology I edited in 2010.

(CAVEMAN)
Drawn with a Pentel Pocket Brush on bristol board. Originally created for Wide Awake Press' '08 anthology, Piltdown, edited by J. Chris Campbell.

EVERYDAY

Drawn with Pigma Micron Pens on copy paper. Self-published as a mini-comic in 2010.

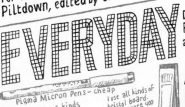

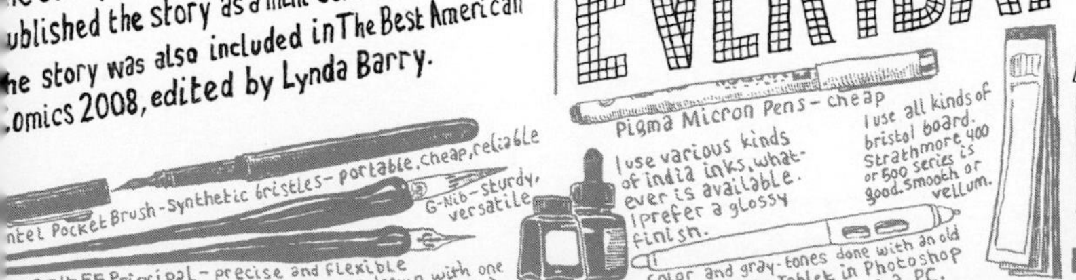
Pigma Micron Pens - cheap
Pentel Pocket Brush - Synthetic bristles - portable, cheap, reliable
G-Nib - sturdy, versatile
Leonardt EF Principal - precise and flexible (the front end-page was drawn with one of these.)
I use various kinds of india inks, whatever is available. I prefer a glossy finish.
I use all kinds of bristol board. Strathmore 400 or 500 series is good. Smooth or vellum.
Color and gray-tones done with an old Wacom Tablet in Photoshop on a PC.

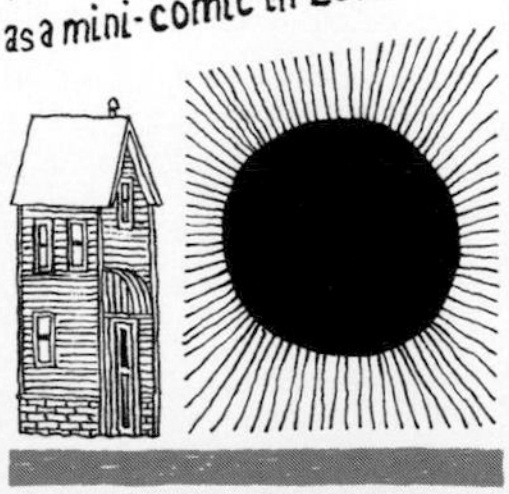

SUBMARINESUBMARINE.COM

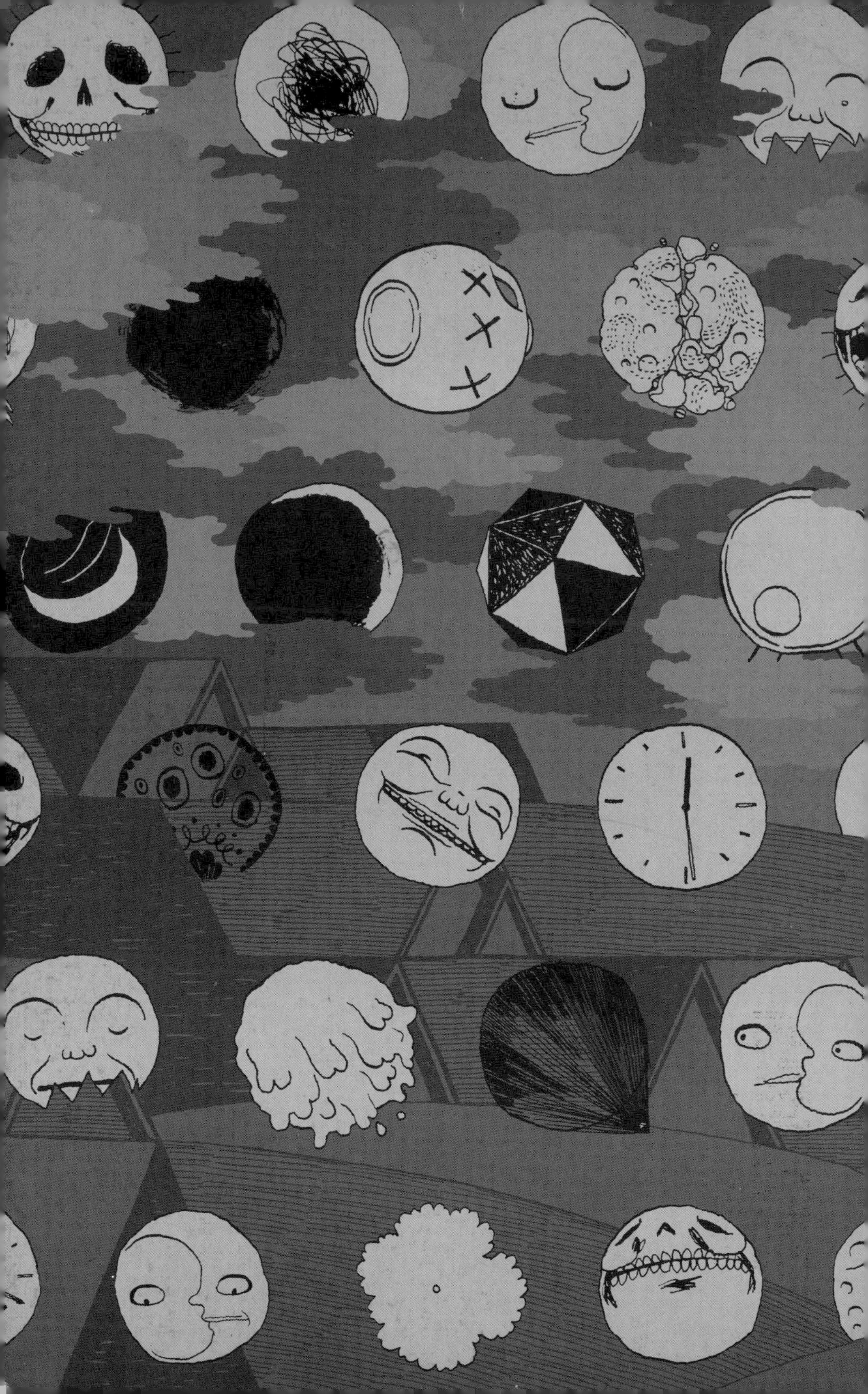